M000282666

BENEATH
HER
SKIN

BOOKS BY GREGG OLSEN

DETECTIVE MEGAN CARPENTER SERIES
Snow Creek
Water's Edge
Silent Ridge

Dying to Be Her

Lying Next to Me
The Last Thing She Ever Did
The Sound of Rain (Nicola Foster Thriller Book 1)
The Weight of Silence (Nicola Foster Thriller Book 2)

BENEATH HER SKIN

GREGG OLSEN

bookouture

Published by Bookouture in 2021

An imprint of Storyfire Ltd.
Carmelite House
50 Victoria Embankment
London EC4Y 0DZ

www.bookouture.com

Copyright © Gregg Olsen, 2011, 2021

Gregg Olsen has asserted his right to be identified
as the author of this work.

Previously published in 2011 as *Envy* by Sterling Publishing.

All rights reserved. No part of this publication may be reproduced,
stored in any retrieval system, or transmitted, in any form or by
any means, electronic, mechanical, photocopying, recording or
otherwise, without the prior written permission of the publishers.

ISBN: 978-1-80019-510-3
eBook ISBN: 978-1-80019-509-7

This book is a work of fiction. Names, characters, businesses,
organizations, places and events other than those clearly in the
public domain, are either the product of the author's imagination
or are used fictitiously. Any resemblance to actual persons, living or
dead, events or locales is entirely coincidental.

For Rebecca, who is neither Vicky nor Cristina,
but her own amazing person.—G.O.

AUTHOR'S NOTE

Some of this story is completely true. And some of it isn't. Like truth, evil comes in all sorts of flavors. Some bitter. Some deceptively sweet. Sometimes it comes with a heavy price. While most people don't invite evil into their lives, the dirty little secret is that an invitation isn't necessary. Locked doors don't matter. Neither do fancy security systems. Evil is kind of amazing when you think about it. She knows how to get inside.

—Gregg Olsen

CHAPTER ONE

Water gushed out of the corroded faucet into the chipped, porcelain tub, pooling at the bottom with a few tangled strands of long, brown hair. The water was easily 120 degrees—so hot that Katelyn Berkley could hardly stand to dip her painted green toenails into it. The scalding water instantly turned her pale skin mottled shades of crimson. Perched on the edge of the tub with her right leg dangling in the water, Katelyn smiled. It was a hurt that felt good.

At fifteen, Katelyn knew something about hurt.

Promises had been made... and broken. Things change. People let you down—even those closest to you. Promises, she realized, were very, very hard to keep.

As a blast of icy air blew in from her open bedroom window, the silver razor blade next to the half-empty bottle of tea tree shampoo glinted, beckoning her. Katelyn fantasized about taking control of the situation—of her pitiful excuse for a life—the only way she could.

She looked in the full-length mirror across the room. The glass was starting to fog as the steam billowed from the tub's rippling surface, but she could see that her eyes were red. There wasn't enough Smashbox on earth to cover the splotches that came with her tears.

"Merry Christmas, loser," she said.

She pulled inside of herself, into that place where there was only a little relief.

The bathtub was nearly full. Steaming. *Just waiting.*

Katelyn had no idea that, not far away, someone else was doing the exact same thing—just waiting for the right time to make a move.

As fresh tears rolled down her cheeks, Katelyn took off the rest of her clothes, threw them on the floor, and plunged herself into the tub.

Downstairs, her mother, Sandra, stood in the kitchen and poked at the congealing remains of a prime rib roast. She yanked at her blue sweater as she pulled it tighter on her shoulders and fumed. She was cold and mad. Mad and cold. She searched her kitchen counters for the espresso maker.

Where is it?

Sandra had a bottle of Bacardi Spiced rum at the ready and a small pitcher of eggnog that she wanted to foam. It would be the last time she took a drink for the rest of the year. The promise was a feeble one, like many of Sandra's. There was only a week left until the New Year. All night Sandra had been watching the bottle's amber liquid drop like the thermometer outside the frost-etched window—single paned because the Berkleys' was a historic home and could not be altered.

Last drink. Promise. Where is that machine?

Her parents, Nancy and Paul, had finally left after their holiday visit, and Sandra needed the calming effect of the alcohol. They always dropped a bomb at every social occasion, and the one they had offered up earlier that evening was a doozy, even by their standards. They'd rescinded their promise to fund Katelyn's college expenses, a promise made when their granddaughter was born. That night at dinner, Nancy had let it slip that they were no longer in the position to do so.

"Sandra, my kitchen counters were Corian, for goodness' sake. I deserved granite. And, well, one thing led to another. A $10,000 remodel, you know, kind of ballooned into that $100,000 new wing. I really do love it. I know you will too."

Katelyn, suddenly in need of better grades, stellar athleticism or richer parents, had left the table in tears and mouthed to her mother behind her grandmother's back, "I hate her."

"Me too, Katie," Sandra had said.

"What?" Nancy asked.

"Just telling Katelyn I love her too."

Sandra had acted as though everything was fine, the way that moms sometimes do. But inside she seethed. Her husband, Harper, had left just after dinner to check on a faulty freezer at the Timberline restaurant they owned next door.

Every single day, even on Christmas, Harper has to find a reason to go to work.

"Katelyn?" she called up the narrow wooden staircase that led to the second-floor bedrooms. "Have you seen the espresso machine?"

There was no answer.

Sandra returned to her outdated, worn-out kitchen and downed two fingers of spiced rum from a Disneyland shot glass. She screwed on the bottle cap, pretending she hadn't had a drink. After all, it was almost like medicine.

To steady my nerves. Yes, that's it.

Katelyn had been taking the espresso machine upstairs to make Americanos the week before Christmas. Sandra had scolded her for that.

"It isn't sanitary, Katie. We don't bring food upstairs."

Katelyn had rolled her eyes at her mother. "Only a restaurant owner would call milk and sugar 'food,' Mom."

"That isn't the point."

"Yeah. I get it," Katelyn said, feeling it unnecessary to point out that she'd been forced to have a food worker's permit since she was nine and could recite safe temperatures for meat, poultry, milk and vegetables in her sleep.

The lights flickered and the breakers in the kitchen popped.

Another reason to hate this old house, even if it does have an extra upstairs bathroom.

Sandra started up the darkened stairs and made her way down the hallway. She could hear the sound of water running.

She called out to Katelyn and knocked on her bedroom door. *No answer.*

Sandra twisted the knob and, at once, a wall of icy air blasted her face. Katelyn had left the window open. The lights were out too. Sandra flipped the switch up and down more times than she needed to, to prove the obvious. The room stayed dark.

Lights from the neighbor's house next door spilled onto the wooden floor.

Sandra gripped the sill and pulled the window closed, shaking her head at her daughter's escalating carelessness. It had to be forty degrees in that room. It would take all night to warm it up. She wondered how any teenager managed to survive to adulthood.

"Katelyn Melissa, you're going to catch a cold!"

Sandra walked past the unmade bed—the one that looked good only on Sundays when she changed the sheets. Katelyn's jeans and black Penney's top—a Marc Jacobs knockoff—were heaped on the floor.

What a colossal mess.

The bathroom door was open a sliver and Sandra, still freezing, pushed it aside. Aromatherapy candles flickered.

"What are you thinking?" she asked, her tone harsh and demanding. Katelyn wasn't thinking at all.

The fifteen-year-old was slumped over the edge of the old clawfoot tub, her eyes tiny shards of broken glass, her expression void of anything. Her long, wet hair dripped onto the floor.

Instinct took over and Sandra lunged in the direction of her daughter, slipping on the wet floor and falling. As she reached for the rim of the tub, she yelled, "I could have broken my neck! What's going on with you?"

No answer, to a very stupid question.

Sandra, her heart racing and the rum now gnawing at the walls of her stomach, tried to steady herself in the candlelight. She tasted blood. *Her own.* She'd cut her lip when she'd fallen, and several red drops trickled to the floor. She felt tears, fear and panic as she looked at Katelyn in the faint candlelight. Her *lifeless* daughter. It was so very hard to see with the lights out. Katelyn's dark-brown hair, highlighted by a home kit, hung limp, curling over the edge of the tub. One arm was askew, as if flailing at something unseen.

The other was hidden in the sudsy water.

"Katie. Katie. Katie!" With each repetition of her daughter's name, Sandra's voice grew louder. By the third utterance, it was a scream that probably could be heard all over Port Gamble.

Katelyn Melissa Berkley, just fifteen, was dead.

"It can't be," Sandra said, tears now streaming down her face. She was woozy. Sick. Scared. She wanted to call for Harper, but she knew he had gone. She was alone in the house where the unthinkable had occurred. She slipped again as she pulled at Katelyn's shoulders, white where the cold air had cooled them, pinkish in the still-hot bathwater. Two-tone. Like a strawberry dipped in white chocolate.

Katelyn loved white chocolate. Even though Sandra insisted it wasn't really chocolate at all.

"Baby, what happened?" Instinctively, Sandra turned off the slowly rising water. "Tell me you're going to be all right!"

At first, Sandra only heard dead silence. Then the quiet drip, drip, drip of the tub's leaky faucet. There was no answer to her question. There never could be. Never again.

Sandra shook her daughter violently, a reflex that she hadn't had since Katelyn was a little girl and had lied about something so inconsequential that the terrified mother couldn't retrieve the full memory of what had made her so angry.

As she spun around to go for a phone, Sandra Berkley noticed there was something else in the tub. It was hard to see. It was so dark in that bathroom. Through her thickening veil of tears, she leaned over and scooted the suds away.

The mini espresso machine.

Her eyes followed the electrical cord. Like a cobra that had recoiled, ready to strike, the plug sat upright, still firmly snug in the wall outlet at the side of the tub.

In small towns like Port Gamble, Washington, news travels fast. Within moments of the reverberating echoes of Sandra Berkley's anguished screams, residents had begun to gather outside the tidy red house with white trim and pineapple shutters. Christmas lights of white, green and red sparkled in the icy night air. A passerby might have mistaken the gathering for a large group of carolers.

Port Gamble was that kind of place. At least, it tried to be.

An ambulance siren wailed down the highway from Kingston, growing louder with each second.

That the teenager had died was known by everyone. What exactly happened, no one was certain.

Someone in the crowd whispered that Katelyn had fallen in the tub and split her head open. Another suggested that the girl had "issues" of some sort and had taken her own life.

"Maybe she offed herself? Kids do that a lot these days. You know, one final grasp for attention."

"I dunno. She didn't seem the type."

"Kids are hard to read."

"True enough, but even so, I don't think she was the kind of girl who would hurt herself."

Scenes of sudden tragedy have their macabre pecking order when it comes to who stands where. Closest to the doorway were those who knew and loved the dead girl: her mother, father, a cousin or two. In the next wave were the friends, the church pastor and a police deputy, who was there to make sure that the scene stayed orderly. Beyond that were casual acquaintances, neighbors, even the occasional rubbernecker who was on the scene because it was better than a rerun of one of the various incarnations of *Real Housewives*.

There was a time when Hayley and Taylor Ryan might have been in the grouping closest to the Berkleys' front door. Though they were no longer *that* close, the twins had grown up with Katelyn. As it often seems to be, middle school became the great divider. What had once been a deep bond shared by three girls had been shattered by jealousy and the petty gossip that predictably turns friends into enemies.

What happened among the trio was nothing that couldn't have faded by the end of middle school. The girls could have reclaimed the friendship they'd had back in the days when they used to joke about Colton James's stupid sports T-shirts, which he wore every single day in fifth grade.

"Only a loser would support the Mariners," Katelyn had once said, looking over at Colton as he stood in defiance, his scrawny arms wrapped around his small chest, nodding as if he were defending his team.

But that was then. A million years ago, it seemed. Since then, Port Gamble's kids had grown into pubescent teenagers. Taylor and Hayley, still mirror images of each other, had blonde hair, blue eyes and the occasional pimple. Colton had traded in sports T-shirts for '80s relic rock bands' insignias and was dating Hayley. And Katelyn was dead.

"When was the last time you actually talked to her?" Hayley asked, already trying to piece together what had happened.

Taylor brushed aside her annoying bangs and shook her head.

"Not sure." A puff of white vapor came with Taylor's warm breath. "Last month, I guess."

"Do you think she was depressed? I read somewhere that suicide rates are highest at Christmas."

Taylor shook her head. "Depressed? How would I know?"

"You have a better pulse on the social scene than I do," Hayley said matter-of-factly. "They're saying she killed herself because she was upset about something."

"Was Katelyn still cutting?"

Hayley looked surprised. "You knew about that too?"

"Duh," Taylor said, wishing that she'd brought gloves like her sister had. Taylor's fingertips were numb. "Everyone knew. Dylan, that sophomore with a shaved head and earlobes he's been gouging since Halloween, called her *Cut-lin* last week."

Hayley looked down at the icy pavement and said quietly, "Oh... I was under the impression she had stopped."

Taylor shook her head, then shrugged her shoulders. "I remember her telling people that she liked cutting. Liked how it made her feel in control."

"That doesn't make sense. Cutting made her feel in control of what?"

"She never said."

The crowd contracted to make room for a gurney. Covered from head to toe was the figure of the dead girl. Some people could scarcely bear the sight and they turned away. It felt invasive. Sad. Wrong to even look.

The ambulance, its lights rotating red flashes over the bystanders, pulled away. There was no real urgency in its departure. No sirens. Nothing. Just the quiet slinking away like the tide.

A few moments later, the crowd surged a little as the door opened and Port Gamble Police Chief Annie Garnett's imposing frame loomed in the doorway. She wore a dark wool skirt and jacket, with a knitted scarf around her thick neck. She had long, dark hair that was pulled back. In a voice that cracked a little, Chief Garnett told everyone they should go home.

"Tragedy here tonight," she said, her voice unable to entirely mask her emotions. Annie was a big woman, with baseball-mitt hands, a deep resonant voice and a soft spot for troubled young girls. Katelyn's death would be hard on her, especially if it turned out to be a suicide.

Hayley nudged her sister, who had started to cry. "We probably should go home, Tay," she said gently.

In that instant, shock had turned to anguish. Hayley's eyes also welled up, and she ignored a text from her boyfriend, Colton, who was out of town and missing the biggest thing to happen in Port Gamble since the devastating bus crash. The twins looked over the crowd to see the faces of their friends and neighbors.

One of the paramedics whispered to another.

"Girl was found in the tub with an espresso machine."

Hayley jammed her hands inside her coat pockets. No Kleenex. She dried her eyes with a soggy gloved fingertip. It could not have been colder just then. The air was ice. She hugged her sister.

"I feel sick," Taylor said.

"Me too," Hayley agreed. Curiosity piercing through her emotions, she added, "I want to know what happened to her and why."

"Why do you think she did it?" Taylor asked.

"Did what?" Hayley argued. "We don't know what happened. Not really."

Taylor indicated those in the outer ring of grief, just beyond their own.

"I mean, really, an espresso machine in the bathtub? That's got to be a first ever."

Taylor nodded, brushing away her tears. She could see the absurdity of it all. "Some snarky blogger is going to say this is proof that coffee isn't good for you."

"And write a headline like 'Port Gamble Girl Meets Bitter End,'" Hayley added.

The spaces in the crowd began to shrink as people pushed forward. All were completely unaware that someone was watching them. *All of them.* Someone in their midst was enjoying the tragic scene that had enveloped Port Gamble as its residents shivered in the frigid air off the bay.

Loving the sad moment to the very last drop.

CHAPTER TWO

Some say Port Gamble was cursed from the moment *they* came. The S'Klallam Tribe had made its home on the bay's shores for hundreds of years, finding food from the sea, shelter from storms and the tranquility that eluded other isolated locations along the Pacific's rugged coastlines.

The place, the earth, the universe were in perfect harmony.

The way it was always supposed to be.

And then the early explorers arrived at the jagged edge of Hood Canal, an offshoot of the Pacific Ocean that pokes into Washington with the force of an ice pick.

That was a century and a half ago, a very long time by West Coast standards. The sawmill, located below the bluff on which the town was built, was still the source of most of Port Gamble's jobs and its pungent clouds of smoke. Green hats (those who actually worked in the mill) and white hats (those who told the greenies what to do) coexisted happily in the town's company-owned neighborhoods of centuries-old homes.

Homes that were known by number.

Taylor and Hayley Ryan lived in number 19, the last house in Port Gamble before the highway's march along the bay toward Kingston, the nearest town of any size. A two-story, chocolate-brown-and-white structure built in 1859 that had been added on to at least four times, number 19 was the oldest house in Washington State to be continually inhabited. It was drafty, quirky and certainly loved more than most rentals.

The conversation in that particular house was likely the same as others were having throughout Port Gamble that fateful night.

Maybe not exactly.

The Ryan family gathered around the old pine kitchen table. And despite the fact that it was Christmas night, the subject that held their attention wasn't the gifts they'd received (a Bobbi Brown makeup collection for Taylor and a forensics book, *The Science & History of the Dead*, for Hayley), all they could think about was Katelyn Berkley and how it was that she had come to die that night in the bathtub.

Kevin Ryan, the twins' father, was about to celebrate his thirty-eighth birthday and had taken to doing sit-ups every night and half-hour jogs around town. The girls had never known a time when their dad, a true-crime writer, wasn't poking around an evidence box, hanging out with cops or prosecutors or, best of all, visiting some lowlife killer in prison. Every year at Christmas time, their mailbox was filled with cards from baby killers, stranglers and arsonists.

Have a Merry Christmas!
Don't do anything I wouldn't do!

Their mother, Valerie, worked as a psychiatric nurse at a state mental hospital near Seattle. Hayley thought her parents had a symbiotic relationship, since her dad seemed to rely on her mom as a human wiki when he was trying to figure out the sociopaths he was writing about.

Valerie was a stunning blonde with brown eyes and delicate features. In elementary school, Taylor always thought her mom was the prettiest one in Port Gamble. Over time, she learned that her mother was also smart and accomplished—and that a person's true character is more important than how they look.

Except on TV, of course.

Valerie blew on her hot chocolate—made with real milk, sugar and cocoa powder—scooting the froth to one side so she could drink it without getting a chocolate mustache. "What did Chief Garnett say?"

"Not much," Kevin answered. "I mean, just that it was probably an accident."

Valerie raised an eyebrow and passed out some candy canes. "I don't see how. Honestly, Kevin, small kitchen appliances don't get into a bathtub all by themselves."

Kevin nodded in agreement and looked across the table at the girls, who'd endured a blizzard of text messages from friends about their suspicions of what had happened to Katelyn. "Was she upset about something? Do you guys know anything?"

Taylor hated cocoa but loved her mom too much to say anything. She stirred the steamy liquid with her candy cane. The only thing that could make homemade hot chocolate worse was a candy cane.

"Nah. Katie is—"

"*Was*," Hayley corrected, always precise.

Taylor looked at her sister. "Right. *Was*. Anyways, Katie was super mad about something."

"She allegedly had a boyfriend. I mean," Hayley quickly corrected herself when Taylor shot her an exasperated look, "that's what I heard. But I never met him. We didn't really talk to each other in school."

Kevin sipped his cocoa. "This has nonfat milk in it, right, Val?"

She nodded, turning to the girls and winking. "Yes, honey. Nonfat."

The Ryans rinsed their mugs, and Kevin turned off the oversize multicolored lights that decorated the large, airy Douglas fir that filled the front window of the living room.

"Sure doesn't feel like Christmas around Port Gamble," he said, looking out the window at the street and the bay beyond it.

"I couldn't imagine being without you girls," Valerie said.

That was a little bit of a lie. There was a time when she had come very close to knowing exactly how Sandra Berkley was feeling right then. Hayley and Taylor had come within a breath of dying, an event that no one in the family ever really talked about. It was too painful and too fragile, like a crackly scab that had never fully healed.

No one knew it right then, but someone was about to pick at that scab, and when they did, many who lived in Port Gamble would face fears and consequences they'd never imagined.

CHAPTER THREE

Hayley and Taylor had shared a bedroom in house number 19 all through elementary school. It was big enough to accommodate two cribs, then later twin beds with matching sheets and identical duvets. Theirs was the larger of two upstairs bedrooms in the place they'd lived in since their parents brought them home from Harrison Medical Center in nearby Bremerton.

Their father had used the second, smaller bedroom as his office to decent effect. Kevin Ryan's most successful crime book at that time, *Gorgeous and Deadly*—the true story of a beauty queen who'd murdered six of her rivals by poisoning them with milkshakes laced with rat poison—had been written there.

He always told his girls, "If only these walls could talk... the world would know just how hard it is to tell the truth in a story in which everyone's a liar."

But the walls *didn't* talk.

One afternoon when the twins were in seventh grade, their best friend, Beth Lee, goaded them into asking for their own rooms. She sipped from a sports bottle—though she didn't play any sports—as the trio sat in the Ryans' family room watching a plastic surgery show on the Discovery Channel.

"People at school think you're weird for sharing a room," Beth said before the girl on TV went under the knife for a nose job.

"How could anyone at school possibly know?" Hayley asked.

Beth shrugged her knobby shoulders. "I might have mentioned it."

Taylor rolled her eyes. "'Course you did."

"I'm just looking out for you, Hay-Tay," Beth said, refusing to call the girls by their individual names.

"The other room is ridiculously small. Besides, it's Dad's office," Hayley concluded.

"Take turns. Who cares? It is almost Siamese-twin creepy that you two can't be apart."

Taylor's face went red. "Can too."

"Someone's upset," Beth provoked. "Wonder why that is? Maybe because someone else is right? As usual."

The twins didn't argue, but that night they convinced their dad to move his workstation downstairs. Then they flipped a coin and Taylor got the little room. They hated being apart, but they despised the idea of Beth Lee blabbing at school that they were weird.

Weren't twins supposed to be close, after all?

They moved their beds—headboard to headboard—to the inside wall, where an old power outlet had been plated over on either side. The single screw that held each plate in place was nearly threadbare. It took only the slightest touch to swivel it aside. It wasn't an intercom system, but it functioned like one. At night when their parents were downstairs, the sisters would talk about the things that troubled them: boys, Beth Lee, the weirdos their dad wrote about, the pasta dish that their mother didn't know they absolutely hated and the odd feelings and visions that came to them at inexplicable times. Those were harder to discuss because putting the unthinkable, the unbelievable, into words was extremely difficult.

How does one really describe a feeling? Or how can one know something with absolute certainty that one shouldn't, couldn't, possibly know?

There were differences in the twins, of course. They might have come from a split egg, but that didn't mean they were identical beyond their carbon-copy genetics. Physical similarities aside, the girls were distinct and unwavering in their likes and dislikes.

Hayley leaned toward alternative music. She loved homegrown Northwest bands like Modest Mouse, Fleet Foxes, and old-school Sleater-Kinney—anything off the beaten path, out of the mainstream. While their friend Beth gravitated toward whatever music was hot and trendy, Hayley was more interested in finding meaning and real, genuine voices.

If Taylor measured things in emotion, Hayley looked at ways to quantify life. Analytical in nature, her head almost always overruled her heart. Love it? Hate it? She wanted to *know* it. Her drive to know something at its very root was likely the reason the boy next door, Colton James, fell for her.

Taylor's intelligence wasn't as logic based; it was more intuitive. She liked a color because it made her feel good, not because it made her eyes look pretty. She prided herself on being outspoken and socially conscious—often flip-flopping with vegetarianism, risking ridicule from Hayley. Words came easily to her, as opposed to her shier, more introspective twin.

But despite their differences, something more than mere twinship always bonded them together.

From her bed, Taylor watched a boat decorated with a Christmas tree on the bow glide across Port Gamble Bay toward the mill. It being Christmas night, the scene was deathly quiet. A faint plume of steam rose above the sprawling site with its rusty, tin-roofed shacks, a near-empty parking lot, and logs stacked everywhere like Jenga on steroids. Taylor may have had the smallest room, but it offered the best view in the house. The boat, an old tug, left a trail of foam in its wake. It curled and undulated on the glassy black surface of the water. She sat up and stared at it more intently, her heart starting to beat a little faster.

On the water were the letters:

LOOK

Knowing this was one of *those* inexplicable moments, she turned, lifted the outlet plate, and called to her sister. "Hayley, come here! You gotta see something."

"I'm tired," Hayley said. "I've already seen that hideous scarf Aunt Jolene got you."

Taylor spiked an exasperated sigh with a sense of urgency. "Nope, not it. Come. *Now*."

A beat later, Hayley stood in the doorway and Taylor pointed out the window.

"Yeah, so it's a boat with a pretty Christmas tree." Hayley narrowed her brow and shot an impatient look at her twin.

"Check out the water *behind* the tug."

"Can't you just tell me what I'm looking for, Taylor?"

"Read it."

Hayley glanced at her sister and then back at the bay. She looked more closely and nodded. The word on the water had morphed a little, but it was as clear as if a child had scrawled it on a tar-soaked pavement with a fat piece of chalk.

"What do you think it means?" Hayley asked.

Taylor drew back the curtain to widen the view, and then turned to face her sister. "It's about Katelyn. I feel it."

Hayley's blue eyes, identical to her sister's down to the golden flecks that speckled her irises, stared hard, searching. "What about her? Where are we supposed to look? And at what?"

Taylor shook her head. "Don't know."

They stood there a moment as the December wind kicked up and erased the message on the water.

"That scarf *is* pretty atrocious, Taylor."

"I'll wear it once for Aunt Jolene. Then I'll ditch it on the bus. I'm just saying…"

The night Katelyn Berkley died was the beginning of something that would change everything.

Everything.

Every. Single. Thing.

CHAPTER FOUR

The day after Christmas in Port Gamble was completely out of whack. Certainly, some things seemed the same on the surface. Plastic bags of gift-wrapping and ribbon were stuffed in alleyways or burned on the sly in backyard fire pits. Children re-examined their haul with an eye toward who'd given them the best gift and who'd screwed them over with something that wasn't even worth returning. A few shoppers descended on the town to make the most difficult of returns: handcrafted items. It was hard to say a pair of mittens was the wrong size or the painted jacquard stemware was something one already had.

As the artist accepted the returns, the lies were told.

"I love them, but I have six pairs already."

"I have a matching hat that you might like to go with it."

Pause.

"I wish I had known. I just bought one yesterday."

Nothing was open on Christmas Day. Another lie.

The mittens were, indeed, ugly.

Lies all round. That happened in shops and households all over town.

Sandra and Harper Berkley had a Christmas holiday that not a soul on earth would want. Their daughter was dead. *Gone.* She was in the chiller at the Kitsap County Morgue in Port Orchard, waiting for the indignity of a knife tip down her skin, a saw through her skull and the cool voice of the county's forensic pathologist as she gently picked through the flesh and bone of what had once been a beautiful girl.

And while it was the end of Katelyn's life, it was the start of something else.

Katelyn was Sandra's last great hope. And a kitchen appliance in the bathtub had stolen it from her. She surveyed her situation and dealt with her disappointment and heartache the best way she could.

She threw a poison-tipped dart at Harper.

"You know, if we didn't have that stupid restaurant, you'd have been around more."

He shook his head. He'd expected her attack. "Everyone works, Sandy. Are you really going to blame me for Katelyn's death?"

"Daughters need their fathers."

Harper stared hard at his wife, weighing a rebuttal that would drive the point home without setting her off. "They also need a sober mother."

It was the wrong response.

Sandra balled up her fist and jabbed at Harper. He stepped back, his wobbly wife no match for his still-agile reflexes. When the emotion of the moment cooled enough for her to realize what she'd done, Sandra started to cry.

Harper put his arms around her and cried too.

They'd been bonded by the joy of the birth of their daughter. She'd been the glue that held them together when their marriage was at its most fragile.

As they had lain in bed in the early morning hours after their daughter had died, Sandra cried quietly into her pillow. Her eyes were now red, a color born of agonizing grief and too much alcohol. She wondered how Harper could have found enough solace to actually sleep.

Yet, Harper had been far from asleep. He'd only been pretending, to avoid talking to Sandra. Everything out of her mouth was tinged with anger and blame. Sandra was that kind of person: bitter, jealous, and completely unsatisfied with her lot in life.

Where some might have found pleasure from seeing the joy on others' faces, Sandra merely wondered why God hadn't given *her* whatever it was that *they* had.

A new car.
A bigger house.
Diamonds instead of CCZs.
The happiness that came with relationships.
A daughter who would lift her out of Port Gamble.

Side by side in silence, both wondered if the death of their daughter would bring them closer.

Or would it be the excuse they'd sought to end their marriage?

All over Port Gamble, the young, the old and those close and distant to Katelyn thought about her. As she lay on her bed and typed on her laptop, Taylor Ryan could see the inky water of Port Gamble Bay. She had been overcome by emotion in a way that seemed more painful than cathartic. Her eyes finally stopped raining.

She texted Beth:

): I feel selfish. Seems wrong to grieve for Katelyn and be happy for my life. Accidents happen. Still sad.

On the other hand, Hayley didn't fight her thoughts about Katelyn. She let them tumble from her, texting her ponderings to Colton about what could possibly have led to this very moment.

Katelyn was imploding over Starla. Seems so unfair. Instead of getting help, she was shoved aside like trash. People aren't trash. No one deserves to be treated like that. Katelyn just wanted Starla to like her again. I know some people think that Katelyn had some kind of girl crush on Starla, but that's not true. That's just the kind of thing mean girls say to make everyone laugh.

Night owls Beth Lee and her mother, Kim, were still very much awake in house number 25 on Olympian Avenue. While they watched late evening TV together (something that Kim said provided mother-daughter bonding time), Beth got out her phone and started texting. She was a facile texter, easily keeping an eye glued to the movie and the other on the task at hand. Every once in a while, Kim would chuckle and pat her daughter on the leg, and Beth would pause her texting to make eye contact. The minute Kim looked over at the screen, Beth would start up again.

Might not act sad, but I don't do sad all that well. Makes my eyes puff. School counselor says I mask my pain with sarcasm. Saw Katelyn's mom crying. Just think we all let her down.

As her husband buzz-saw snored next to her, Valerie Ryan said a silent prayer. She wanted to send something out into the universe that would provide some healing. She was a believer in the power of a positive message.

Katelyn, stay close to your mom and dad. They need you and they will never stop loving you. Where we are living now is not the end of things. You aren't dust. You aren't alive only in a memory.

Almost two hundred miles away in Portland, Colton James felt sick to his stomach about what had transpired just a few doors down from his house in Port Gamble. He wasn't stunned about it, like his mother and father were. Colton had seen Katelyn over the past few months as she declined from a reasonably upbeat, occasionally moody teenager to a more sullen and distracted person. He read the text message from Hayley and texted back. Usually he was a brief texter, just a few words or even a solitary letter to convey what he wanted to say. This time he wrote out his thoughts more fully. He wanted to share. He needed to make a point.

Bummed about her. She was acting strangely lately, but always nice to me and my mom. She got my mom's Pampered Chef crap at her house. Made 4 kinds of pizza with my mom. She really liked Katelyn. Said she was special. Wish it didn't happen.

Next door to the Berkleys, Starla Larsen picked up her phone and touched the Facebook icon. There were lots of messages posted about Katelyn on her wall, as well as just about every other wall belonging to anyone who attended Kingston High. She went over to Katelyn's wall. Starla hadn't been there in a while.

Katelyn's profile picture was of the two of them together, taken when they were Girl Scout Daisies. Both little girls were smiling widely to show off their missing front teeth. Starla hated that photograph for the longest time, but just then it brought a sad smile to her face. She decided she should weigh in with a post on Katelyn's wall too. She liked to post snarky things about people and then add a smiley face to act like she was joking when she really wasn't. She knew she did that because other kids expected her to be sharp, funny and a little caustic; it was because of the way she looked—she was better than just pretty.

So sad about Katie. Don't know how I will sleep 2night. The world was never very kind to her. Hugs 2U Katie.

Starla reached for the nail polish remover as she sat there for a while watching the "Likes" come one after another. Several kids posted comments too.

WE'RE THINKING OF U, STARLA. KATIE SEEMED SWEET. WISH I KNEW HER BTR. WORLD SUX BIG TIME. LUV U, STAR! BE STRONG!

Starla looked over at her cache of Sephora nail lacquers set up like a ten-pin bowling alley. In the back she saw the green polish that she and Katelyn had used in eighth grade when they each bought bottles and decided to glam up for St. Patrick's Day. The color was more evergreen than kelly. The memory brought a genuine smile to her face as she turned the Rimmel London bottle in her hands. The color was called Envy.

Tears came to Starla's crystal-blue eyes, brought on by a mix of regret, sorrow and guilt.

I'm so sorry, Katie, she said to herself. *I wish you knew that.*

And finally, not far away, one person got online and started deleting the contents of a file folder marked "katelyn." Inside were copies of emails, messages and photographs that had meant to trap and hurt the girl. Each item had been designed as payback.

Delete.

Delete.

Delete.

CHAPTER FIVE

It was the destiny of a place like Port Gamble. It snowed hard *after* Christmas. The land management company that kept the town in pristine and marketable form would have offered up a virgin (if there was one handy, that is) to have a little snow sprinkle the town the week before the holidays when it had its annual old-fashioned Christmas celebration, "In the St. Nick of Time." But no such luck. It had been cold, wet and rainy. When the snow finally came, it dumped five inches—a blizzard by western Washington standards. If school had been in session, it easily would have been canceled.

Kids in the area were annoyed about the timing of it all as well. Snow was no good to them if it didn't mean a snow day or two. They were *already* on vacation. It was an utter waste of an arctic blast.

Hayley and Taylor trudged through the snow to hang out with Beth Lee for the afternoon. Beth and her boyfriend, Zander Tomlinson, had broken up the day before Christmas and, with Katelyn Berkley's unexpected death, the topic, outside of rampant text messages, had been tabled.

"I had no choice but to drop him," Beth told them, elaborating on her text message:

Dumped Z. Deets later.

Hayley was the first to pounce. "What did you mean you dumped him? Clearly, you had a choice."

Beth, who seemed fixated on a zit on her chin, didn't look at the twins as she spoke. She sat on the floor in front of the fireplace with a mirror in her hand and a pair of tweezers in the other. "I found a really cute dress and I had to have it."

"Yeah?" Taylor said, taking a seat on the Lees' way-too-big-for-the-room brown velvet sectional in house number 25. "Go on."

Beth tightened her chin and picked at her pimple. "I didn't have any money left over. I knew he was going to get me something for Christmas and I didn't have a thing to give him. So I dumped him. Called him from the mall and said I wasn't feeling it anymore."

Taylor shook her head. "You're so not kidding? You dumped him because you spent your Christmas cash?"

Beth looked up. "Yeah. So what? I'd rather hurt him than look stupid or cheap."

"Right," Taylor said. "Looking cheap or selfish is way worse than hurting someone. He really liked you!"

Beth ignored the sarcasm, and Hayley spoke up. "I hate to say it, but you're acting like Starla, Beth."

"I'll take that as kind of a compliment," she said.

"It wasn't meant to be a positive reflection on you or the situation."

"Whatever. Anyway, I heard something about her," Beth said, changing the subject like she was baiting a hook.

Of course, Starla Larsen-centric gossip was always good. She was the Port Gamble girl everyone love-hated.

Taylor leaned forward expectantly. "Are you gonna tell us or what? Just pop that disgusting zit already and spill it!"

"That's so gross," Beth said. "And kind of mean." She waited a beat, watching the twins, measuring their interest in all she had to say. The hook had been set.

Another beat.

"Starla and Katelyn had a major falling-out," she finally said.

"How major?" Taylor asked.

"Big-time. Before she died, Katelyn told her mother that she hated Starla and that she wished Starla was dead or something."

This time Hayley pressed for more. Her father would have been proud. "How do you know she said that?"

Beth rotated the hand mirror to get a better look at herself. "I heard Mrs. Larsen and Mrs. Berkley talking a few weeks ago. They were in the store buying coffee or hairspray or whatever it is women of their age need to get through the day. Mrs. Larsen was defending Starla, saying that it had been a big misunderstanding. But Mrs. Berkley wasn't having any of it."

Beth stopped talking. Her face beamed with a satisfied grin. "Got it," she said, as she held out her tweezers. "Popped and *no* nasty hole. Who wants something to eat?"

Hayley and Taylor, thoroughly grossed out by what they'd seen, shook their heads in unison.

"That's it? Was there more?" Taylor asked, pushing.

"I really didn't listen, Taylor," Beth said, clearly ready to move on from the Starla/Katelyn drama. "I saw that new kid Eli there, and I was trying to get him to notice me."

Taylor smiled to herself and looked at her sister. Despite Beth's constant need to be aloof, pretending indifference all the time, she knew who was who. "Hay-Tay" had always been her way of pretending to put up a wall. So what if Beth was completely self-absorbed? She was also an astute judge of what was worth passing along *and* when. They liked her.

Besides, in Port Gamble there weren't a lot of choices for the mantle of best friend.

"But, Beth, didn't you really like Zander?" Hayley asked. "Of all your boyfriends, he seemed to stay in your good graces the longest."

"And that's no easy feat," Taylor added.

Beth curled up on the couch. "Is this pick-on-me time or what?"

"No, not at all," Hayley said.

Beth shrugged a little. "Too bad. I like it when you tease me. Makes me feel kind of like I'm the third twin," she said, pausing a beat. "The smart one. The *pretty* one."

Both twins knew there was some truth to that. Not that Beth was prettier or smarter, but that Beth was sometimes lonely being an only child. They'd never known a moment when they hadn't had each other.

"You can be whatever you want to be, Beth. But please, promise that next time you'll pay attention when you're in the vicinity of some good info."

Beth smiled. "All right. And I'll make sure that you're two of the top ten people I'll tell first."

Hayley's and Taylor's phones buzzed.

"That must be Mom," Hayley said. "She's spamming us with mass texts."

Taylor looked at the message from their mother and closed the phone. She looked a little upset, but she tried to hide it as she slid the phone back into her pocket.

"What's up?" Beth asked, watching Hayley as she shut her phone with the same kind of reaction.

"A reporter found out that Katelyn was in the crash," Hayley explained. "She's writing a story about Katelyn, her death and the crash."

Again, the crash.

"Freak! Haven't they milked that one for all it's worth by now?" Beth asked.

"Not from this angle," Taylor said. "Katelyn surviving the crash only to die now makes her death even sadder."

Inside, she could feel her heart rate escalate. The idea of revisiting the crash, talking about it and having others talk about it again made her feel sick to her stomach too. It was funny how the word *crash* could have that strange effect on her. It didn't have to be *the* crash. Just any crash. It wasn't because the memories of what happened were so awful to relive.

It was because neither she nor her sister had any recollections whatsoever of what happened that rainy afternoon all those years ago.

Not a single one.

CHAPTER SIX

What remained of Katelyn Berkley was transferred onto a stainless steel table ringed by a gleaming trough of running water. *Gushing water.* The rushing flow around Katelyn would help eliminate all the blood that would spew forth once deep, hacking cuts were made on her torso. Her eyes were closed and, even more positively and importantly, *she was dead.* And yet, for anyone who knew Katelyn, there was a deserved measure of empathy for the humiliation of it all. Indeed, it was only one of the many indignities that are required when a young, healthy person dies. Strangers would be looking at her body. *Her naked body.* Then they'd begin the practice of cutting her open like a split Chinook salmon as they reviewed and measured the contents of her chest, her stomach and even her brain. In the instance that she took her last breath, she'd unwittingly given herself over to strangers—strangers with blades. If she'd killed herself and sought refuge from pain, real or imagined, she'd made a mistake.

Katelyn didn't fade away or cross over to some kind of nothingness. Instead, she ended up as a piece of evidence, a high beam of light on her, in the county morgue in Port Orchard—a place where she would have refused to be caught dead in… unless she were really dead.

And there'd be no say in it, wherever she was.

While no one seriously suspected foul play in Katelyn's death—there wasn't any reason to, really—the Kitsap County Coroner's Office protocol required the most invasive of techniques before

Sandra and Harper Berkley could lay their only daughter to rest in Port Gamble's Buena Vista Cemetery. And, what with reduced holiday staffing and ensuing police investigation, it would take a while.

Rest. As if rest were even possible since her parents were unable to stop arguing long enough to make sure that their baby was remembered for all the love she'd given them, rather than the pain she'd left them to endure.

There she was, on the pathologist's table, her green painted toenails facing up, ready to relinquish any last shred of modesty. Katelyn Melissa Berkley had died a horrible, tragic death in the bathtub of her Port Gamble home. She'd arrived by ambulance late, late Christmas night, and, like some leftover holiday ham, she'd been held for three days in the cooler of the county's basement morgue in an old house on Sidney Avenue, next to the Kitsap County Courthouse.

With her assistant looking on, county forensic pathologist Birdy Waterman passed an ultraviolet light over Katelyn's skin. She started with the dead girl's neck and moved the beam down her small breasts and stomach.

"There's some cutting on her arms. More on her stomach. New ones on her arms," she said in a matter-of-fact voice that was a mask for her emotions. Among the things that Dr. Waterman loathed above all others was a child on her stainless steel table.

"Cause of death?" asked the assistant, a faux-hawked newbie to the office named Terry Morris.

Dr. Waterman shook her head. "No, no," she said. "I'm sure you'd like to wrap this up so you can go text someone or something, but here we do things right, methodically, and by the book." She looked over her glasses with a kind look.

No need to make the new kid hate me. There's plenty of time for that later, she thought.

"Let's get there one step at a time," she said, returning her unflinching gaze back to the dead girl.

She pointed to the cuts on Katelyn's thigh and frowned. They were the newest. *Fresh.*

"Not deep at all," she said.

"The girl was f-ed up," Terry said.

Dr. Waterman was of the Makah Tribe, with a medical degree from the University of Washington in Seattle; she was a serious woman who thought that death deserved respect one hundred percent of the time. She glared at Terry. He was going to be a challenge. But she was up for it.

"You don't know me well yet, Terry. But I don't talk like that. And I don't want my assistants talking like that."

"It isn't like the dead can hear," he said.

She shot a lightning-fast look at him with her dark eyes and immediately returned her attention to Katelyn.

"How do you know?" she asked.

Terry, a young man with large green eyes, maybe too large for his small face, rolled them upward, but kept his mouth clamped shut—for a change. He was learning.

Death by electrocution is exceedingly rare. Dr. Waterman could recall only two other examples of such cases in the county. One involved a Lucky Jim's Tribal casino worker who had become electrified when he was working with some faulty wiring that fed power to the slot machines. He had assumed his coworker had cut the power source.

It was, Dr. Waterman had thought at the time, *a very unlucky way to die.*

The other involved a pretty, young Bremerton woman who was out walking her Dalmatian after high winds pummeled the region, dropping power lines and blacking out half the county. When her exuberant dog ran ahead, the woman used the moment to tie a loosened shoelace. When she bent down, her knee made contact with a thousand volts of electricity from a power line obscured by fallen tree branches.

Katelyn's case was different, of course. Her death was the result of a household appliance coming into contact with the water in her bathtub.

Dr. Waterman pointed to obvious burns on the right side of Katelyn's torso. "The contact with the voltage was there," she said. The burns were severe, leaving the skin so red it was nearly cooked.

"Yeah, I see," Terry said, not wanting to get slapped down for any editorializing or joke making. It took a lot of personal restraint for him not to say, for example, *Watt are you talking about?*

Next, the cutting and the sawing. The noise of a human body being violated by steel is horrendous—even for those who do it every day. The saw Birdy Waterman used emitted a noise somewhere between a Sears electric carving knife and a small chainsaw. Some medical examiners pipe music into their autopsy suites, turning them into hell's concept of a downtown after-hours club. *Way after-hours.* Others turn up the volume on their playlists during the internal exam. Not Birdy Waterman. She hummed a little and watched her assistant's green eyes turn a little greener.

"Some fractured ribs here," she said, indicating faint lines where the bones had mended.

"Abuse?" Terry asked, peering over the pathologist's shoulder to get a better look.

Dr. Waterman shook her head. "Medical history from the father says that Katelyn was in a bus accident when she was five. No other hospitalizations."

Katelyn's heart and other organs were removed from her body, weighed, measured and examined.

What Birdy Waterman saw confirmed her suspicions. Katelyn Berkley's heart had stopped beating because of trauma resulting from the electric shock.

"So is it a homicide?" Terry asked. "Accidental death? Suicide?"

Dr. Waterman raised the plastic shield that had kept the spatter of blood and tissue from her face.

"The girl had emotional problems," she said, indicating the scars from the cuts the victim had made on herself. Most were old and faded, but some were quite new. "And while it is highly unlikely that she tried to kill herself with the espresso machine, it appears that's what happened."

"So how are you going to rule?" Terry asked.

Dr. Waterman took more photos and removed her green latex gloves and face mask, which were splattered with brain matter and bone chips.

"Accidental," she said. "The police saw no evidence of foul play at the scene to indicate homicide. And the parents don't need to live with the added heartache of wondering what they did wrong—even if they did something wrong. She's dead. It's over."

She started toward the door of the shower and dressing room.

"You can close. No staples. Small stitches, Terry. She's a young girl. I don't want the funeral home to think we do the work of a blind seamstress. Katelyn…" She paused and looked at the paperwork that came with the body. "Katelyn Melissa Berkley deserves better. She's only fifteen."

"So? She's dead," Terry muttered under his breath, hoping the woman with the sharp scalpel and soft heart didn't hear him.

But she did.

"I'll remember that when I see you on my table," she said.

If there was a case to be made for waiting out the geekdom that is middle school before writing someone off as a complete loser, Colton James was Exhibit A. During the summer between middle school and high school, Colton had morphed into something of a hottie.

Colton was one-sixteenth S'Klallam, the native people who'd lived in Port Gamble when it was called Memalucet. He had tawny skin, a mass of unusually unruly dark hair and the kind of black eyes that looked almost blue in the sunshine. He'd been the skinny boy who dragged the girls to the edges of Port Gamble Bay in search of crabs, oysters or anything else that might be good to eat. He joked that he did so because he was Native American, but really it was because his parents didn't always have much money. Colton's dad, Henry, was an Inuit fisherman, often in Alaska for the season, and his mother, Shania, was a woman who suffered from agoraphobia. She almost never left the house. People whispered that Shania James was a hermit and that she was lazy and too fat to do anything.

None of that was true, of course. The truth was far more sinister. Shania had been carjacked in a Safeway parking lot in Silverdale when Colton was two. With Colton secured in his car seat, the man who held Shania captive did things to her that she never talked about. Not to the police. Not to her family. At least, not that anyone had ever heard. Only the Ryans had a clue that Shania had been the victim of a violent crime; once, when Kevin was mowing the lawn, she had called over to him from the window.

She had held a copy of his book, *Innocence Delayed*, and waved it at him.

"You got it right, Kevin."

"What's that, Shania?"

"The author's note in your book. That's what. Sometimes people can't get over things done to them. Dr. Phil is wrong. We can't always get better."

"Screw Dr. Phil," Kevin said.

Shania gave a slight nod of agreement. She closed the window and disappeared into the house.

Colton had always been the boy next door, literally. Hayley and Taylor never knew a summer's day when they didn't chat with Colton, get into some harmless trouble at the Port Gamble General Store or sleep out under the stars.

He in his yard; they in theirs.

And then all of a sudden he seemed to have grown up. Both Hayley and Taylor noticed it. The girls found themselves attracted to him, a quasi-brother or sidekick at best, in a way that was unsettling and peculiar.

One day when he was out in his backyard washing the old Toyota Camry that his mom never drove but couldn't get rid of, Colton called over to Hayley. She'd just come home from the beach in a tangerine bikini top and faded denim shorts, all sticky and smelling of sunscreen. Her hair had lightened, and the bridge of her nose was sprayed with brand-new freckles.

"You want to help me dry?" he asked.

She didn't want to, but because he had his shirt off, she'd found reason enough to cross the yard and pick up a chamois.

It turned out it was more buffing than drying, but Hayley didn't mind. She stooped down low and started on the wheel well.

"I was thinking," Colton said, his teeth all the more white as they contrasted with his deeply tanned skin, "maybe you would want to go out sometime."

"You want to go out with me? What do you mean *out*?" she asked.

"Out."

"You mean like on a date?"

"Call it whatever. But, yeah," he said, now crouching close to her. "What do you think?"

What Hayley really thought was that it was strange. She liked Colton. She always had. Taylor liked him too. They'd even talked about how he'd changed and looked older, stronger and sexier, which trumped all previous feelings they had had that he was like a brother to them.

"What about Taylor?" she finally asked.

Colton laughed. "I'm not into that."

Hayley narrowed her blue eyes. "You're not into what exactly?"

"Never mind. I was asking *you* out. Just you and me."

Hayley wanted to drop the chamois and rush home to ask Taylor if she minded. She hoped she wouldn't. She knew she *might*. Her mind was reeling.

"Yes, I would like that," she said. "When?"

He smiled broadly. "How about tomorrow night? Want to see what's playing in Poulsbo?"

Hayley didn't answer right away. The only movies out were dumb romantic comedies, but she didn't want to turn Colton down.

Colton immediately caught her vibe. "Nah, never mind. There's nothing but trash out. Let's bag the movies and do something else."

In that moment, Hayley Ryan really saw Colton James as someone more special, more in sync with her than just about anyone she could name.

"It's a date," she said, turning her attention to the car but watching Colton in the reflection of the shiny hubcap. Her thoughts were a jumble just then and she couldn't make sense of her feelings. There was no doubt she was jubilant over the fact that he had asked her out, but as she touched the car and moved the chamois in small circles against the chrome, she felt tiny pricks of sadness in her fingertips.

What was it, she would always wonder, *about that car that made me feel that way?*

The night Katelyn died, Hayley thought about that feeling she'd had back when they were polishing the Toyota and planning that first date. The energy that came to her was similar to something she was feeling now.

She also thought of Colton, whom she texted the minute she heard the news about Katelyn. He was in Portland with his dad's relatives and wouldn't be home until the day after school started. His mother had to be coaxed out of the house for the trip.

Hayley: thinking of Katelyn. Sad, sad, sad.

Colton: sorry. What happened?

Hayley: not sure. No one really knows. Suicide? Accident?

Colton: sux

Hayley: miss u

Colton: u2

When Taylor caught Hayley texting Colton, she just rolled her eyes.

Sometimes those two were just SO annoying.

CHAPTER SEVEN

Moira Windsor knew that greatness was never going to come from writing for the "What's Up" section of the *North Kitsap Herald*, but at twenty-three, she'd been saddled with student loans and no prospects for a better job, at least until the economy bounced back. Whenever that was supposed to happen, no one seemed to really know. Moira was also being strategic. She knew that a toehold in a real journalism position was a must in building the credibility that she was sure she could spin into a spot next to Savannah Guthrie on *Today*.

A slender redhead with a nice figure that she used to her advantage, Moira waited outside house number 19, composing her thoughts before knocking on the Ryans' front door. Even though it was freezing outside, she unzipped her jacket a little to showcase what God and a Victoria's Secret push-up bra had given her. She peered through the six panels of rippled glass that ran alongside the solid, painted door. She pulled back and planted a smile on her face as footsteps approached.

Kevin Ryan, wearing gray sweatpants and a ratty, stained Got Crime? T-shirt that Valerie had tried to discard by stuffing it into the bottom of a Goodwill bag more than once, swung open the door and smiled.

A little cleavage always works. Moira had learned that technique trying to get men to reveal things that they ordinarily might not. All told, Moira had about an eighty-seven percent success rate with it.

"Mr. Ryan? I'm with the *North Kitsap Herald*. I'm a huge fan. Can we talk?"

Kevin studied her, then looked at her eyes. He'd seen that purported "huge fan" look before a dozen times. She was young, excited. Like most reporters who sought an interview, this one probably was more interested in advancing her dream of writing books than in interviewing him about anything he'd been doing.

"I'm sorry," he said, hesitating a moment. "I didn't catch your name."

"Moira Windsor," she said with the kind of confidence that suggested he ought to know who she was. "I'm with 'What's Up.'"

Kevin never turned down a chance for publicity, but he had one cardinal rule on the subject: *Never do any media unless you have a book to sell.*

"Right. Moira, I'm sorry, but I didn't get a heads-up from anyone at the *Herald* that you'd be visiting. I don't have a book coming out."

"I'm a huge fan of your work," she repeated.

"You said that already," Kevin said as politely as possible.

Moira fidgeted with her purse and pulled out a slim reporter's notebook.

"Actually," she said, opening the notebook, "I wanted to talk to you about Katelyn Berkley. I apologize for not having the whole background yet. My editor called me and told me the basics. I'm all about research, so bear with me. Go ahead, now tell me."

Valerie had warned him that a reporter was snooping around, but Kevin didn't like where the impromptu—no, *ambush*—interview was going.

"Why would you want to write about her? It was a personal matter. A family tragedy."

Moira ignored the warning that she felt was mixed into his response. "Yes, a suicide or an accident. I get that."

"Of course you do," he said. He could feel his adrenaline pulse a little, and he willed himself to stay calm. He might need her one day for publicity, but not that day, not about that subject. "And as far as I know, your paper doesn't cover personal tragedies."

Moira nodded. "This one is different."

If Moira was going to press the point, Kevin was going to let her. "How so?" he asked, clearly testing her.

"I think you know why."

He did, but he stayed firm in his refusal to say so. "No, I don't."

"Katelyn was in the Hood Canal Bridge crash."

Kevin glanced away for a second, his awareness no longer on the annoying young woman standing in front of him but on his girls, who were just steps away from the door.

"I guess she was," he said. "So what?"

"Well, so were your daughters... and now they are the only surviving children of the accident."

Kevin's jaw tightened. "We don't talk about the crash."

"The paper really would like to do something... you know, coming on the heels of Katelyn's tragic death and the ten-year anniversary of the accident."

A child's death plus a ten-year anniversary equaled a newspaper reporter's one-two punch for a spot on the front page.

"I'm sorry. Can't, *won't*, help you."

"I can mention your last book."

"Thanks, but no thanks. Please do yourself a favor and, more important, the people of this town a favor, by not pursuing this."

"I can't do that, and you of all people should understand. You've always been about the truth, haven't you?"

Kevin Ryan nodded, his casual smile no longer in place. "Please go, Ms. Windsor. We're all out of patience here."

He closed the door harder than a polite man might have done. He couldn't help it. The ten-year anniversary of the crash was looming and with each minute passing, it brought a deluge of hurt and more confusion.

No one knew what had caused the crash or why only three girls and one adult had survived.

"Who was that?" Hayley asked as her father turned around.

"Reporter," Kevin said.

"Why was she talking about Katelyn?"

"Looking for a story, that's all."

"Oh," she said.

Kevin started toward the kitchen, but Hayley's words stopped him like a rope of razor wire.

"When are you going to talk to us about the crash, Dad?"

He turned around, his heart beating faster and his face now flushed. "We've talked about it already."

"Really, Dad? I still have questions about it," Hayley said.

"Look," he said, clearly not wanting to have another word about it with Hayley, Taylor or probably anyone else, "can we just table it?"

Now Hayley's red face signaled her own frustration. "Table it for how long? Are we not going to talk about it for the rest of our lives?"

Kevin refused to answer. Instead, he put his hand up as if the act could really just push it all away. Dads all over the world thought they could win an argument with a teenage girl. Those dads were pretty stupid.

"Sorry, honey," he said. "But not right now. Please don't ask again."

Sometimes good needed a hand in dealing with evil. Both Taylor and Hayley knew that statement to be truer than the fact that their eyes were blue or that their dog, Hedda, a long-haired dachshund, was a bed hog of the highest order. They did wonder, however, if it had always been that way in the outside world. Sometimes it seemed that beyond the borders of Port Gamble, people were caught up in so much conflict, so much hate, incessant evil—whatever word a person would choose to call the ugly that was routinely done to each other.

The Ryan twins had a slightly warped front-row seat to evil and the criminal justice system. As a little girl, their mom lived in a prison run by her father, and she now worked as a psychiatric nurse. Their dad made his living writing about murderers. What they unequivocally knew from their parents was that there were two kinds of evil: accidental *and* intended.

The twins, and especially Taylor, could empathize with those who were accidentally evil, like the drunk driver in Seattle who staggered behind the wheel and plowed into a group of teenagers waiting to get into a club. At least there was hope for those who were truly sorry.

However, the girls felt no mercy for those who perpetrated evil intentionally. Their souls were dark and always would be.

CHAPTER EIGHT

Hayley Ryan could feel a twinge of panic as she turned into the alley that ran behind the houses on Olympian Avenue. She *felt* it in her bones. Her father always told her and her sister to listen carefully to what their hearts and minds might be telling them.

"There's a reason your hair stands up on the back of your neck," he had said, affecting his best *Investigation Discovery* voice, an octave deeper, but still Dad. "It's a warning to be careful. Trust your feelings."

"Hair standing up anywhere is gross, Dad," Taylor said.

Kevin Ryan would not be denied his point. "Maybe so," he replied. "But survivors of a serial killer are the ones who heed the feeling and act on it. Saving your life, Taylor, is never gross."

Hayley smiled. It was a slightly tight grin, the kind meant to contain a more overt response, like an out-and-out laugh. She and her sister had grown up with a father who made his living telling the stories of the vilest things people do to others. In doing so, he never missed the opportunity to push advice on how to survive even the scariest, most dangerous situation.

"See that guy in the camo jacket over there?" he asked the twins one time when the family was shopping at Central Market in nearby Poulsbo. "Say he's a serial killer and he corners you in this parking lot."

Valerie rolled her eyes upward. "Why does everyone have to be a serial killer?"

Taylor piped up. "Because they're the best, right, Dad?"

"Yes, the *best*," Kevin said, nodding at what he knew was a tiny dig. "The best in terms of sales for books, but more important, they're the best in making sure their victims are never left alive to tell their stories."

"Let's get back to the camo guy," Hayley said, eager to continue the role-play. "What about him?"

Kevin lingered by the car door and spoke quietly, watching the kid with the carts, trying to keep his eye contact on his girls. Eye contact, he always said, was very, very important. "Say he helps you to your car and when you open the trunk he pushes you inside."

"Easy," Taylor said. "Jab his eyes out with the car keys."

"I would scream as loud as I could," Hayley said, sure that her response was the better of the two. After all, car keys might not be handy—especially if you're a teenager and don't have a car or even a learner's permit.

Valerie shifted on her feet, eager to get going. "You shop somewhere else," she said flatly.

Kevin made a face at Valerie. "All except your mom's are the right answers. But there's one thing to remember above all others."

The girls waited. Their dad was big on the cliffhanger. Sometimes his sentences ended in such a way that the pause invited more curiosity, a kind of verbal begging to turn the page.

"You only have one second to save yourself," he said. "And that's before camo guy is pushing you into the trunk. If the trunk goes down on top of you, well, you're probably as good as dead."

"Only one in a thousand abducted girls lives if taken to a new location," Hayley said, recalling a dinner table conversation.

"Right," Kevin confirmed, satisfied that the day's spur-of-the-moment crime safety lesson had yielded the correct response. "And I can't have either of you girls be the one who doesn't make it."

The camo guy who'd been the focus of the girls' attention was about thirty-five, with pockmarked skin and scraggly red hair. He smiled warily in their direction as he pushed his cart toward his truck. He certainly looked creepy.

"I bet he lives with his mother," Hayley said.

Taylor nodded. "Yeah, probably."

Those lessons and countless others came back to Hayley as she made her way home from Beth's house, four days after Katelyn died.

It was undeniable. The feeling. The damned hair standing up.

Someone was watching her, tracking her. It was that strange feeling, that compulsion that causes someone to suddenly cross to the other side of the street.

Some girls actually courted the feeling and found some kind of bizarre romanticism in being stalked. The Ryan twins never felt that—not once, and especially not when their dad had had a stalker and the fallout from the woman's twisted fantasies had been devastating to the family. Years later, it was still remembered—quietly so, but nevertheless never forgotten.

Hayley saw nothing that evening as she hurried home on Olympian Avenue. She just had the feeling. She didn't really *hear* anything. It could have been the winter wind or an animal moving in the half-frozen ivy.

Whatever it was, it nipped at her consciousness and it chilled her to the bone.

A moment later, a thread of a thought sped through her mind. It was about Katelyn, Starla and Robert Pattinson, of all people.

Hayley was sure she didn't get it all right. *Robert Pattinson?*

CHAPTER NINE

New Year's Day at the Ryan household smelled of coffee, orange juice and maple syrup. Valerie had sliced a loaf of brioche and had the already eggy bread soaking in a mixture of eggs, cream, cinnamon, and nutmeg. Taylor loved the way their mother fixed French toast. It was the best breakfast thing she made, by far. Hayley was more of a waffle girl, but French toast with maple syrup and peanut butter was pretty hard for her to resist too.

While the French toast sizzled in a foamy sea of butter on the stovetop griddle, Taylor noticed her parents' mugs were low on coffee and she topped them off with a splash more.

"Couldn't sleep last night," she said, returning the coffee carafe to the heating element.

Valerie turned from the griddle. "I know, honey," she said. "I woke up thinking of Katelyn too."

"A terrible tragedy," Kevin said over the morning's *Kitsap Sun*.

"An accident like that should never, ever have happened," Valerie said. "Honestly, what in the world was Katelyn thinking?"

"An accident? Who says?" Taylor asked.

Valerie stacked three pieces of French toast on a plate and handed them to Taylor. "Your dad does."

Kevin set down the paper. "I talked to the coroner. This one's going to fall under the 'tragedy' heading, a freak accident. That doesn't make things any better, of course, for the Berkleys."

Hayley, who had been mostly silent, spoke up. "Do you know if suicide has been completely ruled out, Dad?"

Kevin's lips tightened and he shook his head. "They don't think so. Anything is possible, but only her history of…" He stopped, to search for the words. "Her history of emotional problems could be an indicator of suicide, but the evidence they've gathered doesn't point to it."

Hayley weighed her father's words. "But if they aren't sure it was a suicide and it could have been a freak accident, couldn't it just as easily have been a homicide?"

Kevin shook his head. "I don't know, honey. I don't think so. But really, we might never know what happened to Katelyn."

Hayley looked into her sister's eyes. There was no need to speak. Both of them knew what the other was thinking.

Oh yes, we will.

Beth Lee accepted that she would never be tall. Her parents were both short. She knew her wisp of physical presence might cause her to get shunted off to the side. Sure, she had great hair—black and thick, and near-mirror reflective. Besides the fact that she was the only Asian in her elementary school, she had seldom stood out. At her mother Kim's insistence, Beth wore long pigtails and ribbons that matched her outfit until fourth grade, when she could no longer take it and took scissors to one side.

Her mother ripped her a new one when she got home and made her go to school for a week looking lopsided.

"You want to stand out, so now you do," Kim Lee had said.

After her DIY haircut and resulting humiliation, a line in the sand had been forged, Hells Canyon deep. Beth Lee would never let anyone, not her mother, not her best friend, tell her how to look or dress. She didn't want to be the dutiful daughter, the brainy Asian, the girl who was anything different than the others who lived in Port Gamble.

Hayley and Taylor Ryan were her best friends, though she seemed to consider them a single entity. Hay-Tay were the only ones in town who didn't try to mold her into something she wasn't. They simply let her be. If Beth wanted to be a vegan for a month, fine. If she wanted to go Goth and wear a dog collar around town, the Ryan twins didn't make a big deal out of it.

Lately, she'd taken to shopping exclusively at Forever 21 in the Kitsap Mall in Silverdale, where she purchased outfit after outfit. She never saw a dress or shirt with a nonfunctioning zipper that she didn't proclaim so totally *her*.

The only other Port Gamble woman who shopped regularly at Forever 21 was Starla Larsen's mother, a woman about whom others gossiped, saying that she never saw a zipper she didn't want to undo.

Beth remarked on it. "Saw Mrs. Larsen at Forever."

"Was she shopping for Starla?" Hayley asked as the two sat on her bed waiting for Taylor to come upstairs with snacks so they could eat, chat and waste the last few days before school restarted on January 3.

"Shopping for herself," Beth said. "Same as always. She wears club clothes to work, I guess."

Taylor entered the room carrying a couple of Diet Cokes and a can of Ranch Pringles.

"Who wears club clothes to work?" she asked.

"Starla's mom."

"Did you talk to her?"

Beth took a second. "Not really. I pretended I didn't see her, but she nabbed me by the checkout counter."

"Did she say anything about Katelyn?" Hayley asked.

"Something about how she saw it coming. Katelyn was a sad girl. Whatever."

Taylor looked upset. "'Saw it coming'?"

Beth shrugged. "I didn't ask. I wanted out of there. I was afraid she was going to corner me and force me to come in for a haircut."

"If she saw something was wrong, if she saw it coming, then she should have done something about it," Hayley said.

"I guess so. Can we talk about something else? All this talk about Katelyn is kind of boring me."

Taylor looked at Hayley, her eyes popping. Neither one of them knew how it was that Beth Lee could possibly be their best friend.

But she was.

CHAPTER TEN

Before leaving for work at the hospital, Valerie Ryan made cookies, *fresh*—not Christmas retreads that had been moved from platter to smaller plate as their numbers declined. She boxed them up in a Tupperware container for the girls to run over to the Berkley place. There was no bow or ribbon. It was a gesture, not a gift, to the family down the lane who'd suffered the cruelest blow in a season meant for joy and togetherness. Valerie watched a row of cars head down the highway that morning, looking for places to park as Harper and Sandra gathered in their grief with family members and close friends.

The girls planned on paying their respects at Katelyn's memorial service later in the week, but their mom's cookies needed delivery.

Bundled up in North Face jackets, Taylor and Hayley slipped out the back door to the alleyway that was the shortest route to the Berkleys. Taylor wore Aunt Jolene's hand-knitted scarf, a sad-looking strip of yardage in search of a color palette that didn't suggest—as Taylor aptly assessed it—"a color wheel of different kinds of barf." The air was bone-chilling, with the added jolt of a damp wind blowing off the bay, coating the shrubbery in a glistening sheath of ice. The weatherman had blabbed about an ice storm coming, but since he was seldom on target with his forecasts, no one really prepared for it.

The girls noticed right off that Mrs. James's hundred-year-old camellia was encased in ice.

"She's going to be way disappointed when she gets back from Portland and sees that no one put a blanket over it," Taylor said. "She's so possessive of that dumb bush."

Hayley looked over the shimmering emerald form of the shrub and said, "I think it's pretty."

"You think everything is pretty, Hay."

"Well, not everything," she clarified, pointedly indicating Aunt Jolene's scarf. "But yeah, a lot of things can be pretty. You just have to look at things the right way to see their beauty."

"Mrs. James doesn't own that bush. Nothing in this town of renters belongs to anyone."

"That could be said of anything, Taylor. Whether you rent and live in Port Gamble or buy and live in a house in Seattle, ultimately you're just visiting."

Taylor changed the subject. "This is stupid. Bringing cookies over to our dead friend's house? Lame."

"Yeah, but Mom wanted us to, so we're doing it."

"Right. Because she thought it was a good idea. Like we can't come up with our own?"

"I think that's the point. We wouldn't be going to the Berkleys if Mom hadn't made the cookies."

"Natch," Taylor had to agree.

Sandra Berkley pulled open the front door and faced the Ryan twins. It had been a while since they'd seen Mrs. Berkley outside of the family's restaurant, the Timberline, a breakfast and burger place with good food and a sign over the counter: "Unattended Children Will Be Given an Espresso and a Puppy."

Neither could be sure when was the last time they'd come over to visit. It might have been back in middle school. Katelyn had sort of slipped away insofar as their friendship was concerned. For most of Port Gamble Elementary, they had been in the same circle of happy little girls that once filled the front row of Ms. Paulson's second-grade class. Mrs. Berkley had been their Daisy Troop leader. She was different then, prettier, more serene. Watching her and the other moms of Port Gamble, Hayley and Taylor understood as well as any young girl that with beauty came power. This was before Disney princesses could get what they wanted without having to resort to kicking serious butt.

And yet, kicking butt, the Ryans knew from experience, definitely had its own set of empowering charms.

Mrs. Berkley, on the other hand, had let her strong points fade since the crash. Gossip all over town had it that she was a big drinker, and there was little in the way of excuses one could conjure to suggest otherwise.

When she opened the door, she didn't speak for a moment. Her hair was a black octopus, her makeup was raccoon-smudged and her bird legs shook under her crumbling frame. She was the sum of animal parts, like a mutant cross-breeding experiment gone completely haywire.

Hayley and Taylor, shivering on the doorstep, proffered the cookies.

"Come inside," Sandra said, a sharp waft of booze emitting with her breath.

Hayley looked at Taylor, then back at Mrs. Berkley.

"We don't want to be in the way," she said, pushing the cookies at the dead girl's mother once more.

Mrs. Berkley took the container and smiled faintly.

Was it wistful? A sad smile? A reaction to the kindness of Valerie Ryan?

"I was hoping some of her good friends would come by. Katelyn's friends meant so much to her."

The twins stepped into the house, and before they could say something about the fact that they hadn't seen much of Katelyn lately, they were in the middle of a swarm of relatives and friends who had convened to support the family during the most difficult of circumstances.

"These are two of Katelyn's best friends," Sandra Berkley said to an older woman with thin lips and a wattle neck whom the girls presumed to be Katelyn's grandmother, Nancy.

"Hayley?" the grieving mom asked, pointing tentatively. "And Taylor, right?"

She was wrong, but it didn't matter. After all, they were suddenly "best friends" of the girl they no longer really knew.

"They've brought some treats," Sandra said.

"This isn't a party." The older woman sniffed.

Hayley didn't know what to say. Even though she had agreed to bring them over, she had thought the cookies were a crappy idea in the first place.

"My mom made them," Taylor said. "They were Katelyn's favorite whenever she hung out at our place. Always had at least two."

It was a good save. Taylor was like that. She could always be counted on to think fast on her feet. If Mrs. Berkley was so deluded as to think that she and her sister and Katelyn were the best of friends, she could go along with it.

"Katelyn never knew when to quit. If she hadn't been eating all the time she would have made cheer," the grandmother said.

"That's enough, Mom," Sandra said, shooting what had to have been a practiced glare in the direction of a woman who'd clearly been more interested in bitching about something than grieving.

And yes, both girls thought, Katelyn had put on a few pounds. She wasn't mom-jeans fat, but she was a few cookie trays short of it.

"Really sorry about Katelyn," Taylor said.

"Sorry doesn't do much for a broken heart," the grandmother said.

Hayley didn't take the bait. Instead, she smiled at the older woman, took her sister by the arm and mumbled something about wanting to talk to Mr. Berkley.

Hayley led her sister into the living room, where most of the people belonging to the cars with out-of-state license plates were talking in quiet, anguished tones. The dining room chairs had been pulled from the big mahogany table and were arranged along the wall to provide necessary, but awkward, seating. The table itself was covered with an array of bowls of pretzels, chips and platters of pinwheel sandwiches Hayley recognized as a Costco deli product.

Costco? Wow, that's really sad, she thought. She hoped if she died her parents would at least have Subway cater a gathering in her memory.

Harper Berkley, it was clear, had been crying. He was a tall, balding man with caterpillar brows that could use a good waxing. His eyes were red-rimmed and his formidable presence had been Shrinky-Dinked by the circumstances. He looked so small, so sad. A woman neither girl recognized patted his shoulder.

"We're very sorry about Katelyn," Hayley said.

"We're all in shock," the woman said. "I'm Harper's sister, Twyla. Katelyn's aunt."

As identical twins, the girls were genetic anomalies, not idiots. They knew that the dad's sister would be Katelyn's aunt. But now was probably not the time to point it out.

"These cookies were Katelyn's faves. Just wanted to drop them off," Taylor said.

"Yeah, she really liked our mom's cooking," Hayley echoed.

Harper thanked them with a quiet nod. To say anything was probably too painful. Sometimes one word can lead to a dam burst.

"Thank you for coming," he finally choked out.

Taylor and Hayley stood there a second in uncomfortable silence before retreating toward the front door. Both wondered how it was that with the inevitability of death, no one really had anything to say about it. It was as if one of life's pivotal moments—the final moment—was devoid of potential small talk. Death was a big, fat period to most people. Over and out. Dark and cold. A void.

By the staircase, Hayley felt a tug.

Taylor whispered, "Gotta go up there." She looked up the stairway's too-narrow risers toward Katelyn's bedroom.

Hayley shook her head emphatically. "No, we are most certainly *not* going up there. Aren't you as creeped out by all of this as I am?"

"You mean the Costco sandwiches? Or that our supposed BFF is dead?"

Taylor started up the stairs, turning to her sister with one last look. "Hay, either you can come up with me, or you can make small talk with them." She pointed back at the living area. "Remember the tugboat on the water? We're supposed to 'look.' Well, we're here. We might as well."

"You win. I'm coming," Hayley acquiesced as they crept up the uncarpeted wooden risers, careful not to make much noise. Old houses like that one did a fine job in the noise department all on their own. Downstairs, they could hear Katelyn's grandmother complaining about something. A harsh, mean voice always travels like a slingshot.

Katelyn's door was ajar. Taylor didn't remark on it, but she noticed a faint black rectangle, an indicator of old adhesive residue on the door. She remembered how they'd made nameplates after touring a signage shop in Daisies. Katelyn's, she remembered, was the standard issue of any preteen—KATIE'S ROOM: BOY-FREE ZONE!

Things had changed big-time since then.

They went inside, and Taylor closed the door behind them.

"What are we doing in here, anyway?" Hayley asked.

"Not sure," Taylor said. "Why do you need a reason for everything? Reason is something people say to make sense of things that don't make sense."

"Okay," Hayley said, with a slight smile, "now *that* doesn't make any sense."

Taylor didn't care. "Bite yourself," she said.

The posters and color scheme had changed dramatically since they'd last stepped foot in Katelyn's bedroom. Previously, Katelyn had surrounded herself with bright walls, purple bedding and pictures of horses and orcas plastered everywhere. All of that was gone. The walls had been painted a dark, foreboding gray—a rebellion from Port Gamble's newly enforced white interior décor edict for its historic homes. Katelyn's animal posters had been replaced with images of wan, sad girls and ripped guys with Abercrombie abs. They were hot, hard and probably without a single brainwave firing inside their bleached, tousled heads. Hayley and Taylor didn't have any qualms about the way those guys looked, but like most girls in Kitsap County, they'd never seen one in the flesh.

Okay, maybe one. But Colton James wasn't blond.

Without saying a word, they walked toward the bathroom.

Taylor knelt down next to the tub. It was a big old clawfoot, the exact same vintage as the tub in their house. It had not been re-enameled like the Ryans', however. The surface of Katelyn's was more cream than white, pitted in spots that made it appear dirty. Taylor could imagine Mrs. Berkley telling her daughter to "use some damn elbow grease!" when she told her to clean it.

Or was she imagining it? Sometimes she didn't know where her thoughts came from. Other times, however, Taylor was absolutely sure they came from a source outside of herself.

Hayley left her sister alone. She was drawn toward a small desk next to Katelyn's unmade bed. A lamp with a breaching orca as its base, some black markers, and a couple of small, framed photos caught her eye, but she dismissed all of that. Even though those items had a definite personal connection with their dead friend, they didn't beckon for her to touch them. Her fingertips were hot, moist. There was a feeling in her stomach, knotted like a bag of jump ropes, that made her feel queasy—not throwing-up sick, but the kind of feeling that comes just before the onset of the flu. She was a little light-headed too. Her heartbeat pushed inside her rib cage.

This wasn't the first time she'd experienced being drawn to an object. Neither twin could explain the sensation or the visions that sometimes came afterward. They had little control over it.

It was Katelyn's laptop that had lured Hayley to come closer. She drew a deep, calming breath and touched the keyboard. Nothing. She closed her eyes and ran her fingers over the screen like a blind girl might do with a book in Braille. She could feel her heart rate surge a little more. It was a peculiar feeling that had more to do with fear than excitement.

Something. She felt something. She imagined the folds of her brain tightening around *something.*

Taylor put her hand on her sister's shoulder, and Hayley spun around.

"Holy crap, Tay! I hate it when you do that."

"Then keep your eyes open. Time to get out of here."

Hayley shook her head and felt the keyboard once more. "I'm almost there. I need just a second more."

"Now!" Taylor said without any ambivalence in her voice.

Hayley pushed back at her sister. She didn't want to leave. Not just then. "We can't leave yet. I'm not ready."

"You don't get it, Hayley," Taylor said, her voice rising louder; loud enough to drive the point without alerting the odd cadre of mourners downstairs. "We're not wanted here."

Hayley had thought the same thing, especially about Katelyn's grandmother, but she needed more time.

"This is where Katelyn was murdered," she said.

Taylor's eyes widened. "Murdered?"

"That's the feeling I'm getting. You try it."

As Taylor nodded and braced herself, the bedroom door swung open. Both girls screamed.

"Who said you two could come up here?"

It was Katelyn's mom, wobbling in the doorway.

"Sorry," Taylor said, unconsciously inching back, away from her. "We just wanted to—"

Hayley interrupted her sister. "To be close to Katelyn."

Sandra Berkley looked over at the laptop, which was still open and emitting the telltale glow that it was in use.

"Were you trying to read her private journal?" Sandra's eyes were rheumy, and it was obvious that it was more than the effects of a mixed drink that had brought her to tears that day.

Taylor snapped the lid shut. "No. No. Not at all. We didn't even, um, *know* she had a journal."

Hayley nodded briskly. "We had no idea Katelyn wrote anything down," she said.

Sandra walked over to the window and looked out across the yard to the Larsens' place. Her eyes lingered for a moment before she turned around to face the girls.

"Oh," she said, as if searching for the words. "It was stupid, really. The ramblings of a silly girl, I guess. I never read it."

It was an odd way to refer to a dead daughter. *A silly girl.*

Hayley couldn't take it.

"Katelyn wasn't *that* silly, Mrs. Berkley," she said. "On the contrary, she was a sad girl. I think we all know that."

Wow. Taylor couldn't believe her sister said that. Quiet and sometimes a little reserved, Hayley usually kept things much closer to the vest.

"We're leaving now," Hayley said, and the pair brushed right past the surprised woman. They hurried down the steps, no longer trying to tread lightly. Everyone in the living room looked up, but the girls didn't say a word to any of them.

"You sure told her off," Taylor said proudly as they went outside.

Hayley allowed the flicker of a smile. "Yes, well, we just had to get out of there, didn't we?"

Taylor nodded.

"I really don't believe that Katelyn's death was just an accident. There's more to it," Hayley said, though she didn't have to say it out loud.

Taylor didn't need to reply either, but she did. "I know. Felt it the night she died."

"Tay," Hayley said as she glanced at her sister's bare neck, "I think you might have forgotten your scarf."

Taylor smiled. "Like hell I did. That's our excuse to go back. It may be the ugliest rag in Port Gamble, but it's getting us back into that house."

As they walked through the alleyway toward home, neither Taylor nor Hayley were aware that a pair of eyes was riveted to their every move. *Studying them.* Wondering from a dark place just what the twins' rekindled relationship with the dead girl's family was all about.

CHAPTER ELEVEN

Kingston High was one of those schools built with a tip of the architectural hat to its location. That was usually the intention of school district review boards, but it rarely worked as well as it did in Kingston. Just eight miles from Port Gamble, Kingston was a rolling rural landscape dotted with subdivisions and family farms that dipped at its very eastern edge to Puget Sound. The front entryway of the school was reached by crossing a footbridge over a shallow ravine of sword ferns, cedars, and winter-bronze cattail stalks.

By the time Hayley and Taylor graduated from the middle school just down the road, Kingston High was only four years old. Classrooms were segregated into pods, each known by the dominating color of its paint scheme. Rough-hewn cedar planks artfully lined portions of the interior corridors, and wide expanses of pebbly finished polished concrete swirled in browns and greens like a Northwest stream. In the mornings, the espresso stand adjacent to the student store, the Treasure Trove, did Starbucks-style business, sending a geyser of steaming milk into the air as it caffeinated one teenager after the next. Even those who didn't need coffee got in line—like Beth Lee, who never arrived at school without a Rockstar drink in her purse and a triple tall latte from Gamble Bay Coffee. She'd pay a visit to the student-run coffee stand after lunch for her always-needed midday pick-me-up.

Each pod featured its own teacher's resource room, with their cubicles all crammed with the things they didn't want to take home.

Some teachers put up baby pictures of their children. Students who saw them often remarked how surprising it was that one teacher or another had found someone to have a child with.

"Did you see that photo? The kid looks completely normal. Almost cute," one girl, a willowy redhead in overalls, said as she made her rounds, dropping off the latest *Buccaneer Broadcast*, the school newsletter.

"Yeah," said her friend, a pudgy junior wearing tights, short-shorts, black patent leather ankle boots, and an inch of mascara on each clumped-up eyelid. "I was hoping she couldn't have kids. You know, for the kid's sake."

"Totally," Redhead said.

Most of the congregating among students was done in the common area between the classrooms in any given pod. Along one wall were lockers of varying sizes—larger for those who were lacrosse team members and had unwieldy pads, sticks, and gear; smaller for those who didn't have anything they needed to store but wanted a place to linger.

It was far from status quo the first day back from winter break. Katelyn's death gave the school guidance counselors the opportunity to go into grief-counseling mode. And while they were genuinely sorry to lose a student, it sure changed up the onslaught of "I could be pregnant" or "school is too hard and I want to drop out" sessions that tended to bunch up after the holidays.

The day back from a break marked by a teen's death meant a seemingly endless train of sobbing girls into the counselors' offices.

Most started the preamble to their crying jags with the same words: "I'm so upset about this. It isn't fair. She's the same age as me."

Hayley, Taylor and Beth didn't give voice to the same concerns as others. They were sick about what happened and felt they had a genuine connection with the dead girl. Their friendship with Katelyn might have evaporated since middle school, but they still felt a keen loss.

"I hated a lot about her," Beth said in the commons. "She had no style. She wasn't exactly fun anymore. Still, who knows, maybe she'd have turned into someone cool if she hadn't died."

"There was something always a little sad about her," Hayley said. "I feel like we all kind of dropped her when maybe we shouldn't have."

Taylor agreed with her sister. "I know I did."

Beth scowled and rummaged around in her purse for some lip gloss. It had been five minutes since her last application. "You two are such goody-goodies. She didn't want to be friends with us. She was too wrapped up in being Katelyn of the *Starla & Katelyn Show*. Didn't that get canceled after one season?"

"More like fifteen," said Taylor, not even trying to be ironic.

A junior the trio barely knew came up just then. "Sorry about your friend," she said.

All glossed, Beth answered, "We're devastated. We can't talk about it."

"Take care," the girl said. "Sorry."

Beth looked at Hayley and Taylor. "Did I seem devastated?" she asked. "Just a little?"

"Just a little," Taylor said as the three went off to class.

Later that morning, the Treasure Trove espresso stand put up a small sign asking for donations for Katelyn's family. The school principal, a petite woman with dangerous nail-gun heels, kindly told them it wasn't an altogether good idea.

"But we wanted to help," said the kid foaming the milk.

"Yeah," said the girl pulling the espresso shots. "She was a soy drinker, totally organic. You have to respect that."

"Yes," the principal argued, "but the manner of her death…" She attempted to choose her words carefully. "Katelyn died of, because of…" she said, looking at the big Italian espresso machine.

"Oh," said the foamer. "I get what you're putting down."

The shot girl apparently didn't. "Huh?"

"An espresso machine killed Katelyn," the foamer said. "She was electrocuted in the tub."

Finally, the look of awareness came to the student's face. A light switched on. The coffee girl got it.

"Yeah," she said, quickly pulling down the sign. "We shouldn't collect money."

The principal gave the pair a quick nod and walked away over the shiny polished surface to her office at the front of the school. She looked through the windows of the first pod's reception area. A small group of girls, some who might not even have known Katelyn but who got caught up in the sad drama of a dead girl, had amassed.

Taylor Ryan was one of those girls, waiting to talk with the grief counselor. She understood that Katelyn's death was a tragedy and there was no bringing her back, but the pain of it was a knife point to her heart.

She wanted to tell someone that she could feel Katelyn's presence all around her. She felt that whatever had happened to Katelyn in that bathtub had the hand of another person in it somehow.

She just didn't want her sister or Beth to see her there.

Later that afternoon, Hayley and Taylor slowed as they walked in the vicinity of Katelyn's locker. A few members of the Buccaneers' cheer team congregated nearby, chatting about their holiday. Tiffany, a senior, had a tan and was bragging about her "awesome" Hawaiian vacation and the hot swimsuit that she bought in a boutique in Maui. When the twins approached, she smiled.

"She was a friend of yours. Sorry," she said.

"She was a friend. She wasn't a really close one, but thanks," Hayley said.

As the cheer squad moved aside, they revealed the beginnings of a makeshift memorial. A few grocery-store bouquets past their pull dates were slumped on the gray linoleum floor. Someone had taken a photo from Katelyn's Instagram profile, blown it up and written in very careful print:

RIP, KATIE!

The fact that they'd used an exclamation point was odd, but most of the kids in school couldn't punctuate anything properly, so it probably wasn't meant to signify that Katelyn's resting in peace was something exuberant. Hayley thought it could have been worse.

Yay! Katie's on permanent break!
Have a fun time in heaven!
You go (dead) girl!

Hayley stopped her train of thought as the buzzing of the other girls abruptly ceased. Starla Larsen, wearing black pants and a black cashmere sweater, joined the group in front of Katelyn's locker.

"Sorry about Katie," Taylor said. She resisted the urge to actually give Starla a hug because in that moment it just didn't seem right.

"Yeah, we both are," said Hayley, who didn't hug Starla either.

Starla, for the first time in recent memory, looked terrible. Terrible for her would have been pretty good for a lot of other girls. Starla Terrible was quite noticeable, nevertheless. Her skin was pale—in fact, very pale, especially next to the ultra-tanned senior, Tiff.

"It was a big shock," she said, making a sniffling sound, although it didn't appear that she had any need for a tissue. Though she had first-class designer bags under her eyes, it was pretty clear she hadn't been crying. "We weren't as close as we once were, but I loved her very, very much."

Tan Tiff put her arms around Starla. "Let's go somewhere we can talk and grieve," she said to the others hanging around Starla. "I want to show Baby Girl the photos from my trip too."

"Thanks, Hayley, Taylor," Starla said, disappearing down the hallway.

Hayley turned to her sister. "Is it just me or what? Starla had dropped Katie. Those two haven't spoken for months, and she's saying she *loved* her?"

"Guilt, maybe?" Taylor suggested.

Hayley thought for a moment. "It could be guilt, or maybe it's revisionist history."

"Dunno," Taylor said. "She looked tired for sure, but sad? Not so much."

"She didn't look sad at all," Hayley agreed. "She doesn't seem one bit upset, and what's this 'Baby Girl' crap?"

"Cheer talk," Taylor said, inserting her finger in her mouth, the universal sign for puking. "Worse than the twin talk we made up when we were little."

Hayley laughed and the girls blended into the mass of Axe-drenched boys and makeup-laden girls moving like a single living organism into the doorways of classrooms.

"Please remind me never to go to another pep rally," Hayley said.

"Gotcha." Taylor slipped into her life science class, and her sister went on to English.

Both were wondering the same thing: *What was up with Starla?*

The winter afternoon sky turned into dusk as Taylor trailed her sister down the stairs from their bedrooms. Hayley had just run home to grab a textbook.

"Off to hang out with Colton again?" Taylor asked. Her tone was unmistakable. The little lilt on the last word turned the question into a snipping judgment.

Hayley turned to and stared. She did not have a smile on her face. In fact, she could not conceal her brewing anger. That first day back at school, Hayley had spent every minute between and after class with her boyfriend. And Taylor took every opportunity to complain about it. The incessant questioning about Colton had become more than an irritant.

It was worse than a flea bite that never went away.

"What's gotten into you, Taylor?"

Finally, another chance to be direct, and Taylor took it. "Maybe the fact that all you ever do is hang out with him. What about Katelyn? And the 'look' message? We're nowhere with it. What are you two so busy doing all the time, anyway?"

Hayley clearly didn't like what she was hearing. "What is that supposed to mean exactly? If you're accusing me of something, I would prefer it if you'd just spell it out."

Taylor held her ground. "You know."

"Colton and I are just hanging out."

"Hey, I'm your twin. Don't lie to me. Save it for someone who doesn't give a crap," Taylor spat out, trying to bury her jealousy.

Hayley wasn't buying it. "Look," she said, "there's a lot going on around here that we don't know. The two of us need to stick together to figure it all out. In the meantime, I would appreciate it if you'd please lay off the Colton jabs."

With that, she turned the knob of the back door and was gone.

CHAPTER TWELVE

Jealousy, annoyance, whatever it was, reverberated between Hayley and Taylor with a vengeance. Maybe it was because they had come from the same egg, or maybe it was because even after the womb they spent so much time together. Whatever the case, the girls shared and experienced intense emotions simultaneously. The energy was almost a twin-sense, telegraphed to each other silently through the air like sound waves.

Didn't everyone feel that way? Didn't everyone understand the transference of emotion in the same manner?

They didn't, of course.

Hayley's ability to capture feelings and images came to her differently from Taylor's. The older sister by less than a minute, Taylor could immerse herself in water and infuse her brainwaves with the past thoughts of others. Hayley's pathway was more tactile. The transmission that came to her often came through her fingertips. It was as if she could touch an object, a person—dead or alive—and capture an instant in the real, present world.

She'd touched Katelyn's laptop, and the exchange of the moment had taken place.

Two days after school had started, Hayley sat at the kitchen table, her parents gone somewhere, her sister upstairs reading her latest *US Weekly*. She drank a glass of water because water always helped the process. She shut her eyes and tried to recall the images that had flashed too quickly through her head in Katelyn's room.

She needed to see it all in slo-mo in order to understand it. She waited. She did what she and Taylor called "hope and focus."

In a moment, the images came. There was a computer. Hayley could tell that a person was typing on one machine and sending the words to Katelyn's shiny silver laptop. She watched fingers glide over the keyboard as if each grenade being dropped were a mere powder puff. One fluent keystroke after another. There was very little hesitation because the writer of the message knew exactly which words to use.

Cullant: i'm not a total stalkr but i've bn watching u, katelyn.

Hayley watched as the pair typed.

Katiebug: u sound lk a perv.

Cullant: not @all!!! It does sound pervy 2 watch someone. Lol. Truth is if u weren't so hot—i 100% mean that in the right way—i would just ask u out.

Katiebug: ru a freak or what?

Hayley sipped the tepid tap water, and then let a flood of it down her throat.

Cullant: no. Just a guy who doesn't want 2 get shot dwn by the hottst girl @khs. That's u, katelyn. U know, u really r.

She could feel that Katelyn knew every reason why she should just stop the online conversation and maybe report the guy to someone. But Katelyn wasn't exactly sure, however, *who* the boss of the Internet was anyway. It didn't seem like there was an Internet

police either. Every day her email inbox was stacked with ads for
Viagra (gross), breast enhancers (not!) and offers from Nigerians
to share their fortune (tempting, but no thanks).

Hayley was irritated by the digression, though she completely
agreed with Katelyn's thoughts. She hoped and refocused on more
of what she was after, and what she was seeking came forth.

Instead of telling someone or giving the boy on the other side
of the computer screen the big kiss-off, Katelyn, who'd never felt
lonelier in her life, answered him.

*Katiebug: thx, i guess. But i don't know anything bout u. Ur
not like that phantom of the opera guy. Ru?*

Cullant: don't like opera. Boring.

Katelyn shook her head and typed.

*Katiebug: lol. Meant the broadway musical. Freak w/a burned
up face falls 4 a woman & doesn't want her see his butt-ugly face.*

Cullant: i'm tld i have a nice butt.

Katelyn smiled. The guy hitting on her was actually kind of
funny. Maybe a little clueless, but amusing, nevertheless. The boys
at Kingston were in one of two camps—either a slacker or a jock
who measured his muscles in the reflection of the school's crowded
trophy case. None seemed to understand for a single nanosecond
that *talking* to a girl was hotter than a Dirty Girl Scout drink, a
blanket and a quickie down at the beach.

Far, far, hotter.

Cullant: i want 2 meet u.

Katiebug: dn't know if i'm rdy. 2b w/u in person might be more thn i cn handle.

More than she can handle? She could handle plenty. That is, if someone gave her something to sink her teeth into... er... hold. Whatever!

Katelyn started to type just as her mother entered the room. Sandra Berkley had been drinking since five that afternoon and she was clearly feeling the effects of the alcohol. She'd switched to vodka earlier in the year because she was under the erroneous assumption that it didn't have an odor. Of course, it didn't have the sweet smell that wafted out of a whiskey drinker's mouth, but it did carry the hard-edge scent that reminded Katelyn of Listerine. Minus the minty freshness, of course.

"What do you want?" Katelyn asked, sending a perceptible glare in the direction of her nosy, drunk and all-too-predictable mom.

"That's no way to talk to your mother, Katelyn."

"You haven't acted like my mother since I was seven," Katelyn said from behind her laptop. She'd swiveled on the edge of the bed so that her mother could see only the back of her computer.

Sandra brushed her dark, limp hair from her forehead in a display of dramatic effect that was meant to show impatience and tolerance at the same time.

"Must we always go there?" she asked, slumping on the foot of the bed.

Katelyn closed the chat app on her laptop, just in case her mother's vision was less blurry than she expected it to be.

"I guess so," she said. "I guess we must. Where's Dad? Shouldn't you be downstairs fighting with him?"

Sandra wrapped her arms around her shoulders, trying to convey that she was freezing or maybe a little vulnerable.

In reality, Katelyn was sure that her mother was merely trying to steady herself. She'd overdone it, like she always did.

"What are you doing online?" her mom asked. Sandra put her hand on the laptop, but Katelyn flicked it away.

"Homework. What do you think?"

"Don't get lippy with me," she said.

Katelyn let out a sigh. It was exaggerated, but with her mom drinking too much, emotions sometimes had to be painted with very, very broad strokes. It was the only way to ensure that something, *anything*, got through her mother's alcohol-induced haze.

"I'm not lippy," Katelyn said. "I'm just tired, Mom. Tired of you not trusting me."

The images faded and Hayley fought hard to hold on to what she was "seeing."

Suddenly Sandra reappeared. This time she was wearing jeans and a sweater, and her hair was clipped back from her face. She was angry and she stood to leave. "I won't ever trust you after what you did last fall."

She spun on her heel, shot her own glare in the direction of her daughter and left the bedroom.

Katelyn sat there seething.

Last fall. There would always be that to throw in her face.

*

Taylor came into the kitchen to get a post-hanging-out-with-Beth snack. A slice of cold leftover Hawaiian pizza sounded good just then. And since she was the only one in the house who'd eat it, there were *always* leftovers for her. She glanced over at her sister and the empty water glass.

"Hopeful and focused?" she asked, a little more quietly than needed. They were, after all, home alone. "Anything?"

Hayley looked up and nodded. "Yeah, although I'm not sure what it means or if it really has anything to do with Katelyn's death."

Taylor took her pizza from the refrigerator, grabbed a too-long streamer of paper towels, and slid into a chair facing Hayley.

"What did you get?"

Hayley drew a deep breath and exhaled. She was wiped out from the experience of seeing the conversation play out over Katelyn's laptop.

"She had an online hookup," Hayley said. "Did you know that?"

Taylor picked at an errant piece of pineapple and shook her head. "Who?"

"I have no idea," Hayley said. "It felt kind of deep, kind of personal."

"Personal how?"

"Katelyn seemed really interested in him. She was really happy. It was like that boy was the only thing that lifted her heart. I didn't get all the information. Her mom interrupted them."

Taylor nodded. "Her mother is the worst."

"Her mother's *mother* is, that's for sure," Hayley said, remembering the visit with the family after Katelyn died.

Hayley closed her eyes and tried to replay the last part of what she'd felt.

Taylor was impatient, something she was pretty good at being. "Well?"

"Give me a second, okay?" Hayley said.

Though Hayley kept her eyes shut, Taylor could see them move back and forth under their clamped lids. She finished her pizza and wondered when Hayley had started to wear that hideous frosted slate-gray eye shadow, but she didn't say anything. She waited. Not everything could be rushed to meet the schedule of a ticking clock.

Hayley opened her eyes. "Something happened last fall," she said. "I'm not sure what it was, but it was something big. Her mom said she had 'trust' issues with Katelyn."

"Like what? What did she do?"

"I have no idea. She didn't say, and I didn't get anything to point us in the right direction—except a reference to last fall."

"Last fall?"

"Yeah. They said something about last fall," Hayley repeated.

"What happened? Where was she in the fall?"

"I can't really think of anything. We didn't see her much. Remember, she and Starla were always practicing for cheer?"

Taylor nodded. "Ugh, I hated that. With a passion. We could hear them jumping up and down and yelling from our backyard."

"That's right," Hayley said. "I remember it was intense."

"Maybe it was related to cheer?"

"I doubt it, but there's one person who might know."

Taylor gave her sister a knowing look.

Starla Larsen—Port Gamble's It-girl. She'd be worth a visit. It would have to be at her house, not at school. Since she had picked up her pom-poms, Starla was too cool to acknowledge any of the old Daisy Troop girls she'd known forever.

They were a step way too low on the popularity ladder.

Later that evening, Taylor's phone vibrated with a text from Beth.

Beth: Saw weirdo over by K's house.

Port Gamble was not a big town, but it had plenty of weirdos.

Taylor: What weirdo?

Beth: Segway guy.

Taylor: What was he doing?

Beth: dunno. Segwaying. Like always. He gives me the creeps.

Taylor: My dad checked him out. Harmless creep.

Beth: Perv.

Taylor: Not a perv.

Beth: He just hovers round there. Right?

Taylor: What if he was K's fake bf?

Beth: That's really gross. He's like 40.

Segway Guy was closer to fifty, but Taylor let it go. One of Beth's fortes was her ability to underestimate everything.

Even so, Taylor did think Segway Guy was a little creepy. Seriously, riding around in a Segway without at least a little irony about the spectacle?

CHAPTER THIRTEEN

Taylor Ryan filled the old, white clawfoot tub with too much water, nearly sending a small wave over its rolled edges. Since childhood, she always wanted the water as deep as possible—deep enough to dive down and hold her breath. *One, two, three.* Her record was 177 seconds. Her sister's was about the same. She was fifteen now, and getting into the water on that night had nothing to do with trying to set a new record. Hayley had tried to find out more about Katelyn's death, and Taylor wanted to dip her toe into these waters herself.

Literally.

The air in the bathroom was cool, and the steam from the bathwater collided with the mirror. Taylor noticed the circular motions she'd left on the surface of the glass the last time she'd been stuck with bathroom cleaning duty. She undressed, folding her favorite Hollister jeans, pale pink cami, and cream-colored merino wool sweater into a neatly squared stack on top of the toilet seat. Slowly, she stepped into the hot depths of the bathtub. Her hair, no longer as blonde as it had been in the summer, was pulled back in a messy ponytail. As she slid down to cover her body, she could feel the water wick slowly up her backbone, like hot fingers along each of the knobs of her vertebrae.

The water shut out all of her senses. No sound. No air upon her face. No sight. Just the stillness of a blanket of hot water. Taylor let it all go. She had been thinking of Katelyn all day, and her sister had brought them a bit closer to finding out what had happened. That evening, the water, the sensory deprivation, the forced concentration held the answer to questions that she and Hayley had asked over and over since their visit to the Berkley house.

What happened to Katelyn?

Like the flood of images that sometimes came to Hayley through touch, what transpired underwater with Taylor couldn't be explained—at least not to anyone's satisfaction. Not that either of the twins ever tried to come up with the reasons for it or how they discovered it. In truth, they really weren't sure of its origin. It just happened, like the random way things happen in nature.

All on their own.

They talked about it through their bedroom outlet intercom, but only occasionally, and always with great respect—respect that came from the fear of whatever it meant, whatever was happening to them.

Or where it came from.

Sometimes Taylor practiced immersions, but with the discretion that comes with keeping something secret. One time, Valerie came in and found Taylor floating under the surface of the bathtub, and her mother had screamed.

"Are you okay? What are you doing?"

The words came at the girl with a rifle-shot of panic that startled her so much, it had almost made Taylor ashamed of being naked.

Now, she lay perfectly still and dropped below the surface. Quiet. Focused. A surge of feelings that somehow translated into images emerged. What visual cues came at her were never from a memory of her own. These memories belonged to others. Sometimes they came in a steady stream, like swirling orbs linked up in a video shooting gallery game. They moved quickly. So fast, in fact, that she experienced a kind of upper neck pain akin to whiplash. Looking, following, trying to see whatever it was.

Other times the images were more static, without a sense of urgency.

Five seconds into the immersion.

Though her eyes were closed, Taylor felt tears underneath her eyelids. In front of her she saw a horizontal box of white light. Along the left side were tiny rows of black.

Ants on an envelope? That didn't make sense at all.

Twenty seconds passed.

She turned her head in the water and imagined her eyes open, staring hard at the white block in front of her. The ants had moved. In fact, the ants were moving across the blank field, shifting in and out of focus.

What is it?

Forty-five seconds elapsed.

Her lungs were beginning to strain a little. It had been a long time since she'd held her breath for a minute or more.

I'm not ready to stop, she thought. *And just what are those nasty ants doing?*

Her hands floated toward the surface, a reflex to grab onto the edge of the tub and pull herself out. Taylor ignored the impulse and willed her body to stay just where it was.

A minute and fifteen seconds.

They weren't ants, but letters.

Okay, Taylor thought, *what are they saying?*

Seven words spun by and she grabbed at them. The first five were easy, but she kept failing on the last two.

LEWD HOT ROD KOALA FURL

Three minutes underwater.

Taylor's lungs were going to explode. She strained as hard as she ever had.

I'm not giving up, she thought as she fought the physical compulsion to rise up and breathe.

Katelyn's dead. She's got a messed-up family. She didn't need to die. I need that last part of the message. She wants me to have the words! Give me those words, Katelyn!

The last two pounced at her.

SELF IVORY

Taylor clawed at the surface of the water, her eyes open with the kind of fearful look that beach lifeguards know all too well. She wasn't drowning. Even so, more than three minutes without a breath underwater was frightening beyond words. Coughing, choking on oxygen, Taylor pulled herself to the side of the tub and tried to breathe.

What was Katelyn telling her?

CHAPTER FOURTEEN

There were ways to figure out what messages Katelyn had left behind. That was if, presumably, the words transmitted under the waters of the bathtub were truly from her. Taylor knew that the seven little words she had received underwater probably didn't mean what they said. They were only a clue to put her on the right path. Figuring it all out was the hard part.

When Hayley and Taylor had first started receiving messages, they played around with index cards. Even with a half-dried Sharpie, Taylor had better handwriting, so it was she who wrote down each word in crisp black printed letters. Whenever they'd unscrambled the true meaning of each message, they tore up the cards and flushed them down the toilet—despite the historic district's rule against the disposal of anything other than toilet paper and "personal waste," as it taxed Port Gamble's sewage system.

"Isn't this personal waste?" Taylor asked, looking down at the confetti of index cards.

Hayley nodded. "It is *personal*—though we're not always sure what person we're hearing from. And it is waste, but I think we could come up with a more eco-friendly way."

"E-occult-friendly. I like that. We should copyright that one."

Hayley gave her sister an irritated look. "It has nothing to do with the occult."

"Kidding," Taylor said.

"I hate it when you make comments like that. It makes all of this seem so ugly."

"Maybe it is."

"It isn't ugly. It comes from someplace good. I feel it. So should you."

"I'm not like you, Hayley."

The comment was funny, and both girls laughed.

After that, they had settled on using their parents' Scrabble game, a handmade relic from their mother's childhood, to twist around and rearrange the letters that came to them. Kevin and Valerie shared a deep love of words. Whenever the twins were lying on the thick, powder blue Oriental carpet in the parlor playing Scrabble, it brought a smile to both parents. They could see that their daughters were engrossed in a different version of the game, but in a day of video-this and Internet-that, they didn't say a single word about how they played.

Flames crackled in the fireplace, and the smell of their parents' nutmeg-laced eggnog wafted through the drafty house. It was the last gasp of leftover cheer in a holiday that had pulsed with an undercurrent of sadness. The family dog, Hedda, was curled up between the girls and the fireplace.

"You girls want some company?" Kevin asked as he entered the room, mug in hand.

"We're good, Dad," Taylor said. "Just messing around."

Kevin looked a little disappointed. He had work to do on his latest book and a distraction, apparently, was not in the cards.

"Okay, I'm going to rewrite the discovery of the victim scene."

"That's always my favorite part of your books, Dad," Hayley said.

He smiled. Those girls had been born into a life of crime. They had never known a moment when blood-spatter analysis, gunshot residue or chain of evidence was not a part of the family's dinner table conversations.

Valerie Ryan always tried to push dinnertime topics toward ponies, peonies or something lovely, especially when the girls were young. She did so as a mother, seeking to protect her children from the things that hurt deeply, things that pointed to the darkest side of humanity. It was easy to understand why she tried—and why she failed.

Valerie had grown up on McNeil Island, the home of Washington State's oldest penitentiary. Her father, Chester Fitzpatrick, was the warden (though, later, the governor changed the position's title to superintendent, to better reflect a more clinical, institutional approach to incarceration). She'd grown up in what any outsider would consider a lonely, desolate place to raise a child. For Valerie, it was a town, and the guards, staff, and prisoners were its citizens. As a little girl, she watched wide-eyed as the Friday afternoon chain arrived—man after man tethered together to step off the prison boat to make their way past the big white house that her father, mother and sister called home. Valerie, a pretty towhead like the daughters she'd one day have, was riveted by the stream of men, faces haggard, angry or resigned, wondering what they'd done and how they'd done it.

And some stared back at her. Occasionally, the looks in her direction caused her to turn away. A few times they'd even made her cry. It wasn't fear that caused the tears, though her father and mother thought so. It was something else. She wasn't sure what it was until many, many years later.

Valerie found some things about the institution that were beautiful too.

The razor wire coiled over the almost-tree-topping fences was a braid of tinsel at Christmastime. The bars over the windows that looked over the deep blue of Puget Sound were a steel version of cat's cradle. Nothing, young Valerie came to believe, could match the splendor of the hallway that ran from her father's enormous office down toward the cellblock. The shiny gold-hued-by-age linoleum was Dorothy's yellow brick road.

One day, she knew, it would lead her away from there.

"I'm going up to read now," Valerie said, casting a wary eye at the handmade Scrabble board Taylor and Hayley had arranged in front of the fire.

"What are you reading?" Hayley asked.

Valerie smiled and acknowledged the paperback she was carrying off to bed. "A murder mystery. Is there anything else?"

"Not lately," Taylor commented as their mother disappeared down the hall.

No words were said about the Scrabble game or why they'd chosen it that evening instead of the Xbox console with its collection of video games, which had been a Christmas present. There was really no need to explain.

Valerie understood her girls in a way that most mothers couldn't. There was a time when she was just like them. Even as a grown woman, she could still tap into the feelings she held when she was a young girl. It was more than her compassion that made her such a good psychiatric nurse or a mother, though she joked that the skills were interchangeable.

The twins picked out the tiny squares of pale, smooth wood.

"Let's break it down," Taylor said.

Hayley, who was busy turning all the letters so they were facing up, nodded. "All right. Why don't you call them out?"

"Lewd hot rod," Taylor said. "Sounds nasty."

Hayley laughed. "Lewd anything would, but adding hot rod is particularly, well, you know."

Next, Taylor set the appropriate letters in front of her, studying each as if they might literally speak to her.

She collected the T, H, E first.

"You're the new Vanna White," Hayley said.

"Huh?"

"You know, the helper on *Jeopardy*."

"You mean *Wheel of Fortune*." She moved the O, L, D next.

"The old…" Hayley said, pulling up the final four letters. "W, O, R, D."

Taylor looked at the unscrambled letters. "'The old word'," she said.

"Maybe Katelyn was a teen hooker," Hayley surmised. "You know, the oldest profession in history? There are lots of those girls in Seattle and Portland."

Taylor looked at her sister and shook her head. "Don't think that's it."

The next words, KOALA and FURL, stared up at the teens.

This time, Taylor took on the task of moving them around. In a few moments she'd arranged the letters into LAURA FOLK. Taylor shifted away from the fire. "Never heard of *her*."

"I don't know of anybody named Laura Folk either. Maybe she's a senior or something… but I think we know everyone from Port Gamble and Kingston. That's one of the supposed good parts of living in a small town."

They looked down at the tiles. Taylor carefully slid them aside and then laid out the last two words: SELF and IVORY.

"Maybe ivory is the color of something we need to know and self is about us."

"You like it when the words need no interpretation, Hayley."

"It *is* easier when you don't have to read into anything or extrapolate an inference from the words."

"Nah. These words aren't in the right order," Taylor said, moving the pieces around until it read: I'VE FOR SLY.

"That sounds stupid. It doesn't even make sense," Hayley said.

"Maybe I remembered it wrong?"

"Maybe you did. Or maybe it has nothing to do with Katelyn."

"I'm not going back into the tub."

"Well *I'm* not. I'm not as good at it as you are."

Kevin went past the staircase and called over to them. "What are you two arguing about? Hayley, did you come up with some esoteric or scientific name to get a triple word score?"

The girls looked at him blankly, having never played the game the way it had been intended.

"Something like that, Dad. We were just about to call it a night anyway."

"All right. Maybe I can play next time. You never ask me."

Hayley smiled as she moved the wooden tiles back into the box. "Okay, next time, for sure."

They turned off the lights, followed their father to the creaky stairs, and said good night.

From the outlet cover opening, Taylor whispered to her sister, "This isn't right, Hayley. Something's wrong."

"What do you mean *wrong*? We're doing great."

"I feel it."

"Well, I feel tired. Let's let it sit and see what comes up."

Taylor knew what that meant. Both girls did. They'd wait until something came to one of them. Something they could never directly ask for, but they knew it beyond a shadow of a doubt when it arrived.

That's just the way things were.

CHAPTER FIFTEEN

Miranda "Mindee" Larsen was a hairstylist at Shear Elegance in downtown, or rather, what approximated downtown Kingston, only a short drive from Port Gamble. Until recently, Mindee had been first chair in the salon for four consecutive years, a designation of power and excellent performance. She blamed herself only a little for her recent shift from first to second chair.

It had finally sunk in that the owner, a hard-bitten, humorless woman with blue-black hair named Nicola Cardamom, was never going to let her buy into the business, despite their agreement to the contrary. When Nicola wooed Mindee from a salon in Bremerton, promises had been made.

"A woman with your talent," Nicola had said, "should be front and center."

Mindee fell for it and packed her scissors, clippers and color kit. Things weren't great with her husband and she needed something to build upon. Just in case.

In time, Mindee finally understood how empty a promise could be. She'd been stuck in neutral for too long, and if things at home hadn't been as complicated as they were, she simply would have quit. Doing head after head, day after day, for a lying boss like Nicola was exasperating and demoralizing. She found herself angry at everyone.

A few times she purposely let the tips of her sharp scissors nick a customer's ear.

"You shouldn't have moved!" she scolded.

The customer, ear bleeding, knew she hadn't and decided never to return.

In the past year, Mindee had seen her client base drop. That's when Nicola moved her to second chair, and took the number-one spot for herself.

Mindee imagined taking her scissors to Nicola's lipo-sucked stomach, but she didn't, of course. Instead, she continued styling hair, doing colors and quietly and oh-so-discreetly bad-mouthing Nicola.

"I'm not sure where she is," she told one longtime customer, a devoutly religious woman from Poulsbo. It was a lie. She knew Nicola had a dental appointment that morning. "Don't make me tell you what I think she's doing. I don't even want to go there."

Just a drop of poison. Nothing more. Mindee never said anything specific. She didn't have to. She knew the power of suggestion, the impact of a hint dropped at the right time. The customer was a member of Living Christ, a mega-church. She was also an incorrigible gossip. A woman with a big mouth and a ready-made audience was a terrific and useful weapon.

The Larsens—Mindee and her two children, fifteen-year-old Starla and thirteen-year-old Teagan—lived in house number 21, right next door to the Berkleys. The two families had been friends for years. Close and trusted friends. After her husband, Adam, disappeared, Mindee increasingly relied on Harper Berkley to help with whatever heavy lifting she needed. Though nothing ever happened between them, there was talk. Small towns need barely a whisper to get things moving in the wrong direction.

Starla and Katelyn had been best friends forever back then. They'd grown up side by side, from Barbie to bras, and no one doubted that when one or the other got married, the maid of honor duties had already been secured.

That was never going to happen. Not now.

On the morning after Katelyn's sudden death, Starla refused to get out of bed. She was racked with hurt, guilt, even some shame. She and Katelyn had had a falling-out several months back over, of all things, making the cheer team at Kingston High School. They'd tried out together as freshmen, and Katelyn again the year after when she didn't make it, working on routines in the fenceless backyard that the two families shared as if it were their own private park.

Most people in Port Gamble seldom used their front yards anyway. If they did, they'd end up having to give a nosy tourist a mini history lesson on their house, the mill, the school or whatever it was the interloper wanted to know. While it certainly wasn't Colonial Williamsburg, with its phony blacksmiths and chambermaids running around with beeswax candles and a request for "all ye gather 'round," it was annoying residing in a living museum like Port Gamble.

The only Port Gamble residents who could escape incessant scrutiny were the 115 people in Buena Vista Cemetery. And, of course, they were dead.

Starla was a hot blonde. Not model pretty, but more like reality-TV beautiful. Almost everyone knew that her mother was a colorist and assumed that Starla's shimmering golden hair had a lot of help. There was more to be coveted than just her pretty face. In fact, in the world of teens at Kingston High, a pretty face was only as good as the boobs that went under it. At least, most girls knew that's where the boys' eyes seemed to always land.

Like a fly on a slice of cherry pie.

Starla had hit puberty earlier than her best friend, and by the time they got to Kingston Middle School it was clear that Katelyn was never going to quite measure up. Although she was pretty, she was just a shadow of Starla's beauty. Nobody had the power that Starla commanded by the mere virtue of just breathing and being. When Starla didn't have time to have her 7 For All Mankind jeans altered, she rolled up the hems—and all the other girls in her class did the same thing.

Almost all of them. Katelyn resisted.

When Mindee cut Starla's bangs for the last time, *ever*, the other girls followed suit. Even the older ones thought Starla Larsen was the real deal. No one could say for sure what direction Starla would go. Music? Acting? *America's Got Talent*? There was a reason why they called her SuperStarla—and she allowed it.

She was, no doubt, going to put Port Gamble on the map.

It was funny, some would later say, how it was her decidedly less glamorous former BFF who actually put the place on the map. Yet it would never be funny how she did it.

Not far from Port Gamble, Moira Windsor pecked the headline of her story onto her faded keyboard:

DEATH OF A SURVIVOR

It was absolutely perfect. Sensitive. Moving. Even a little shocking. Everything she thought her story would be. If she could just get the interviews. She wasn't asking for all that much. She needed the story. Why was Kevin Ryan being so damned difficult?

Moira looked at her headline once more. She loved the idea of plucking the heartstrings of her readers—while giving them a story that only she could tell. Plus, she needed to find out more about these girls. The Katelyn story was an entrée into something a lot bigger, a toehold into a tale so fantastic that she was surely going to get that spot next to Savannah Guthrie with a single flick of her finger. She had been leaked a tip—and if it was true, it would blow Katelyn's death story out of the water. These stupid twins were all that separated her from her coveted success in uncovering the truth. That job would be hers. She deserved it. She wanted it bad. And Moira always got what she wanted. *Always.*

She dialed Kevin Ryan's number. He answered the phone on the second ring.

"Hi, Mr. Ryan," she said. "Moira Windsor here."

There was silence for a beat, before Kevin said anything. "Moira," he said coolly, "I thought I was clear the other day."

Moira drummed her chipped nails on her out-of-town aunt's kitchen table, where she'd set up her office.

"You were, but I was hoping you'd change your mind. I really want to do a good job. You were young once. You know the importance of a good story, how it can help you."

Kevin hesitated again as he contemplated an answer that would shut her down and get her to go away. "I don't want you writing about something so personal and tragic," he finally said.

Wrong answer.

"Look who's calling the kettle black," Moira retorted. "You've made big bucks off writing about crime victims and their families. Always there with the personal detail."

"This is supposed to win me over? You really need to work on your technique, Moira."

"How about your wife? Maybe I could talk to her?"

"Maybe you should just go away."

"Your girls? They're fifteen, almost adults. They can decide if they want to talk," she said.

"Stay away from them," he warned, his voice louder than necessary. "Stay away from my family."

Moira fired back. "That sounded like a threat."

"Not a threat. Just a request."

Kevin hung up. He wondered how many times he'd made someone else feel like Moira Windsor had just made him feel: defensive, angry and worried.

CHAPTER SIXTEEN

When Starla was called out of Washington State history class last fall, she had no inkling Katelyn Berkley, her soon-to-be former BFF, was responsible for the bomb that would be dropped over her perfectly highlighted head.

After Starla was confronted by the principal, her boyfriend, Cameron Corelli, drove her home and screeched his rebuilt Bimmer to the curb. Starla mashed Cam's face and jumped out of the car. She strode angrily past Katelyn, who had lingered in the front yard waiting for her return. Starla had no idea Katelyn had wanted to say so many things but couldn't.

Sorry.

Didn't mean it.

Forgive me.

Or... *You deserve it, bitch.*

Starla didn't even return Katelyn's gaze. If she had, she might have seen a trace of sadness, remorse. It was as if Katelyn were a sheet of glass and Starla Larsen looked right through her.

Katelyn was nothing.

Starla had no clue when she stomped past her friend that Katelyn would sequester herself in her upstairs bedroom. That she wanted to cry, but no tears came. That she knew her betrayal was so great, Starla would never forgive her. That she loved Starla and hated her.

Starla would never know that Katelyn kept an online journal in which she admitted to giving the principal the incriminating photo out of spite. Because she wanted to be just like Starla, but couldn't be—and was losing her.

Starla would never know any of this because in a few short weeks, Katelyn would be dead.

"She did what?"

Mindee Larsen had just come home from work, smelling of hair product, toxic chemicals and her pack-a-day menthol cigarette habit. She threw her oversize purse onto the kitchen table and looked directly into Starla's eyes.

"You heard me, Mom. She reported me to the school cheer coach. It was total crap, and it's all Katie's fault."

"Yes, I heard that. I needed to hear it again because my brain isn't knitting the information together. Why would she do that? You're her best friend. Start from the beginning."

Starla wanted to say something about her mother's inappropriate knee-high boots and shimmering top, but she thought better of it. She wanted her mother to know what she was up against, and as far as advocates went, her mom was basically all Starla had.

"The beginning of what? When we were best friends?"

"*Today.* What happened today?" Mindee went to the refrigerator and filled a glass of wine from the boxed sangria that always commanded most of the top-shelf real estate.

"Okay, you don't have to be so bossy," Starla said, sliding into a dining chair while her mother took a seat across from her.

"I'm a mom," Mindee said, adding without a scintilla of sarcasm in her voice, "bossy is what I do."

"Can I have a sip?" Starla asked, mostly to needle her mother. She hated any wine that could stain her teeth. Sangria was right in the middle with a rosé, her buzz wine of choice.

Mindee shook her head. "No. You *can't.* Now, tell me what happened."

"All right," Starla said. "From the beginning…"

*

It was 1:30 p.m. on an early fall day the week before homecoming in the very middle of state history class, a requirement that brought most students to the brink of the abyss called boredom. Teacher Relta Cox liked to "celebrate" the lives of people who had made their mark on Washington, but the reality of it was that students sitting in front of her didn't care one bit about early explorers, native people, or pioneers who settled the region back in the days when it was called Oregon Territory. They might have been more engaged if the discussion veered toward the ritzy house that Bill Gates owned near Bellevue, or how much dope Jimi Hendrix smoked on any given day, or some tidbit about Starbucks when it was cool and not just a Denny's that served only coffee drinks and pricey pastries.

The rest of the stuff, forget about it.

A boy from the principal's office, who no doubt asked to be the bearer of the message since it was going to Starla Larsen, entered the classroom, spoke with the teacher and then handed some paper to Starla. She looked down, shook her head and got up to leave. The girl knew how to own the room. She wore a leopard print tank, black Capri pants and a gold choker that looked very, very expensive. Her purse was a black Michael Kors that her fans knew was her go-to bag. Starla's outfits made her the best-dressed girl in school. Starla scanned the classroom as her long legs moved toward the door to the hall. Her eyes lingered only a second, and on only one person.

Katelyn Berkley! She'd made good on her threat.

When Starla arrived in the principal's office that afternoon, her fears were confirmed. Seated across from Principal Andrea Sandusky was the cheer coach, Lucy Muller, a young woman with long, dark hair, a bad overbite and the kind of strong, lithe body that suggested her past as an Olympic gymnast hopeful. As a high school principal, Ms. Sandusky never smiled anyway, so her grim face offered no tip-off of what was to come.

"Starla, I've asked Ms. Muller here because a situation has arisen that calls into question your ability to stay on the cheer team."

"What is it?" Starla said, trying to not crumble. Even being somewhat prepared was not enough to ensure that she'd be able to keep it together. She had wanted nothing more than to be the youngest Buccaneer varsity cheerleader captain in the history of the team. She'd been the only freshman to make the squad and was well on her way. The honor would surely be hers. She deserved it.

Not everyone deserves all good things, but I deserve this. This is mine!

"We have high standards here at Kingston," began the principal, who apparently had just finished a spinach salad because her left front tooth was covered with a fragment of a mossy green leaf. "We're proud of our students and consider them to be ambassadors of our school in the community."

"Yes, Ms. Sandusky," Starla said, trying not to look like she was staring at that green tooth, but she was. "I know. I get that. I am the best ambassador for this school."

Andrea Sandusky rolled her tongue over her tooth and sucked. *Got it.*

"I thought so too. But something has come to our attention that has given us great concern about you." She stopped and picked up a manila folder. In a flourish that would have impressed most defense lawyers, she pulled out a single 8-by-10 photograph. Then, as if it were laced with poison, she set it on her scrupulously neat desk, faceup. It depicted Starla with a beer bottle in one hand and a cigarette in the other.

Starla shifted in her chair. "I can explain that."

"I'm sure you can, but explanations don't really count for much when there is incontrovertible proof." The principal tapped her unmanicured fingertip on the photograph, which, on closer examination, appeared to be a laser print, not a photographic print.

Lucy Muller, who'd up to that point seemed to check out of the meeting, finally spoke, whistling through her overbite like a piccolo. She was fired up and on the defensive. Starla, as her name implied, was the cheer team's future star.

"I want to go on record now," she said.

"This isn't a courtroom," Principal Sandusky said.

"Right," the coach said, acknowledging that she'd overreached in her language. "I want to go on record that this morals offense, while serious, does not meet the requirement to remove Starla from the squad."

Principal Sandusky didn't appear to be too convinced. "Oh, really. Smoking and drinking?"

Starla knew better than to say a word. It wasn't easy for her to keep her lips shut, but this time reason won out over the need to always jump into the fray.

Lucy Muller picked up the flimsy photograph. "It is a violation, but look at the date stamp on the border. The bylaws say that an offense is only punishable if the person violated rules *after* she had been uniformed as a member of the Buccaneers' cheer squad."

Ms. Sandusky studied the date: the year *before*.

"You're underage now," she said, obviously miffed. "This kind of trailer-park behavior is unacceptable, and we have a zero-tolerance policy at Kingston High. What were you here, fourteen?"

Starla didn't say a word. She didn't even move her lips.

Coach Muller did, or rather, whistled. "In case you didn't know," she said, now lapsing into a slight Southern accent, "I was raised in Mobile Manor Estates near Louisville. I think we should consider leniency."

The principal's face went a shade of red. Not scarlet, but very close. The last time Starla had seen that same color was on a pair of Christian Louboutin shoes. It was, she thought at that very inappropriate moment, her very favorite color in the world.

"I will take that under advisement," Principal Sandusky said, looking first at the cheer coach and then over to Starla. "See that this doesn't happen again."

Starla nodded. She hated the woman, yet somehow she managed to smile just enough to signify that she understood and was still a very congenial person.

"I promise," she said. "Thank you, Ms. Sandusky."

*

Mindee finished her first glass of wine and returned to the refrigerator. By then, Teagan had come into the kitchen in search of dinner. He had enough food stains on his shirt to make the casual onlooker think he'd already eaten or was wearing a cool graphic tee.

"We're having tuna noodles tonight. The *good* kind. The kind with potato chip crumbs on top," Mindee told Teagan as she flicked him out of the room.

Starla wondered how anything with potato chip crumbs could be considered "good." Her mom was a terrible cook. She didn't mind enough to say anything. To keep her weight down, she'd taken to purging two nights a week. Only two, because she was sure that didn't meet the wiki guidelines indicating a serious problem.

"First of all," Mindee said, "you can only drink and smoke at home. If that photo was taken anywhere but here, you're going to have your butt handed to you right here and now."

"It *was*," she said. "Promise."

Mindee didn't question her daughter's veracity just then. That usually brought more drama than she could handle on a glass and a half of wine.

"Second of all," she went on, "I am so pissed off at Katelyn. I could just kill her!"

"I know. Me too. But, Mom, really, I am kind of sad for her."

"Sad? We can show her sad."

"Look, she's a nothing. She didn't make the squad again—she didn't even have a chance. She's a clumsy brunette. When I think about it, she doesn't even have a boyfriend. She never, ever, has."

Mindee grabbed a kettle, a can opener and a can of mushroom soup. "She hurt you, honey. She tried to take your spot. Get me the StarKist. Two cans."

Starla got up and went to the pantry. "Coach Muller would never have put her on the team. She laughed at her like the other girls did. *I did.*"

Mindee fastened her eyes on Starla's. "If she's so damn jealous because of what you've got, then let's give her something to talk about."

Starla looked confused. "I don't get what you mean."

Mindee poured a bag of egg noodles into the just-boiling water.

"Let's get her a boyfriend," she said.

Again, a confused expression appeared on Starla's pretty, pretty face. "I still don't understand."

Mindee indicated her empty wineglass. She didn't worry about it being her third glass. She'd read somewhere online that three a night was not a serious problem.

"You don't have to," she said. "All you have to do now is get me the open bag of chips and crunch some up. Teagan gets cranky when he doesn't eat. I can't stand cranky preteens and all the drama they bring. We'll take care of Little Miss Troublemaker after dinner."

Mindee Larsen had no idea of the drama she was about to unleash. Neither did Starla. On his worst day ever, Teagan Larsen couldn't even come close to being *that* bad. Sure, he *might* try. In a home with two contentious females and Jake Damon, his mom's boyfriend, the boy had to try.

CHAPTER SEVENTEEN

Taylor Ryan couldn't sleep. It might have been the jitters that came with being back at school after a long break. Kids were bragging or complaining about their Christmas gifts or where they went on vacation. Some complaints were deserved. Outside of Port Gamble were a number of mobile homes tucked in trailer parks or by themselves behind Douglas firs and big leaf maples. Some were hidden from view for a very good reason. The poor of Kitsap County, sometimes referred to as Kitsappalachia, were one group: people with drug or alcohol problems, mental illness or something that forced them to live in circumstances that were far from ideal. Then there were the others, the criminals—the "rough crowd" as Valerie Ryan called them—who chose to hide out in the country so they could cook meth, grow pot or do other things that led only to trouble.

"Trouble always begets more of the same," she had told the girls on more than one occasion. "When you see trouble, don't run to it like a moth to a flame. The moth gets burned, remember."

And yet, that's exactly what Hayley and Taylor did. Their mother knew it, of course, and her admonition was a warning with little teeth; it was nothing more than a reminder to be very, very careful.

"You poke at evil with a stick," Valerie had said, offering chilling advice they'd never forget. "Never use your fingers."

Taylor went downstairs quietly that night, although she didn't need to be so light on her feet. She could hear her father snoring, and she knew that her mother probably had earplugs in and her head under a pillow.

Maybe under two.

She made her way to the kitchen and rifled through the refrigerator, but she wasn't really hungry. She filled a glass with tap water and walked to the windows with the rippled glass that were original to the 1859 house.

The bay was a black void, with only the faint shimmer of waves at its rocky edges. A bird called out abruptly somewhere in the darkness. The finality of its cry chilled the teenager. The scream of an animal in the dark almost certainly meant its gruesome demise.

Taylor wondered about Katelyn and if her soul had crossed over, if Katelyn's soul had been lifted to the place where there is an absence of all pain. She and her sister were blessed in many ways, but there was never a time when either could understand fully why it was that their empathy for the dead was so deep, so profound.

"Katelyn," she whispered, leaving a misty fog on the window-pane, "what happened to you?"

Her fingertips touched the cold glass for a second, not long enough to leave more than a few dots on the fogged, uneven surface. She resisted the impulse to draw a heart. It was a strange feeling just then, strong and confusing.

"Tell me when you are ready. Tell me, if you can," she said haltingly.

Taylor and her sister knew people would think their gifts were faked, like bad sideshow psychics, carnival mediums and the pack of middle-aged men that paraded around cable TV talking with the dead like some nitwit's idea of an otherworldly cocktail party.

"Wow, he guessed that someone in the audience has a family member with the first letter J in their name," an unimpressed Beth Lee had said one time when she was over watching TV at the Ryans'.

"Yeah," Taylor said. "Pretty stupid."

"I love how they always say that dead people have unfinished business to attend to," Beth said. "Like whatever you're doing when you croak needs to be put in order."

Hayley caught her sister's eye. Beth was a lot of things—vegan, Goth girl, fashionista—but she didn't really understand that there was truth to some of what those TV shows were playing up.

"Do you really think that once we die, you know, there isn't anything more?" asked Hayley.

Beth rolled her eyes. "Oh, don't go all religious on me."

"It isn't about religion," Hayley said. "It's about our spirit. I think there is something here, something more."

"I'm not saying there isn't," Beth replied flatly. "I just haven't seen any evidence."

Taylor spoke up. "Have a little faith."

Beth looked over at the TV. "Dr. Phil is coming on. I have faith that he'll still be a chub despite his exercise and health books."

The show intro cued up and the TV host with the bald head and mustache appeared.

"Look," Beth said, "I was right. *He is.* I must be psychic."

Hayley and Taylor laughed, but inside they knew that no matter how hard they might try, no matter how much those closest to them might want to believe them, some things could not be explained.

Maybe it was more than that. Maybe some things *shouldn't* be explained.

The twins locked eyes. They both knew that that was the truth, absolute and unqualified.

CHAPTER EIGHTEEN

A few days after the cheer squad results were posted, Katelyn and Starla sat out on the Larsens' rickety old back porch glider and watched Teagan as he tried to keep their attention on a rope swing that Adam Larsen had put up the year he vanished. The swing was a replacement for one that had rotted, and as a replacement, there was no need to go through the cumbersome process of sucking up to the property management company that kept things Stepford-pretty in Port Gamble.

Starla offered Katelyn a smoke from a pack of Vogue Superslims Menthol that she'd stolen from her mom and tucked behind a cushion on the porch glider.

"I didn't know cheerleaders were allowed," Katelyn said.

"They're not. But they're also not allowed to get fat, and smoking helps. I don't want to be bent over a toilet because I ate something I shouldn't. It's better not to eat at all. Smoking is very, very helpful."

Katelyn lit her cigarette from the ashy red tip of Starla's smoke and kept her eyes on Teagan.

"He won't tell, will he?"

Teagan was a wiry, fearless boy who seemed to delight in the attention of the older girls. He noticed the smoke.

"Are you watching me? Katelyn?" he called over from the rope.

"No, he won't tell," Starla said, before calling across the yard to her annoying brother. "We're watching you, you little brat."

"How can we *not* watch him?" Katelyn said, pulling a long drag through her cigarette. She was proud that she wasn't coughing, but, of course, she didn't say so. "He swings around like a crazy version of Tarzan."

"Tarzan was a dork," Starla said. "His best friend was a monkey."

Katelyn smiled. She stifled her desire to correct her friend by letting her know that a monkey and chimpanzee were not of the same species. Not any closer than man and monkey.

Instead, she changed the subject.

"I like your hair a lot," she said.

Starla fussed with it with her free hand. "I hate it. My mom cut it, and she's not much of a stylist."

Katelyn wanted to touch Starla's hair, so golden and pretty, but she didn't.

"I don't know," she said. "I think it's hot."

"You *would*. I mean," she said, eyeing Katelyn with a cool look, "you don't have to try as hard as I do to keep things going."

It was a dismissive, snarky remark that on the surface seemed like a compliment, but both girls knew it really wasn't.

"Nothing's easy, Starla," Katelyn said.

"I get that. Sorry," she fake-apologized.

Katelyn reached down to pet the Larsens' cat, Bobby, a vicious Manx, and, in doing so, the length of her arm was exposed.

"Jesus, Katie, what happened to your arm?"

Katelyn sat up ramrod straight and tucked in her arm like a chicken wing. "Nothing," she said.

Starla bent closer. "Bullshit. Let me see." She pulled on her friend's wrist to wrestle her arm from her body.

Katelyn didn't put up much of a fight. Not really. She let her arm go limp as Starla pushed up her sleeve to reveal three small parallel cuts just below the elbow. The freshly scabbed-over redness popped against the whitest part of her skin.

"I wondered why you were wearing a sweatshirt on a day like today. You haven't started up again, have you?"

"Your cat scratched me," Katelyn said, her tone defiant and pleading at the same time, begging Starla to notice that the bloody mess had taken over once more.

Starla shook her head, her eyes worried. "If the cat was named Katelyn, I'd say so."

Katelyn turned away, easing her arm from her friend's not-so-tight grip.

"You're cutting again, aren't you?"

Katelyn kept her focus on Teagan, performing his Tarzan spin on the rope.

"No, I'm not."

"Don't lie. We're practically sisters."

Weeks before, the comment might have resonated as being slightly genuine. But not then.

"Is it because you didn't make cheer again?" asked Starla.

"A little, I guess," she admitted.

Starla dropped her cigarette and crushed it with the toe of a tacky Candie's sandal she'd borrowed from her mother's closet. "I thought you stopped that," she said.

"I guess I didn't." Katelyn faced Starla before snuffing out her own butt. "Can we not talk about it? Please."

"It isn't normal and you know it."

Katelyn had let loose a deep, throaty laugh at Starla, the ethereal beauty, the one all others wanted to be like or be with.

"*Normal?* What could you possibly know about normal?"

"You need to go to a shrink," Starla said.

Katelyn's expression flatlined. "You need to butt out."

Starla shook her head. "Seriously, you need help. Does your mom know?"

Katelyn got up off the glider, her inert expression turned to anger.

"You tell her and one way or another I'll never speak to you again," she said.

"Like *that* would ever happen." Starla stood her ground. "We're tight, remember?" Starla said, knowing that it wasn't really true. She never had time for Katelyn anymore. Now, she saw her only from her bedroom window or on the rare occasion when they met on the street on their way home, like that summer afternoon they spent on the porch glider.

Katelyn had bristled at the lie. Starla was no longer a friend. She was no longer anything. She was the enemy and, as far as Katelyn could tell, she was unstoppable. If Starla had viewed Katelyn as a backup dancer in her laser-fantastic arena show, she was wrong.

Dead wrong.

CHAPTER NINETEEN

Hayley and Taylor found their father in his tiny office, which was decorated with paperback book covers that were so hideous they really couldn't pass for art, even though they were professionally matted and framed. Kevin Ryan was bent over his computer. Approaching middle age, Kevin was holding his own in the looks and cool department—at least on the dad scale, which every teenager knew was not so demanding. His hair was no longer styled in a foppish dad style but was cut short. He shaved off the porn-star mustache that he'd worn throughout most of the girls' younger years. His gray eyes looked up from the computer screen, and he grinned at his daughters.

Kevin always welcomed an intrusion.

"You talk to the police today?" Taylor asked.

He took his hands from the keyboard and swiveled around in his black leather office chair. "I talk to the police almost every day. It's kind of my job." He grinned.

Taylor pulled up a chair and scooted it closer to her father's desk. Hayley took a space next to Hedda, who was lying on her back, dead-opossum style, in the small window seat.

"We know, Dad," Hayley said. "Did you find out anything about Katelyn?"

Kevin didn't answer right away. He clicked the SAVE icon on the screen and took off his glasses, which he said he needed only for "computing" but the girls knew otherwise. Next to him was a printout of a Kitsap sheriff detective's report.

Katelyn's name and the date—twelve days after her death—were smudged across the top.

"Look," he said, "I want you to understand that what I'm about to tell you isn't the kind of information anyone really needs to know. But I've trusted you with important stuff before, haven't I?"

Their father could have been referring to a number of things right then, but more than likely it was the story of Donita Montero, a woman who'd abused her children before murdering one in a coin-operated washing machine in Duluth, Minnesota. His book, *Clean Getaway*, did not disclose the sexual abuse of the surviving daughter. While another author might have included it for shock value, Kevin Ryan took the higher ground and didn't even tell his editor about it. To confide in an editor was, without a doubt, like opening the door a crack.

A crack was all it took to ruin someone's life.

"Dad," Taylor said, "we were friends with Katie. We want to know what happened to her. What *really* happened?"

Kevin weighed her request carefully. "They thought it was an accident at first, but it is possible—maybe even likely—that she killed herself."

"Killed herself?" Taylor shook her head. "Doesn't add up, Dad. She wouldn't have done that."

"She got some bad news the night she died," he said.

"What bad news?" Hayley asked from the window seat.

"Her grandmother had promised to fund her college expenses but told her that night that the money was gone."

Hayley got up, and Hedda, astonishingly spry for seventeen, jumped to the floor. "I doubt she would have killed herself over that. College is years away. Anything could happen between now and then. She could get a scholarship or win the Lotto. She could even get a student loan."

Kevin nodded in agreement. Hayley was right. "That's what Chief Garnett told me. Nothing further is going to be done with the case. They're closing it as an accident, a freak one at that. Better than having Sandra and Harper live out the rest of their lives thinking that they could have done something to save their daughter."

There was no arguing that one. Instead, the twins took in each word with the respect and solemnity that they knew their dad, a kind of purveyor in tragedy, would expect of them. There could be little doubt that Chief Garnett and their father believed that digging around Katelyn's tragedy would only yield hurtful results.

It wasn't the twins' fault that they were driven to do so.

Others could never see what they saw or felt.

Others simply didn't get the messages that they did. In a very real way, others were actually kind of lucky.

Outside, barely out of the cutting chill of the weather, Moira Windsor stood under the green water towers at the entrance of the main business district of historic Port Gamble. She'd taken up smoking to be more reporter-like, and she was actually enjoying the buzz of the nicotine. It calmed her. It soothed her at a time when she really needed it. She'd accosted Sandra Berkley earlier in the day as she left the Timberline restaurant. Sandra barely said a word to Moira, but what she said left no doubt about her feelings about an interview.

"You bloodsucking bitch, leave my baby alone!"

"That was harsh! I'm sorry about your daughter, but I'm on a deadline!"

Sandra could have killed the reporter right then, but she didn't.

There'd been enough death in Port Gamble.

For a second, Moira felt a little embarrassed, but on further reflection she dismissed it when she realized that no one else had seen the encounter.

She'd left more messages for the Ryans, but there were no return calls.

What do I have to do to get somebody's attention? she asked herself as she snuffed out her cigarette, ignoring the sign to dispose of trash in the proper receptacles.

The more people pushed her away, the harder she'd push back.

She heard a dog yelp somewhere in the distance, and she smiled.

CHAPTER TWENTY

Unlike Inuits who purportedly have an unbelievable number of words to describe snow, teenagers in Port Gamble have only four to describe rain: almost all the time.

Those who don't live there could never comprehend the incessant downpours that come in fits and starts all year long. Spring. Winter. Whatever. Rain falls like a curtain over the town. On those rainy days, anyone looking from the General Store to Buena Vista Cemetery could see nothing but a white wall before them. Not even a tree is visible. And forget the scenic view. During the heaviest downpours, the bay and the canal blend into one large, seamless cloud. Oddly, only the most overt nerd townie or tourists carry umbrellas. No one loves the rain in Port Gamble, but residents live there in spite of it. They refuse to let it stop them from doing what they need to do.

There were never any rain delays for school sports events. Never did a June bride plan a wedding on the bluff overlooking the sound without the benefit of tents. No camping trips to the Olympic Mountains were canceled over inclement weather. No picnics were moved inside.

As Kevin Ryan told his girls over and over, "You're not the Wicked Witch of the West. You won't melt if you get wet. Trust me."

It was raining, of course, when Taylor and Hayley stood out in front of their house waiting for the school bus. In a few months they'd be sixteen, and if there was any justice in the world, their father would help them buy a car.

Girls like Starla Larsen with older boyfriends managed to halt the cycle of abuse that was the bus ride to Kingston High School. The driver, Ms. Hatcher, liked to keep perfect order on "her" bus. She was a driver. Not a mom. She didn't want to be a hugger. She made one touchy feely kid sit behind her on the window seat in her blind spot so she never had to engage with him, next to a boy from house number 27, who wore a raccoon tail on a back beltloop as a fashion statement.

Other kids sat in the usual order. In the front were the geeks, the crybabies and the kids who just wanted to get off the bus as soon as the doors swung open. The couples and the druggies sat in the back. The middle section held everyone else.

Beth Lee was seated in the middle—one of the few kids to actually migrate toward the center of the bus since leaving elementary school. Beth had so many incarnations that she easily could have found a spot anywhere. Hayley and Taylor scooted into the seats next to Beth.

As the bus pulled away, the girls rolled their eyes at Segway Guy, the man who lived in house number 91 along the water and who for some strange reason chose the most embarrassing mode of transportation known to man as his preference to get from point A to B.

"Freak," Beth commented. "Even the rain doesn't stop him."

"The rain stops no one," Hayley said, deadpan. "Not even Segway Guy."

"Where's Colton?" Beth asked. "Home exhausted?"

"From what?"

"From doing it with you." Beth spoke loudly, not so much to overcome the noise of the idling bus and Ms. Hatcher's tendency to over-press the accelerator pedal as she waited for her turn to merge onto the highway, but to increase the opportunity for someone to overhear. Anyone who saw her could figure that. That day Beth Lee's impossibly black hair was spiked with so much Elmer's Glue that someone could hang a coat on it. No doubt once they got to school, someone probably would try.

Hayley motioned for Beth to lower her voice. "For your information, he was out of town all winter break. And in case you were wondering, you're gross."

Beth smirked a little and touched the tips of her hair. She made a pained expression that was either meant to signify her sharp hair spires or that she'd been quietly told off by one of the girls whose names she used interchangeably. "Just asking. I figured that you did it by now. Probably told your sister, but not me. People leave me out of everything."

Taylor spoke up. "She hasn't told me anything." She looked at her twin. "You didn't, did you? I mean, I would have known if you had."

Hayley scowled a little. "That's none of your business, but no, I didn't, and no, I won't tell you when we do."

Beth glossed her lips with some overly fragrant strawberry lip balm. "So you're going to?"

Hayley shook her head, her face now a little more pink than she could ascribe to the cold weather. "I didn't mean *that*. I meant, *if* we do. Unlike some girls around here, I'm actually in no big rush."

Beth deflected the remark by changing the subject. Beth was like that. Taylor once wondered if Beth's ancestors invented fireworks because she seemed to totally get off on lighting fuses and standing back to watch the fun.

"I heard some news," Beth said as the bus lurched down the highway toward Kingston.

"Do we have to pull it out of you?" Taylor asked.

"Right, we know you're so discreet," Hayley chimed in, unsuccessfully trying for a little payback.

Beth put her lip balm in her purse and scrolled through her text messages.

"My mom told me that her friend Lu at the Timberline said that Katelyn got into big trouble last fall. Something that made her mom and dad furious. I couldn't hear it all."

Hayley narrowed her focus on her best friend. "I thought you said your mom told *you*."

"Guilty. Big deal, I was eavesdropping. So what? The information is good."

"What did your mom say, exactly?" Taylor asked.

"I'm Asian. That doesn't make me a Sony recorder."

"Right," Taylor said. "But what did she say?"

Beth thought for a moment, extracting every word for her friends who always annoyingly insisted on precision. "She said, 'If I were Katelyn's mother I'd have done the same thing. What girls won't do these days for a boy.'"

"What boy was she talking about?" Hayley asked.

Beth sighed. "I don't know," she said, clearly bored with the subject of Katelyn's imaginary love life. "I really don't care. But I thought you two might."

Beth Lee anchored her trademark black Doc Martens on the green linoleum floor in front of the lockers in the Red Pod at Kingston High School and flipped through her texts. The school administration didn't allow the use of electronic devices during class, and teachers had gotten pretty good at catching the kids who tried to strategically place books to block the view from the front of the classroom. One violation got a slap on the wrist (not literally, of course, because that would be abuse and abuse was so very, very out of bounds), but two violations meant confiscation of the device and required an irritated parent to personally retrieve it from the principal's office.

That day Beth's fashion sense was subdued. Her top was a small men's chalk-striped suit vest that left her arms bare, and her jeans were old-school acid-washed. She looked a little like a 1980s reject, but she didn't care.

While a sea of kids trudged past her, she methodically scrolled through her messages, ignoring her mother's notes, which were always signed LOL. Beth didn't have the heart to tell her it did not mean Lots Of Love.

Be home late tonight. You'll have to make your own dinner. Lol. Mom.

She'd moved on to Instagram when Hayley arrived.

"Where's the other one of you?" Beth asked.

"Maybe Taylor's in the bathroom?" Hayley guessed. "I don't know."

Beth held out her phone. "Who is Moira Windsor?"

Hayley looked on and shook her head. "I don't know. I've never heard of her."

"Says she's a friend of yours; she's following me."

Taylor joined them.

"Who is Moira Windsor?" Beth asked her.

Taylor shook her head. "Dunno."

Beth looked at the twins. "Do you two always say the same thing?"

Hayley laughed, but it was a nervous laugh. "No, and no, we don't know her."

By then Taylor was looking at her Instagram account.

"Get this," she said. "This Moira person says she's following me because she's *your* friend."

The three girls looked at each other.

"Stalker!" they all said in unison.

Beth put her phone back into her purse.

"Hey, that was cool," she said. "This time I got to say the same thing. Someone's rubbing off on someone." She let a beat pass. "Not sure I like that."

Hayley and Taylor didn't say anything more about Moira as they peeled off in different directions for their respective classes. Taylor had art, Hayley had life science and Beth was toying with getting out of PE because it was table tennis and she felt it would be racist to make her participate. She hated to sweat, and the excuse seemed a plausible way to get out of suiting up.

Forcing me to play because I'm Asian is offensive, she imagined herself saying to the coach, a nice woman who never offended anyone.

Kim Lee would be mortified by her daughter's actions, and Beth would pretend to sulk after she got a talking-to.

Her mom might notice her then. That would be good. It was all she really wanted.

Hayley and Taylor knew Moira's name. They'd heard their father talking to their mother in the living room again about the pushy reporter, but it was a conversation that ended abruptly when they approached.

What was that all about?

CHAPTER TWENTY-ONE

Number 19 was eerily quiet. For a change, their father's some-times-jackhammer snoring couldn't be heard. Hayley and Taylor had talked through the outlet about what they were thinking and feeling. Not surprisingly, Katelyn remained heavy on their minds. She was probably in the thoughts of many in Port Gamble before they slept. Those who were religious likely included Katelyn and the Berkleys in their prayers. All wondered just how it was that a girl could die in a bathtub with a household appliance as her killer.

Hayley and Taylor went to sleep hoping that a clue would come to them.

Something did.

Taylor's last thoughts before slumber were pleas to whomever or whatever controlled her dreams to let Katelyn come to her.

Then she was in the corner of Katelyn's bedroom, watching, *feeling* all that was happening.

The illumination from the laptop's screen sent a cool white spray of light over her face as Katelyn sat on her bed, hoping for more conversation with the boy she was falling hard for. She wasn't disappointed. The chat window was open for only a second before he appeared online to talk.

Cullant: why won't u meet me?

She took a second before answering. Being too quick would signal desperation.

Katiebug: cause i don't know who u r.

His typing was slow as he hunted and pecked his way across the keyboard, stopping, correcting.

Cullant: that's the point in meeting someone.

Katelyn was nearly sixteen. She was nobody's fool. But she was undeniably lonely.

Katiebug: thx for the nice things you've said. But 4 all i know, you are some old man in port orchard & u get your rocks off by going after teen grls.

Cullant: lol. That's good. Like i've ever been to port orchard.

Katiebug: k. That was a low blow. LoL.

Cullant: a perv is fine, but port orch? Ur hitting below the belt.

Katelyn laughed; it wasn't an LOL, but an actual genuine laugh. She liked this guy. *Whoever he was.* She needed someone to like. She'd felt so abandoned, so lost. Nothing had been going right. Her grades had slipped precipitously from the year before. It was as if she'd been free-falling and there was nothing to land on. And as lame as it was, she felt her only hope was the guy on the other side of her computer screen.

Katiebug: when ru sending a pic?

Cullant: what kind of pic do u want?

Katiebug: now u really r beng a perv. U know, the kind u might give your mother.

A short pause was followed with some more typing.

Cullant: k. Just so happens i took a new 1 today. Here it comes.

She waited for the image to upload in the window of her messenger app. One pixel at a time. The wait was excruciating.

Katelyn's eyes lingered over the photo as it came into crisp view. It was a casual shot, not of the quality pulled from some male model site on the Net. The boy had dark hair, blue eyes. Hot.

Katiebug: that's u?

Cullant: yup. That's me. U like?

Katiebug: if dat's really u, i do.

Cullant: it's me.

Katelyn knew there were other stupid girls out there who'd fall for some Internet guy, but she wasn't that type of a girl. Even if she was, even if she allowed herself a little fantasy, it was something that she needed right then. She wanted the attention of someone special because she no longer felt special herself.

Katiebug: let's talk tomorrow.

Cullant: K.

Katiebug: bye.

Cullant: TTFN.

Katelyn set down her phone. She went into her bathroom and looked at herself in the mirror in a way a stranger might: critically, with an eye to pick her apart in the meanest way possible. She wasn't really fat. She had good skin. Her hair was cute. Cute-ish, anyway. When she really processed what she saw in her reflection, she knew that she should feel better about herself. But she just couldn't get there. She could blame it on any number of things—her parents and their stupid restaurant, living in Port Gamble and probably the worst of it, not making the cheerleading squad.

When it came right down to it, it was all Starla's fault. She was to blame for everything wrong in Katelyn's world. She never could have imagined a betrayal from someone who had been a part of her life for nearly as long as she could remember. Yet it had happened. It came swiftly and irrevocably. It was like Starla's cold indifference to her had literally frozen her out of the life she'd imagined.

Katelyn pulled her clothes off, one item at a time, until she was naked, except for her bra and panties. She sat on the edge of the clawfoot tub and reached for the razor that had been calling to her all day. The cold metal blade's handle felt molded to fit her fingers and hers alone. Although it had become increasingly difficult to find the right place—a place that could not be seen by anyone but her—she managed to find a fresh spot on her upper right thigh. She drew a deep breath, like the kind she'd done when she'd tried to smoke cigarettes with Starla when they were kids.

When they were still so very, very close.

With a steady hand and a practiced technique, Katelyn Berkley cut. It was slow, deliberate. Even strokes. One. Two. Three.

She watched the blood ooze and closed her eyes to savor the feeling that came with the cut. The release was better than she imagined sex might be. She wondered *when* she would have sex.

And if it would be with the boy she'd met online.

It came to Hayley Ryan in a dream, the way a lot of things did. She was in the middle of the food court of the Kitsap Mall in Silverdale. All around her were the people of Port Gamble. Her family. Her neighbors. Mill hands whose names she didn't know because they lived in Little Boston or on the other side of the Hood Canal Bridge, but whose faces were very familiar. Beth. Colton. Starla. Even Segway Guy. No one seemed to be talking to each other, though the noise of their voices fought with the sound of dueling blenders at the Orange Julius counter. She watched herself wait for Taylor's smoothie—raspberry and banana. All around her. The noise. The people she knew. The girl behind the counter made change and handed it to her. She didn't recall ordering anything and was going to hand the money back to her sister, who was sliding a straw through the "X" cut through the plastic lid.

When she held out her hand, she noticed something peculiar about the dollar bill crumpled in her palm.

Hayley looked down, closer. Written over George Washington's unattractive green face:

THE CAUSE OF HER DEATH IS AMONG YOU

For a second, all sound stopped. It was instantaneous. Hayley looked up from the money and then quickly scanned the crowd in the food court.

Everyone from Port Gamble was there. For a moment, she even thought she saw Starla's dad, Adam Larsen, who'd been gone a couple of years. He waved at her, and then he vanished. All of them did. Gone, like the smoke from a birthday candle.

The next morning, while the twins put on makeup in the bathroom mirror, Hayley told Taylor about the dream.

"Weird. I hate bananas, and you know it," Taylor said, running brown mascara over her fair eyelashes.

Hayley knew her sister was playing with her. "I thought it was strange, too."

"Seriously," Taylor said, "I had a dream sort of like that last night too. Not exactly, though. Mine wasn't set in the mall. It was in Katelyn's room. Same idea. The feeling that the person responsible for Katelyn's death is right here, among us."

Hayley thought a moment, checking herself in the mirror.

"I know you're not going to tell anyone about our dreams, or whatever they are. But if you ever feel tempted, please leave out the part that I was in the food court in my dream. It sounds so lame."

Taylor put her makeup into a small pink and black makeup bag.

"Are you kidding?" she asked, heading down the hall. "If people think you're a dork, then that'll transfer to me. Half the people around here think we're the same person. As far as I'm concerned, the mall dream never happened."

But it did.

CHAPTER TWENTY-TWO

It was the morning of her former best friend's funeral. Starla Larsen stood in front of the mirror in her Kingston High cheer outfit. The dress was red, trimmed in gold with a narrow white edging. It was a color combination left over from the days when cheerleaders were wholesome and when it didn't matter what color their pom-poms were—as long as they shook them with enough persuasive vigor when the team put some numbers on the scoreboard.

It was clear that no one back then took into consideration what a girl like Starla Larsen could bring to the uniform.

Starla knew.

White and black would be better, she thought as she turned in the mirror. *White and black don't compete; they enhance.*

She had a point. Starla usually did. She was that kind of a girl.

Because of her looks and somewhat overly seductive personality, Starla was an easy target for the B-word. If gossip ever got back to her, Starla merely looked blankly at her informant.

"Really? Wow, I never even noticed *her*. Wonder why she feels that way?"

It wasn't easy for most girls to look as hot as she did, and Starla almost felt sorry for them. It was true that she was blessed with her mother's and father's good looks, but it took more than genetics to change things in the physical world.

She was good at embarrassing girls, teasing boys and making things worse. Those, along with her undeniable in-your-face beauty, were her gifts.

Starla's teeth were white, her eyes glacial blue and her hair spun gold. Those things were easy to alter. Sure, teeth could be whitened, and she routinely did that. Her eyes, thankfully, were the right hue of blue. Not blueish. Not gray. Intense icy, icy blue. Certainly, her hairstylist mom helped her with her hair. That was more out of convenience than the fact that Starla thought her mom really knew what she was doing. Starla read enough fashion magazines and watched enough Style TV to understand that the cut was more important than the color.

Her mom almost never cut her hair.

Starla had it all, and she was only a sophomore. That, she was certain, had to be some kind of a freaking record.

The only downside in Starla's world, besides her anxious little brother, Teagan, and her omnipresent stage-mother wannabe, was her mom's boyfriend, Jake Damon. Even at almost thirty, Jake was eye candy, to be sure. He had a decent chest—pecs, not boobs—and arms that looked muscled but not overly gross when he purposely flexed around the house doing some chore that Starla's father would have done without making such a show of it.

Yeah, she thought, *Jake is the perfect guy for Mom. She still thinks she's in her twenties, and Jake is stupid enough to go along with it.*

Starla's mother came into her room and planted her four-inch pumps into the floorboards like she was nailing something down for posterity. Mindee was a sight as always. Her hair was gooped up with so much product, Starla wondered how her mother's pencil neck could support it. Mindee wore a simple black dress, her asymmetrical hair clipped with a questionable matching black bow, but Starla didn't say a word about it.

This time it was Mindee's turn to be critical.

"You're wearing that to the memorial?" she asked, indicating the cheerleading uniform with a jab of her fingertip.

Starla faced the mirror again and carefully re-glossed her lips. "The squad is going to be there. All in uniform."

Mindee shook her head disapprovingly. "I don't know about that, Starla."

"We aren't going to do a cheer, Mom."

Mindee pulled her heels from the floorboards and walked closer, touching Starla on the shoulder.

"I didn't say *that*," she said. "I was thinking, you know, about how Katelyn felt about you being a cheerleader. It seems inappropriate."

Starla pulled away. She wanted to say something about her mom's boyfriend being inappropriate, but she held it inside. After all, the day wasn't about her, her mom or Jake. It was about Katelyn Berkley and her suicide or accident.

Or whatever. Starla didn't care. Dead was dead, no matter how someone got there.

Teagan, a preteen with the pink flush of emerging acne and a modified Bieber haircut, wore black jeans and a sweater. He'd been unusually quiet for the past week, and Starla took his hand. It was clammy, but she didn't mind. She liked having Teagan around to use as a human shield between her mother and her boyfriend.

"Let's go. Let's go say goodbye to Katie," she said.

"I guess so," he said, dropping her hand. "I don't need you to drag me there."

Starla and Teagan started down the stairs, their mother behind them. At the landing was Port Gamble's answer to a jack-, or in his case, a Jake-of-all-trades, master of none. Jake Damon was the town's handyman. Until he took up with Mindee Larsen, most women would have said he was reasonably handy—with or without his toolbox.

Or something like that.

Jake smelled of beer, which was how he usually smelled. He looked Starla up and down and raised a brow in that creepy way he had when he was drunk and thinking he was sexy.

"Go, Buccaneers," he said, nodding like a dashboard bobble-head.

Starla wanted to ignore her mother's squeeze, but she couldn't hold her tongue. "Why don't you go off somewhere and Buccaneer yourself?"

Jake clenched his fists. The large veins on his arms stretched against his skin, and Starla thought he was a bigger jerk than she ever could have guessed.

"Did you say what I think you said?" he asked, stepping closer.

"You heard me," she said, giving proof to all doubters that pretty could also be tough. "I said Bucc You!"

Mindee yanked on her daughter's hand. "Starla! What a mouth you have."

"Let go of me," Starla said, twisting away. "I didn't say anything *that* bad."

Mindee looked at Jake pleadingly. "She's grieving; let it go."

"She's a pain in the ass," he said in his Bud breath. "But sure, I'll let it go."

The four of them slipped on their coats and started out the door. The church was only a short distance away and they decided that, despite the cold weather, they'd walk. There wouldn't be any conversation—just hurried steps through the cold led by a very pissed-off cheerleader.

While Katelyn Berkley's friends and her parents waited patiently for the cause of death to be determined—and for grandparents Nancy and Paul to return from a four-day cruise to Ensenada they refused to cancel—her body had been kept on ice under Birdy Waterman's watchful eye. Finally, two weeks after Katelyn's death, it came time to bury her. Her casket was carnation pink and ivory, a color combination more appropriate to an ice-cream store than to the final resting place of a girl who eschewed such colors in favor of the drab tones that she wore in the months before her death. Behind the casket, on the church altar, were photographs of the dead girl's life: Baby, Girl Scout Daisy and Sullen Teen. All of Katelyn's iterations of life stages were on display, along with a few things she'd made: a candy dish she'd glazed in purple and black at one of those coffee and pottery shops, a painting of a forlorn moon over the tar-colored waters of Port Gamble Bay and a letter opener made in shop class that looked suspiciously like an old-fashioned barber's razor blade.

No one said anything about that. *How could they?*

The church was full, though not particularly because of Katelyn's popularity in the community. It was true that she was well-known because of her omnipresence at the family's restaurant, busing tables, helping the cooks, sitting at the counter reading a vampire novel with a half-naked boy on the well-turned cover. Indeed, the swelling size of the crowd at her memorial service had little to do with Katelyn specifically. People were there because of her youth. Nothing, all ministers know, brings out mourners like the death of a child. Katelyn might have been more than halfway to adulthood, but she was still a little girl.

A very dead little girl.

Hayley, Taylor and their parents sat in the third row, two rows back from the Berkley family. Colton James sat behind the Ryans, and three rows farther back were Beth Lee and her mother, Kim. The order was as it had been the night of Katelyn's death: the closer the relationship with the deceased, the nearer to the casket.

Occupying the seats across the aisle from the Berkleys were Starla and her family. Next to them mourned the rest of the Buccaneers cheer squad.

Taylor whispered to Hayley, "Look, it's the pom-pom posse. If you ask me, Katelyn's spinning in her grave now."

"She's not in her grave yet," Hayley corrected.

"Ya know what I mean. She hated it when Starla ditched her for cheer."

"She hated it even more that she didn't get on the team."

Valerie put her finger to her lips but thankfully didn't follow the gesture with the librarian's shushing noise.

Someone pushed a button and a CD recording of an abbreviated verse of Celine Dion's bombastic classic, "My Heart Will Go On" from *Titanic*, tinkled aloud.

Hayley kept her mouth zipped, but she couldn't help but think she'd rather be dead than have that song played at her memorial. And in which case, even if she were dead, she still didn't want Celine, Mariah or Whitney piped into *her* service.

*

Valerie Ryan gripped her husband's hand as they looked up at what had to be the saddest sight in the world: the pink casket in the front of the Port Gamble church, a place in which historically the denomination changed with the tide and the whims of the mill boss's wife. St. Paul's was home to an Episcopal congregation then, but it had once been a Lutheran, Catholic and even a Baptist church. It didn't matter. The faithful went regularly, no matter what religion the wife had decreed for the town. Taylor and Hayley cried, not in the way that close friends shed a stream of tears, but tears born of a shared moment of tragedy. Some who lined the spaces in the old oak pews sobbed because they loved Katelyn. Others cried because of the overwhelming sadness that comes with a young life lost.

Valerie's own tears came from memories of when her girls were small, memories from the darkest time of her adult life.

The event had been long ago, but the feelings of hopelessness and the fragility of life came to the mother easily while the minister talked about Katelyn's abbreviated life. Valerie's own girls had been side by side in Seattle's Children's Hospital for thirty-one days after the crash, their eyes fluttering, scanning under eyelids both parents prayed would open. The hospital wouldn't allow another bed in the room. Apparently, fire codes were more important than an aching heart of a mother or father. So Valerie brought a foam mattress from their home in Port Gamble, and she and Kevin took turns sleeping on it in the space between the girls' beds.

"Why aren't they waking up?" she asked, over and over.

"We really don't know," said the doctor, a pleasant, bespectacled man with nicotine-stained fingertips. "It isn't physiological."

"Why do you keep saying that?" Valerie caressed her girls, gently touching their cheeks to remind them that wherever they were right then… *wherever their minds were*… that she was with them and she would never leave.

"I'm sorry," the doctor said. "Sometimes medical science doesn't seem very scientific."

Valerie positioned herself between the two beds. Twin beds. Hayley's and Taylor's beds were tucked into a web of tubes and wires. "I just want to know what you're going to do to get them to…"

"Snap out of this," Kevin said, entering the room with two cups of coffee and a granola bar for Valerie, who'd stopped eating. The worry for all three of his girls was evident on his face—haggard eyes, dark circles. And as tired as he appeared to be, he never once wanted anyone to think he wasn't grateful for what he had. Other parents had lost their children.

Hayley and Taylor had been spared.

But for what? What kind of life would this be if they never woke up?

The Ryans' prayers were answered, of course. The girls did recover and they did get out of that hospital and back home where they belonged. It was true that both parents knew their daughters were not the same as they had been before the bus crash that almost killed them, but they never talked about it. Not really. It was easy to avoid because the change was invisible.

In the church pew alongside her grieving family, Valerie pushed those memories aside. She looked over at Sandra and Harper Berkley in the front row. Harper had his face buried in his hands;

Sandra had tilted her head and was resting it awkwardly on his shoulder. Valerie could imagine how they were feeling sitting there, thinking about how cruel life had been to them.

Katelyn had survived the crash, only to be snatched by death as a teenager. There was something very, very wrong with the world.

Valerie just didn't know how wrong.

*

Her tear-soaked tissue kneaded into a near-perfect sphere, Hayley looked on while the minister talked about Katelyn… her love of orcas, baseball, Claire's boutique and Cinnabon rolls served hot at the mall in Silverdale. The list made her smile and cry at the same time. She and her sister—she and everybody—had let Katelyn down. *What had they missed? How could it have been prevented?*

She looked at Taylor, her mother, her father. Over at the row of cheerleaders. She noticed how Katelyn's grandmother, Nancy, seemed to just stare straight ahead, while her husband, Paul, let tears roll down his ruddy cheeks.

And without turning too much, because being a spectacle at someone's funeral was the last thing Hayley Ryan wished for herself, she glanced back at Beth and her mom. Colton gave her a quick, supporting nod.

What had they all missed?

And yet it was more than the words spoken about a friend who'd become a stranger that tugged at Hayley's emotions; she could feel something coming to her. Coming at her. Hard and fast. It was more than the emotions of the occasion or the sadness pouring at her from every direction as a teenager just like her was being mourned. That feeling was anguish, heartache, misery.

Instead, Hayley was feeling, of all things, *fear*.

Not from the dead girl in the pink casket—which might have made some kind of sense, given how she'd been abandoned by everyone—but from someone else in the church. Someone wasn't sad at all. Someone was thinking that Katelyn Berkley had brought this on herself.

Hayley leaned very close to her sister and whispered in her ear. "Someone's worried about all this," she said. "About the truth of what happened."

Taylor, her blue eyes welling with tears, nodded. "I know," she whispered back.

In doing so, she happened to catch Sandra Berkley's eye. She looked so sad, so completely broken. She was lost and alone in the middle of a crowded church. Something about Katelyn's mother called out to Taylor.

It was as if she was beckoning her, asking her something.

*

Like a flock of crows against a stainless-steel sky, black processional umbrellas zigzagged along the trail up the hill to the Buena Vista Cemetery. The snow had turned to rain, which fell upon Katelyn's family and a small group of friends from all stages of the dead teenager's life. They had convened to watch her coffin slip quietly into the muddy earth above Port Gamble Bay. Harper, Sandra and even Katelyn's kitchen-remodeling grandmother, Nancy, sobbed like they were at war with one another over who could be the most anguished.

Without question, Sandra was winning. She had her thin fingers interwoven and locked around her heaving chest.

The Ryans were there, too. They'd known Katelyn forever. Beth and her mother were also on hand, their eyes lingering on a small row of graves not far from Katelyn's final resting spot. They knew that place so very well.

Starla's family also showed up. They were joined by Jake, whom Mindee clutched like an accessory, which, of course, he was.

Because his dad was away fishing and his mom incapable of leaving the house, Colton had arrived with the Ryans. Throughout the brief and grim graveside ceremony, he held Hayley's hand like a C-clamp. There was no way he was going to let go. If Hayley had thought she was all cried out, she was wrong. Katelyn might not have been her best friend, but she didn't deserve any of this—not then, not ever.

Taylor's tears mixed with the rain as she stood and looked at the casket while the minister said a few words. Inside, she felt nauseated. She wasn't sure she could hold the contents of her stomach. The feeling was more than just sadness, grief or loss. Taylor could feel the presence of something dark and scary. She'd been deeply troubled since the church service. She had carried that feeling to the cemetery, and it intensified.

What she sensed was terror from someone fearful about being caught—from a person close by.

It can't be.

Whoever had done this to Katelyn, whoever had resigned the teenager to a casket the color of a bakery box, was there... *among them.*

CHAPTER TWENTY-THREE

The excuse for revisiting the Berkley house was the hideous scarf that Taylor had purposely left behind. With her sister off somewhere with Colton, Taylor took it upon herself to do what needed to be done. First, she stopped by the Timberline, but its owner wasn't there. She saw Katelyn's mother in her office behind the hostess station, looking grim as she typed on the keyboard of the old CRT that filled half of her tiny desk. Since Taylor didn't want to talk to her, anyway, she quietly departed for their home next door.

Rain had left the remnants of snow on the sidewalk between the restaurant and house number 23 like a gray Slurpee. With each soggy step, Taylor wished she'd sprayed her lavender Uggs with more water repellent when her mother had suggested it. Hayley *did*. Hayley always did the practical thing. Taylor could feel the cold wetness pick at the tips of her toes, the chill working its way up her legs and the rest of her body.

Harper Berkley answered the door. His face was ashen and the stubble on his chin suggested that he probably hadn't shaved in at least a day or two. His eyes were the saddest Taylor had ever seen. Katelyn was always close to her father, in the way that teenage girls often are. It wasn't because their fathers were so much more wonderful; it was just that mothers always seemed to think that whatever road map they'd taken to get where they were would have been smoother if only they'd listened to their own moms. Of course, no teenage girl really wants to know that her mom had lived a life much like her own—twenty or thirty years ago.

"I'm sorry to bug you, Mr. Berkley," she said.

"Hi, Taylor." Harper was one of the few in Port Gamble, outside of her own family, who usually got the twins' names correct on the first attempt.

"That's me," she said, not sure about what more she should say that she hadn't already. She was sad about what had happened to Katelyn. She was guilty that she hadn't been "there" for her. Seldom at a loss for words, she was embarrassed after the service when it came time for people to file up and say something nice about the deceased, and she was unable to do so.

"What can I do for you?"

She took a breath. "I left my scarf here the other day. My aunt Jolene made it for me."

Katelyn's dad opened the door wider and motioned for Taylor to come inside. "Cold out there," he said. "Let's look for it. I don't know if I've seen it."

He shut the door behind them.

"You'd know it if you had," Taylor said, with a slight indication in her voice that the scarf might be memorable for the wrong reasons. "My aunt is nice, but the stuff she makes us…"

Harper smiled faintly. "I understand."

Taylor looked beyond the foyer. The Christmas tree was still up, lights twinkling and casting a strangely cheery glow into the living room of what had to be the most pitiful place in Port Gamble. Through the kitchen doorway, she could see a mountain of dishes piled up everywhere. No sign of that obnoxious grandmother, which was good. Katelyn's father led her to the hall tree a few steps inside the door, reached over to the top hook, and fished out the scarf, pushing aside a silver and black trench coat. Taylor knew the garment instantly. She hadn't seen it in a while. It was a Burberry knockoff that Katelyn had bought on eBay. She remembered how Katelyn was showing off her purchase by her locker at Kingston High. She was beaming, but not overly so. After all, it was a knockoff, but a pretty good one.

"Oh, Katie," Starla Larsen had said as she passed by the show-and-tell scene. "Another one of your auction winnings? It is so cute. I love the slimming silhouette on you."

"Thanks, Starla," Katelyn said, obviously unaware that her friend had dissed her.

With an LED-bright smile, no less.

Taylor remembered how she had felt when she observed that encounter. Starla was being cruel, needlessly so, and Katelyn just kind of stood there and let her be. Why didn't she tell her to F-off or something along those lines? Katelyn had it in her to push back. But not then. It was as if Katelyn were some kind of abused child, seeking the approval of a parent who never loved her—trying, but failing, then doing it all over again.

As the memory spun back into her consciousness, Taylor noticed a slip of paper protruding from a pocket of the faux Burberry trench.

She looked over at Katelyn's dad and gently touched her throat with her fingertips. "Mr. Berkley, I've got something stuck in my throat. Can I have a glass of water, please?"

"Of course," he said, turning in the direction of the cluttered kitchen.

Taylor lingered a half a second and grabbed the paper. It had been wadded, smoothed out and carefully folded. She didn't know why, but her heart started to beat faster as she unfolded it. Her eyes widened.

In typed, block letters it said:

I'M WATCHING YOU & LIKE WHAT I SEE

DON'T LET ME DOWN

"Coming?" Harper called from the kitchen sink.

Without a second of hesitation, Taylor shoved the paper into the pocket of her jacket and secured it decisively with the pull of a zipper.

"No need," she said, shaking her head. "I'm good. Thanks for the scarf. Take care, Mr. Berkley."

Taylor didn't wait for a response. She wanted to get out of there, right then. She twisted the doorknob and hurried outside into the slushy afternoon, her hand touching the pocket holding the note. Some younger kids were throwing wet snowballs in the field next to what had been old stables—before horses ceded their role to automobiles in Port Gamble. The kids' laughter was wholly at odds with what Taylor was feeling right then.

Fear.

The note was like a heartbeat in her pocket, pulsing, and urging her to get home. Its discovery was huge. It told Taylor that whoever had been talking to Katelyn online, had been close enough to her to give her a written, *real* message.

It wasn't a long walk to number 19 by any means, but Taylor made it there in record time. She called hello to her father typing in his office and ran upstairs to her sister's bedroom. Hayley barely looked up. She was immersed in the forensics book she got for Christmas.

"Taylor," she said, her eyes transfixed to the contents of the page, "did you know forensic science was first used to solve a crime that occurred in 44 BC?"

Taylor knew better than to cut her sister off. Hayley liked to share her little factoids. And there was no sign of Colton, which was kind of a relief. Despite the bombshell in her pocket, a little slack was in order.

"Not since *CSI* went on the air?" she pondered, sure her sister didn't hear her.

"You know, when Caesar was stabbed to death by Roman senators, a doctor named Antistius looked at the body and determined who the guilty senators were. Nobody's sure how, but he did it."

"Fascinating," Taylor said, pulling out the slip of paper.

"Yeah, that's how forensic science got its name. The doctor, medical examiner, or whatever he was, presented his findings in the Roman forum. *Forensics* is Latin for 'belonging to the forum.'"

Satisfied that she'd imparted some amazing information, Hayley finally looked up from the book.

"Gotcha. I'll remember that for *Jeopardy*," Taylor said, "but for now let's deal with something a little more current." She pushed the note to Hayley.

"What is this?"

"Read it."

Hayley unfolded the paper and read, her face growing grim and excited at the same time. "Where did you get this?"

"From Katelyn's trench coat."

"I liked that coat. She looked great in it."

"She did look fab. Anyway, you know what the note means—at least, what I think it means?"

Hayley nodded. "Yeah, it means that the person playing games with Katelyn was close by. Close enough to give it to her."

"It could have been mailed," Taylor said.

Hayley got up and held the paper toward the window. "It wasn't mailed," she concluded, indicating a rectangular smudge of glue. "It was taped to something."

"Her door?"

Hayley didn't think so. "No, then anybody could have found it."

"Like her mom and dad," Taylor said.

Hayley handed over the paper. "Yeah, them. Maybe it was taped to her locker at school?"

"Feel anything just now?" Taylor asked.

"No, did you?"

Taylor shook her head, carefully folding the paper along its original creases. "Should I sleep on it?"

For most, that particular phrase was a call to mull over a problem. For the Ryan girls, it was more literal. "Sleeping on it" meant just that. One or the other twin would put the paper under her pillow and try to sync her dreams to the document, its writer and the recipient. Taylor was better at that than Hayley, having discovered it when a note was left by the tooth fairy under her pillow when she was seven.

She didn't dream about the tooth fairy, of course. Instead, she got the feeling that her parents were behind the dollar traded for the tooth and the note left behind, in teeny, tiny script. She saw her mother squint her brown eyes while writing one minuscule word after another. It was amazing to Taylor that what she'd thought at first was a little note from a faraway land turned out to be a note her mother had written in the kitchen downstairs.

Thank you for your beautiful tooth. It will be the centerpiece of a necklace that I will wear proudly, now and forever. The Tooth Fairy

Taylor had believed for the longest time that what'd she'd seen and felt was only a funny dream. That changed one morning when she was nine and her mother, dressing for a book launch party, asked her to get her earrings from her jewelry box; Taylor found a little metal pill case. Inside, a cluster of small white teeth occupied most of the space.

Although it confirmed there was absolutely no tooth fairy, it gave crystal-clear proof of two things: there was magic in their mother's love and, as far as her girls could tell, Valerie Ryan had unlocked a pathway to information that was not of this earth.

If there was any "specialness" in the family, an understanding of it was only courted once. Just after their first birthday, Taylor and Hayley were studied by University of Washington linguistics researchers documenting early talkers. The twins had started talking in full sentences at ten months, and Kevin, never missing a chance to make a connection with someone who might be an asset later, answered an ad and submitted a video clip of the girls. Unlike some of his other endeavors, it worked. Sort of. A research assistant named Savannah Osteen was assigned to the Ryans, and she came to Port Gamble to tape them for a four-hour period a few weeks later.

Naturally, Kevin had been particularly proud of the girls' unusual verbal skills. Whereas most kids, months older, only pointed and called out one word for whatever it was they desired, Hayley and Taylor actually strung words together in a completely coherent fashion. No "Kitty!" for them; rather, it was, "I want to play with Kitty!"

Other times they called out phrases that made no sense to anyone but them.

That was at ten months.

And while it wouldn't surprise anyone who has studied twins, the Ryan girls did indeed develop a language that was unique to them. Savannah called it the girls' *idioglossia*, a language of their own. Neither Valerie nor Kevin quite understood what "levee split poop" meant, for example, but it clearly did signify something very important because Taylor and Hayley called it out many, many times. Outsiders, like the UW observer, considered it to be a descriptive phrase for a bodily function, with *poop* being the most crucial word. It seemed to be directed at certain *people*, however, not at the contents of a diaper.

Through the course of the observation period, Savannah captured the action on a videotape recorder mounted on a tripod discreetly stationed in the corner of the living room by a Christmas cactus, which once served as a focal point in Valerie's father's office at the prison.

The resulting report submitted by Savannah Osteen to the UW language department focused on the girls' unique language skills, of course, but it also touched on the intricacies of their relationship:

MEMORANDUM
FROM: Savannah Osteen
TO: UW Language Department

Twin A seems slightly more dominant than her sister, Twin B. On at least two occasions Twin A cut off Twin B when she was speaking in the language that they'd developed. In addition, Twin A was somewhat aggressive with the evaluator. A second session will take that into consideration and will mitigate any potential conflict by separating the sisters during the evaluation. Keeping them apart is an optimal protocol for this particular case.

Valerie and Kevin never really got a sense for how the girls performed in relation to other early talkers in the study. A third session was scheduled for about three weeks after the second. Since this one called for the evaluator to join the family for a dinnertime observation, Valerie made her famous planked salmon with balsamic vinegar and shallots. She even sprang for a better bottle of wine—a California Chardonnay—than she would have if she and Kevin were dining alone.

Evaluator Savannah Osteen, however, never showed. She didn't even call to say she wasn't able to make it to the taping session. Port Gamble often felt like the ends of the earth for those who lived there or those who had to come and visit, but honestly, everyone knew phone service worked just fine there.

Kevin called the university the following day to see if anything had happened to Savannah, and her advisor indicated in a some-what curt manner that she was no longer working there.

"She abruptly quit the program," he said. "Didn't give us one bit of notice. Maybe we can reschedule?"

Kevin, the crime writer, was suspicious. He was good at that. It came with the territory. "Hope she's all right. Safe?"

The advisor sighed. "She's fine. Just undependable."

"Really? She seemed to enjoy what she was doing," Kevin said. "She said it was very rewarding, and she thought our daughters could be quite helpful in the study."

"Changed her mind, I guess. Young people today don't stick with anything."

Kevin thanked the man and hung up the phone, a white kitchen wall mount that would stay put for five years before the standards committee of Port Gamble would rule it was not historic and could be removed after the Ryans switched to cell phones. Kevin thought the situation with the UW researcher was a little bizarre and certainly annoying, but ultimately he didn't mind too much. He'd had second helpings of the salmon the night the observer didn't show up. He normally hated leftovers. The sole exception was his wife's planked salmon. Hot or cold, it didn't matter; it was the best thing he ever ate.

Kevin was still relishing the meal when he took out the trash, which was heavier than usual. As the black Hefty dropped to the bottom of the metal garbage can, he heard the sound of glass-on-glass rattling, echoing in the night.

Curious, he tugged at the drawstring and peered into the bag. It was full of baby food jars—all of the same kind.

ABC pasta in organic tomato sauce.

CHAPTER TWENTY-FOUR

Teagan Larsen sat in front of the computer. Next to his keyboard was a bowl of fluorescent-orange microwave macaroni and cheese—the only thing that his mother let him cook for fear that anything else would burn down the house. The computer was set up on a small table adjacent to the sofa in the living room. Mindee Larsen had worried about teens being victims of online predators, and while she was sure Starla was cautious, Teagan wasn't. Since his father had left, he seemed more vulnerable than ever.

Although he'd brought a fork to jab at the sad bowl of pasta, he used his fingers to pick out one slimy, cheesy tube at a time. Each time he did so, he licked his digits with noisy and aggravating abandon.

"Teagan, you're making me sick," Starla said. She sat on the couch.

"Your face makes me sick," he said.

Starla didn't even glance in his direction. "How original, Teagan," she said. She continued flipping through the channels until she landed on *America's Most Wanted*. It wasn't her favorite show, but the idea of ordinary citizens rounding up the scum of the earth appealed to her.

"I wish Jake's photo would show up here one of these days," she said, barely looking over at her younger brother, who by now had started using his fork to eat the mac and cheese.

"I hate him too," he said.

Starla turned down the volume. This was an interesting exchange with Teagan, and she liked what she heard.

"I thought you liked him," she said.

Teagan nodded at his big sister. "I act like I like him because if I don't 'treat him with respect,' he'll beat my butt."

"He'd better not," she said, actually meaning it. Since making the cheer team, Starla had dialed down the pretense of being kind to everyone. She didn't need to be that nice anymore. She was already on top, and that kind of position was very, very powerful.

"You know he was in jail?" Teagan asked.

She didn't. If it were true, why didn't she know about it? Her mom's thug boyfriend was presented to both Starla and her brother as "a dear friend" before both of them realized he was staying over every night in their parents' bedroom.

"How do you know that?" she asked, no longer interested in the creep du jour who was being profiled on TV—a big fat dude who'd killed his mother with a crowbar and then stolen her car (a measly hybrid, of all things!).

They had a creep du jour right there in their house.

"I heard him talking to mom about it. Said something about how he'd had his freedom taken away once and never, ever would allow that to happen again."

"What did he do? Molester?"

Teagan went back to typing on the computer. "Dunno. Maybe. They didn't say what."

Starla paused, weighing other scenarios before settling on the molester theory.

"I don't like the way he looks at me," she said, slumping her head back onto the sofa pillow and wiggling her toes. Her nail polish, OPI's I'm Not Really a Waitress red, was looking a little tired. She'd attend to that later on that evening.

Teagan was only thirteen, but he almost had to laugh at his sister's remark. Starla didn't lift a finger, say a word or take a gulp of air without someone watching her. She lived for an audience—creepy or not. She just did.

He hated her and admired her for that.

Valerie Ryan felt the stream of cold air coming from the kitchen and knew immediately that the back door had popped open. Kevin was no Mr. Fixit, and it didn't even occur to her to call him into service. Instead, she went for the junk drawer next to the stove and retrieved a screwdriver. It wasn't really anyone's fault. The door handle was always loose.

She noticed the girls' coats and shoulder bags on the bench by the door.

They must have taken Hedda for a walk, she thought. The dog was lazy but dependable when it came to doing her business on the end of a leash.

"Hi, Mom," echoed at her, which meant that both girls were right behind her.

"Oh," Valerie said, slightly startled. "I thought you were out walking the dog."

Hayley and Taylor shook their heads in unison.

"Nope. We haven't seen her," Taylor said, suddenly feeling a little worried. Hedda was loved by everyone, but no one thought she was particularly smart. A lot of people liked to chuckle at the slightly dense, long-haired doxie with a dappled silver and black coat, which had made her look old even when they first got her.

"We thought you were," Hayley said.

The three of them went outside in the mid-January frost and stood on the back porch calling for Hedda. Hayley went down the alleyway looking, and Taylor canvassed the road along the bay in front. Their mother stayed put, calling for Hedda to come home.

Their dog was gone.

Deep down, mother and daughters knew that something bad had happened. Hedda was a homebody who didn't go far. She just didn't. Besides that, the little stub of a dog never missed a meal.

Ever.

CHAPTER TWENTY-FIVE

At the time of her death, Katelyn Berkley was no longer close friends with any of the Port Gamble girls she'd known since grade school. It wasn't that the other girls didn't want to be tight anymore. They did. Some even tried. But the more they tried, the more she seemed to retreat. No one really understood why. Hayley and Taylor assumed that it was because of the situation between her parents. When Katelyn was in middle school, the Port Gamble Police made at least two trips to the Berkley residence to defuse what busybodies liked to call a "domestic disturbance." The Ryan twins, having learned from their father's work, knew that "domestic disturbance" was the PC way of saying "knock-down, drag-out argument." There might have been other occasions in which intervention was needed, but no one knew for certain.

The teen gossip line said that Katelyn had been the one to call the police, saying she was fearful that her parents would end up hurting each other.

Hayley felt sick about what had happened to Katelyn in the years since those physical altercations. Katelyn had once told her that things were better at home.

"My mom's getting help," she said.

"What kind of help?"

Katelyn pretended to hold a glass and tipped it to her lips.

"Oh," Hayley said, because the gesture needed a response. But she didn't know what else to say. Sandra Berkley was a sad woman and, like her daughter, she was good at building walls around herself. Alcohol made a great barrier.

Maybe we should have tried harder, Hayley thought.

She fingered the note that her sister had recovered from Katelyn's trench coat.

She'd slept on the little slip of paper the night before, as had Taylor the night before *that*, but nothing had come to either one of them.

Instead, she found her thoughts drifting back to the state of things in the Berkley household before Katelyn's life began to unravel. She recalled the time she heard her mother talking with her father about what was going on over at house number 23.

"Things like that happen everywhere," Valerie had said.

"I know. But, honestly," Kevin said, "I never would have suspected the Berkleys."

"With all you know about violent crime, you ought to know that it thrives wherever it can."

"I feel like the dope who says that their serial killer neighbor seemed so nice, but when they look back on it they can remember a cat squealing and they wonder if he'd just killed it."

Valerie laughed. "It isn't that bad, Kevin."

"No," he said. "I hope not."

Hayley remembered how she'd seen Katelyn the day following a police intervention and asked her if everything was all right.

"I'm fine," she had said. "Why?"

"I don't know," Hayley admitted, feeling like she'd intruded on something private. "If you ever need someone to listen…"

Katelyn had stared hard at her, sizing her up, weighing her somewhat cryptic response.

"I don't need anyone's help," she said, finally and quite firmly. The wall was up, and it was made of brick, stone, steel and tank armor.

Hayley had stood there a second. The words that came from Katelyn were completely at odds with her appearance. She looked incredibly sad, worn down and very afraid.

"Are you sure?" Hayley asked, pushing only a little. "Can I help?"

Katelyn turned away to answer a text message. "There's no problem," she said without looking up. "No one but me." And then she walked off, toward her class, toward the cafeteria.

Somewhere away from Hayley.

Hayley let it go that day at school and regretted it years later. She hadn't pressed her further because it just seemed too private. Later, when she heard that Katelyn was cutting herself, she assumed what everyone who watched daytime TV did about cutters and their motivation to self-mutilate. They did it to control their pain, to let out the hurt one slice at a time.

Hayley hadn't dug deep enough to think about the root cause of Katelyn's problems.

She thought about how middle-school hierarchy ensures that a good number of kids are relegated to loser or outsider status. Katelyn, the cutter, was never really viewed by anyone as a loser. Few knew that secret. Katelyn was engaging. She was pretty. She still had her funny, bright side. And most of all, she still had the ear of her best friend, Starla.

Starla's friendship, no matter how tenuous, was nearly a guarantee that Katelyn could still get a passkey into something better than her miserable life back home or in the restaurant where she worked.

Still mulling over those memories, Hayley looked up as her sister entered her bedroom.

"What's up?" Taylor asked, finding a place on the corner of her sister's cozy bed.

"I was just thinking about Katelyn," she said.

Taylor ran her fingers over the old chenille bedspread that instantly, tactilely, reminded her of their grandmother on their mother's side.

"I know," Taylor said. "Me too."

Hayley studied the folded paper held in her fingertips. Taylor's eyes landed there, taking in its contents, and she wondered out loud, "Do you think we could have saved her?"

Hayley shook her head. To think that they could have done something but didn't was an immense burden. "I don't know," she responded. "But maybe Starla could have."

Valerie glanced down at Hedda's water and food dishes. There was still some reduced-calorie kibble in the dog's white ceramic dish, but it was stale. So was the water. She often complained that she was the only person in the family who thought to keep things fresh. It was only a flash of a thought, the kind that came and went with the bruising realization that Hedda had vanished.

The dog had been a part of the family for almost ten years. The day she had come to the Ryans was a day wrought with unthinkable tragedy and heartache. Valerie had returned home from the hospital for a change of clothes, when Kevin phoned her to say he'd seen on the news that they were recovering the bus. She drove over to the crash site, out of curiosity and the need to be there. She parked the car on the east side of the bridge and made the long walk toward the center of the span. The wind was blowing softly and the craggy Olympic Mountains lifted the sky. It was beautiful, but she barely noticed. In fact, Valerie was in such a state as she stood behind a barricade watching the recovery of the short bus that when a young deputy officer handed the dog to her, she took it.

"She's one scared pup," he said, "but now that she's back with you, look at that tail wag!"

Valerie didn't even think to say the dog didn't belong to her. *Because the dog did.*

The Ryans loved Hedda, though no one else seemed to. They weren't sure of her age, but a vet in Kingston put her at five or six when she was found on the bridge. The suggested age made the Ryans sad, as they knew that under the best of circumstances Hedda would be theirs for only a short time.

And yet, the tubby little dachshund kept going. She was seventeen and really no worse for wear than a dog half her age. Her fur had grayed quite a bit and her hearing had dulled, but her eyes were bright and unmistakably alert.

Valerie picked up the water dish and rinsed it in the sink. She washed out the food dish too. Instead of putting them away, she refilled both and set them on the place mat that the girls had bought at Petco in Silverdale. The mealtime mat read:

DOGGONE IT'S DINNER TIME

Valerie disregarded the words and smiled for the first time in a long while.

The dog might be gone, but she's definitely coming back.

CHAPTER TWENTY-SIX

Talking with Starla at school would never, ever happen. Even though she was only a sophomore, she was always surrounded by gatekeepers, wannabes and hangers-on. Hayley and Taylor knew they had to go over to her house to see her, which always meant the risk of running into Port Gamble's resident sleaze. Not Mindee Larsen—though a case could be made for that—but Jake Damon, a man who left footprints of slime in his wake.

At least, that's what most Port Gamble teenage girls thought whenever he was brought up in casual conversation. Even a blind girl with a halfway decent service animal could detect how Jake's hooded eyes traveled over a female's body, as if he were taking a tour of what he'd like to touch. They noticed how, at the first hint of warmish weather, he'd plant himself along the edge of the bay to smoke and watch the girls as they lay out on blankets to suntan Washington-style—which usually meant a bad sunburn under overcast skies. No one could argue that Jake wasn't good-looking. He was. He had nice eyes and straighter teeth than most handymen, with their picket-fence grins. He had a better body than those whose stomachs overhung dinner-plate-sized belt buckles. Jake never wandered around town in butt-crack-revealing, low-slung jeans.

Taylor and Hayley, however, didn't think Jake was hot in the least. In fact, behind Jake's back the twins referred to Starla's "momster's" boyfriend as "Mr. Yuk," because of the smiley-face tattoo on his right bicep. That undoubtedly was meant to be ironic, as it looked more like a poison-control sticker when he flexed, which was constantly.

When the twins arrived at the Larsen house a few days after Katelyn's funeral, they were relieved to see that Mindee's car, a late-model red Cabriolet with a ragtop she'd repaired herself with duct tape after her husband ditched her, was gone. Also missing was Jake's Toyota Tacoma, a dumb name for a small pickup truck if ever there was one. Who, Beth Lee once wondered aloud, would ever want to drive a pickup named after Tacoma?

It made as much sense as calling a sexy sports car a Boise.

Starla opened the door. She was wearing a pale pink top and dark-dyed jeans. The top, like most of the things she wore around the house, was her mother's. Mindee could be trashy, but she had good stuff among the crap that she'd collected from the middling boutiques at the Kitsap Mall. Starla wore whatever she could hustle from her mom's wardrobe because it meant less wear and tear on her own things.

"Are you two collecting for something?" Starla asked.

Somehow Starla could always manage a few words that rubbed their recipient the wrong way. Next to mounting the top of the human pyramid on the football field, it was one of her best talents.

"That was last year," Hayley said. "By the way, we never did get that money for the breast cancer walk. But that's not why we're here."

Starla made an annoyed face as she one-handedly clipped her tangle of long hair into a messy bun.

Another skill.

"You want to come inside?"

Taylor pushed past the cheerleader. "It's super cold out here. Thanks for inviting us in."

The Larsen house was as it always was—a total mess. Mindee wasn't a hoarder, per se. But she was an incorrigible collector of the kinds of things that Valerie Ryan liked to call "dust catchers." On the table next to the front door was Mindee's collection of Scottie dogs. She seemed to embrace the concept that if one was good, fifty was awesome. Her kitchen was done up with more chickens and roosters than a KFC. The living room was less cluttered, save for the sofa table and its clutch of glass egg-shaped paperweights.

Teagan was playing a video game on the computer in the family room. He brightened a little when he saw Hayley and Taylor.

"Double trouble," he said, trying to be cool.

"Hey, that's clever. Let me write that down," Hayley said, pretending to smile. "You are so funny."

Taylor smiled, trying to defuse her sister's annoyance at the kid she'd babysat a couple of times—and never wanted to again. "Actually, we're twice as nice," she said.

"Whatever," Teagan said as he went back to bombing New York City with a scary kind of enthusiasm.

"What do you two want?" Starla asked.

"I'd like a diet soda, please," Hayley said.

"Water for me," Taylor added.

Starla made a face. "Okay, but I didn't mean *that*. Why are you here? Not that it's not nice to see you, but we really don't hang out anymore. Not since I made cheer."

You have to throw that out as if it were winning the Pulitzer, Hayley thought.

"We're here about Katelyn," Hayley said. "Can we talk in your room?"

Starla eyed her warily. "I guess, but do you still want the drinks?"

"No," Taylor said. "We're good."

They followed Starla upstairs. It had been a couple of years since they'd been in Starla's inner sanctum. The last time they'd been there, she had posters of pop stars and hippy-dippy beaded curtains she bought at Spencer's back in seventh grade.

This time it was completely different. Taylor almost gasped when Starla swung open the door.

The walls looked like mirrors. Everywhere they turned were pictures of... Starla. She was posing in her Buccaneers' uniform (with and without pom-poms) and in some ridiculous evening-wear attire that reminded Hayley of getups she'd seen in kids' pageants on TV. There were even some images of Starla practicing her cheer routine in the backyard.

"Motivation," Starla explained, picking up on the girls' obvious stares. "I read in a magazine that if you surround yourself with the best that you are, you'll get even better. I have a lot more to work with, but you two should give it a try."

You're a real piece of work, Taylor thought, but thankfully she managed to hold her tongue. She and her sister were there for a reason—and an important one at that.

Hayley studied the photo of Starla in the backyard. In the background, off to the side, was Katelyn, standing with slumped shoulders and a sad look on her face.

The reason they were there.

"We wanted to talk about Katelyn," Hayley said. "Do you think she actually killed herself?"

"I don't know. I guess she had a lot to live for," Starla said halfheartedly, as though she was not sure if that was true. She planted herself on a big pink beanbag, the only item that either visitor remembered. Beth Lee had once hurled all over it during a sleepover when Mindee served salmon cakes ("made up of two cans of salmon—the good kind") and Tater Tots. The memory was disgusting, but it still made Taylor smile. Just the idea of Beth retching over a beanbag was awesome enough, but the fact that it was Starla Larsen's made it absolutely *sweet*.

"I heard Hedda went missing. Did she come home yet?"

"No," Taylor said. "Have you seen her?"

Starla shook her head. "Oh, no! What kind of a friend would I be if I didn't call you the very second I saw her?"

You would be a rotten friend, thought Hayley.

A friend like Starla Larsen, thought Taylor.

Like most bedrooms in the historic district, Starla's room was small and there weren't many places to sit. Hayley slid to the floor, resting her back against Starla's white wrought-iron daybed. It had a lemon-and-cherry print duvet and enough ruffled pillows that it seemed it would take an hour to scoot them aside to make space to sleep at night. Taylor swiveled the white and black plastic IKEA desk chair around to face the other two.

"Katie was pretty messed up," Starla said.

Hayley tried to get comfortable by shifting her weight. The hardwood floor was, well, hard.

"Messed up enough to kill herself?" Taylor asked.

"Teen suicide is rampant in this country," Starla said, readjusting her messy bun. "I did a paper on it."

Hayley gave up on being comfortable. "Katelyn was your best friend."

Starla shook her head. She did so slowly and without making eye contact.

"Correction," she said. "And I know this will sound harsh, and harsh is not at all what I'm about, but she was most definitely *not* my best friend. I might have been *her* best friend, but not the other way around."

"All right," Taylor said. "But you knew her better than anyone. You would have noticed it if she was spiraling downward, thinking of killing herself. Right?"

Starla punched at the beanbag to spread its flattened Styrofoam beads. "Look, I've been busy. I feel horrible about what happened to Katie. But if you're looking for me to give you some insight—and I don't even know why you'd care—I can't do that."

"What about last fall? Can you tell us about that?" Hayley asked. "What happened?"

Starla refused to meet Hayley's gaze. "I don't know what you mean."

Taylor picked up the beat in the conversation. "Something happened. Her mother was really mad about it."

"Her mother was always pissed off at something," Starla said. Her tone was dismissive and mean.

"Right," Taylor said. "But what happened, Starla?"

Starla appeared to think for a moment. It was hard to tell sometimes—not because she wasn't smart; she was. She was just very, very cagey.

"I don't know," she said, hesitating a little. It was clear the Ryan twins weren't going to leave her alone without some kind of revelation.

"Tell us, Starla. Katie would want us to know," Taylor said, nearly wincing at her own words. Who knew what anyone would want, especially a dead girl?

Well, maybe she and her sister would.

"It might have to do with stealing that money from the till at the Timberline," Starla said, getting up from the giant pink beanbag.

"What money? What are you talking about?" Hayley asked.

"She took some cash out of the register so she could get away."

Taylor leaned closer. "Run away?"

"Not really," Starla said. "She took the money and caught the Bainbridge ferry to Seattle to see her boyfriend."

"Boyfriend?" Taylor asked.

Starla looked around, refusing to meet either girl's piercing gaze. "Some online guy," she said. "I don't know any more about it."

Again, Taylor pushed. "She never told you his name?"

Starla got up and started walking toward her bedroom door; her very clear signal that the conversation was over.

"Cullen Anthony, I think," she said. "But I don't even know if the dude is real or not. Katelyn had gotten weirder."

"How weird? What do you mean?" Hayley asked.

"She was so, I don't know… it seems embarrassing to admit it, but she seemed so jealous of me."

Like that was some kind of admission she didn't want to make. Starla reveled in the jealousy that swirled around her. She didn't always live in What-About-Me-City, but she'd done a good job finding a spot on the town's main drag.

Taylor picked up on the meat of what Starla had said. "Weirder, how?"

"I don't even think the boyfriend she wanted to meet was real."

"No?" Hayley asked, interested in that repeated disclosure.

Starla continued talking as she walked down the hallway, down the stairs. Teagan was hovering by the entrance to the kitchen.

"It is so sad," she said. "But I think Katie just kind of lost it after she didn't make cheer again this year. I wanted her to… I did everything I could. And when she didn't make it, I had to distance myself from her a little—for obvious reasons."

Obvious reasons? Like the fact that if you were a bigger biatch you'd have to sleep in a kennel at night? That kind of obvious reason? thought Hayley.

Before Starla opened the front door to shove the twins back out into the cold air, Hayley reached into her pocket and pulled out the WATCHING YOU note.

"I don't think she made up her boyfriend," she said.

Starla took the note and warily eyed Hayley, then Taylor.

"What's this?" she said, taking the message.

"What do you think it is?" Taylor said in a voice unable to mask her anger. "Your best friend—or rather, the girl who considered *you* her best friend—had someone in her life."

Starla looked up from the paper and twisted the doorknob.

"I don't know anything about this," she said as the winter air blasted inside. "I'm sorry that we have to cut our visit so short. I have some chores to do before Mom and Jake come home."

Taylor scoffed but said nothing.

Chores? When did Starla go all Little House? Or when did she do anything but worship her face in the mirror?

*

After dinner, Taylor put up a second LOST DOG posting on Craigslist, this time with a photo of Hedda taken by their mother on Christmas Day. The dog was curled up like a kielbasa in front of the crackling fireplace, looking cozy and reasonably alert—at least for Hedda. Hayley created a LOST DOG flyer using the same photo and, by the end of the day, Beth, Colton and the girls had plastered it all over Port Gamble.

None of their friends thought that Hedda was a particularly good-looking or smart dog, because, to be completely fair, she wasn't. Beth, in particular, had been merciless in teasing Taylor and Hayley about the dog over the years.

"I saw a dog just like yours that used a skateboard to get around because it had no legs," she said one time.

"She has legs, Beth," Taylor said a little defensively.

Another time…

"The *Ugliest Dog in America* is ramping up again. It's time that disgusting Chinese Crested with the overbite is given the boot. I was thinking that Hedda has a shot at the title."

"She's not ugly, Beth."

"I'm just saying," Beth said.

As they stapled flyers to the kiosk by the General Store, Beth admitted something that surprised the others.

"I hope we find her. I really, really like that little dog."

"I thought you hated her," Colton said.

"Tells you how much you know about me, Colt. I'm more than what I say," she said, before waving goodbye from the corner and heading home.

Taylor walked a few steps ahead of her sister and Colton, who always found a moment to linger alone together. She looked up at Katelyn's bedroom as they passed the Berkley house. She wondered if Mr. Berkley was watching from the darkened room.

She nodded in the direction of Jake, next door, who, despite the weather and the season, was barbecuing something that actually smelled pretty good.

For meat, anyway.

She wondered if they'd ever learn what really happened to Katelyn on that awful night.

Talk to us, Katie, she said to herself.

As the three of them walked to their side-by-side houses, no one called out to Hedda. There was no point in it. Hedda was half-deaf. There was a more disquieting reason too. The air was so cold that if the missing dog had been outside, she'd have frozen to death by then. The wind blew hard across the water. It was harsh and decisive. Port Gamble on a cold winter's night was no place for a short-legged dog, ugly or not.

Later that night, as Taylor burrowed under her blankets and drifted off to sleep, Katelyn remained on her mind.

And so did someone else. Someone she could not see as her eyes fluttered behind her shut eyelids.

Fingertips moved slowly across the keyboard, stopping and starting as if each keystroke were a separate word followed by a period. Stop. Start. In a way, it was almost like Morse code. Rat. Tat. Tat. It was as though whoever was writing the message used the depression of each key to shoot anger at a target far away in cyberspace.

Katelyn stared at the computer screen, her heart beating faster. She knew she was moving closer and closer to something a little dangerous. But danger was needed. Her life had become pathetic on every front. Her mom was drinking more often. Her dad was growing more distant. Starla, her best friend, could no longer see fit to even smile in her direction.

Not that she deserved a smile, but even so, one would have been welcomed.

A flurry of messages zipped across the screen in the chat window:

Cullant: meet me @sSattle ctr. By that ugly ass fountain. U know the 1.

Katiebug: i climbed in it last may @folk life when it wz really hot.

Cullant: that's lame

Katiebug: i know. My parents lyk that crap. Flutes. Latvian dancing. Whatever.

Finally, this came across her computer screen:

Cullant: only a renaiss fair wud b wrse. Meet me. Let's get away frm evry1—esp parents. Let's get the hell outta here.

She liked that he used the word *parents*, because part of her still held the possibility that he was some old freak messing with her. She'd watched *Dateline* and knew "To Catch a Predator" episodes never failed to showcase some beer-guzzling creep with a sackful of Four Lokos and a pocketful of roofies.

Katelyn hated to admit it, but it was the truth.

Katiebug: no $$$.

Cullant: get some.

She hesitated only a moment.

Katiebug: WHERE?

And then the words that would motivate her to do the unthinkable:

Cullant: FIGURE IT OUT, BABE.

CHAPTER TWENTY-SEVEN

The wood-fired pizzeria in Poulsbo was one of those strange restaurants in that its appearance didn't match its cuisine—like a sushi bar in a log cabin. The tiny building on Front Street was like a lot of the themed edifices there, a Norwegian-style facade with stucco and exposed beams. The Ryans didn't care how the restaurant looked as long as the pizza was good, which, thankfully, it usually was.

The outing was supposed to help cheer everyone up. Hedda still had not returned, and Valerie in particular thought a change of scenery was in order. However, Hedda was just one item on the twins' growing list of worries.

Hayley texted Taylor in the car on the way over.

Hayley: You bring it up.

Taylor: can't u?

Kevin, Valerie and Hayley shared the spicy Portuguese sausage, the Linguica, while vegetarian flip-flopper Taylor ordered a small Herbivore. While they waited for the pizzas to bake, all melty and crispy in the wood-fired oven, Kevin and Valerie talked about the events of the day over a couple of beers. Ordinarily the girls didn't mind hearing such updates. Their mother was very discreet about the patients at the institution. She never mentioned a name or any specifics that anyone could use to positively identify who it was she was talking about. She dropped a few words, however, that usually ensured that the interest meter was going at full speed.

"A screamer today stabbed a student nurse with a plastic fork," she said. "Other than that it was the same crazy, just a different day."

Kevin set down his beer and surveyed the quiet restaurant. A couple two tables away sat side by side, a seating arrangement that was meant to be cozy but always looked like another party had stood them up.

"Mine wasn't much better," he said. "Except my crazy is my editor who thinks my book is going to be done on time. Still can't get the perp to give me an interview. Now she wants the questions in advance."

"You'll charm your way around that," Valerie said. "You always do."

With her sister engrossed in texting Colton, Taylor saw a break in the conversation, and she went for it.

"Mom, Dad, we need to talk about something." Her tone came off as a little strange and she worried for a second that her parents would think she was going to drop some major bomb on them—that she was pregnant, gay, or both.

"What is it?" Valerie asked, clearly anxious as she reached for her drink.

Kevin didn't say a word. This was Valerie's territory.

"Wait, it isn't anything about me or Hayley."

Both parents deflated a little and relaxed in their chairs.

"Of course not," Kevin said. "Didn't think anything was up, not at all."

Our parents are such dorks! Cool sometimes, but dorks! Taylor thought.

"We need your help. We think—" Taylor said, noticing that Hayley had finally put down her phone. She thought Hayley's thumbs must need a good soaking after they'd had such a workout texting. "We think," she repeated, "it's really only a hunch…"

Kevin narrowed his focus on the girls, looking at one, then the other, ping-pong style. "What is it?"

It popped into Hayley's mind right then that they could say Katelyn was gay and pregnant, just as a way of getting out of a conversation that didn't seem to be going as they'd planned. But she didn't.

Taylor took up the slack. "Dad, Mom, we think that someone was playing Katelyn. Messing with her. Mindf—" She wisely cut herself short.

The waiter brought their pies and the family sat in silence for a beat.

"I'll pretend I didn't hear that," Valerie said. She wasn't mad, but a slight reprimand went with the business of being the mother of a teenager. In her case, times two.

"I didn't say the entire word," Taylor said, passing napkins around the table.

"You have a better vocabulary than that," Valerie said.

"So what's up with Katelyn, besides the fact that she's dead?" Kevin asked, a remark far more flippant than he'd meant it to be.

Valerie shot him a look, and then looked over at her girls. "Tell us. We're listening."

Taylor told them about the note she'd found in Katelyn's coat, and how she and Hayley had gone to see Starla and what she'd said about Katelyn's supposed rendezvous in Seattle with her mystery boyfriend.

"You don't think there was a boyfriend at all," Kevin said.

"No, we don't," Taylor confirmed, picking at the crust of her slice.

"I think she thought she had one," Hayley added.

Taylor nodded emphatically. "Someone was playing her."

Kevin swallowed a big bite of pizza. He'd been taking in the conversation, watching his girls and wife as they circled around what had happened to Katelyn and, if, just if, there was some reason behind it. He was a little skeptical.

"All right, I know we run on feelings around here quite a bit, but what proof do you have that something like that was going on?"

"We don't have any proof," Hayley said. "I mean none that would hold up in court, if that's what you're asking."

It was kind of a dig, but he let it slide.

"If you think someone had been pushing her, abusing her," he said, "then we need to know who. And we need proof."

"Not everything has to end up in court," Valerie said, eyeing her husband. She'd have preferred a more supportive approach with the girls.

"Who would play a cruel game like that?" he asked.

Neither girl had an answer.

"No idea," Taylor said.

"But we want to find out. It isn't right, Dad," Hayley added.

He nodded.

No, it wasn't.

"But you need proof. Something more than a feeling," he said.

Neither girl said so, but both knew that the answer to their father's challenge rested back with Starla Larsen. She had been close to Katelyn and she had to know what Katelyn's state of mind was at the time of her death. She'd also be the best bet for knowing the source of the taunts, but if she knew, she wasn't talking. Indeed, she'd blown them off at the pink beanbag interrogation in her bedroom.

Just as the family was leaving, Kevin excused himself to talk to a pretty young woman with red hair who'd been sipping wine of the same hue all night at another table.

"A fan," he said, exchanging looks with Valerie. "Give me a minute."

Valerie and the girls headed out the door. As they crossed the parking lot, Taylor caught a glimpse of her dad and the woman through the restaurant's window.

Kevin was animated, but not in a happy way. He was moving his hands to make a point. Even from that distance, Taylor could see the vein that popped in his temple whenever he was angry. It looked like he was scolding the young woman. She didn't seem the least bit put off by whatever he was saying.

When he returned to the car, he had a worried look on his face.

"What was that about, Dad?" Taylor asked.

Kevin exhaled—a sure sign that he was angry—and turned the key to start the car.

"Nothing," he said.

"You look really upset," Taylor said.

"People always expect you to give them a free book, and when you don't, they get mad," he said.

Valerie exchanged a quick look with Kevin and turned on the car radio, a not-so-subtle signal that the conversation was over.

From their places in the backseat, Hayley turned to Taylor, pointed to her phone and started to text.

Hayley: who was dad talking 2?

Taylor: that wz no fan. 2 young 4 dad's bks. Wndr wat pissed him off so much?

CHAPTER TWENTY-EIGHT

The words churned in her head as Taylor lay in her bed staring into the darkness of her tiny bedroom. She knew that whatever she and her sister had hoped to find in the letters that came to her underwater was still there to be unscrambled. The letters by themselves were absolutely correct. It was the order that was all wrong. Maybe they'd tried too hard to make sense of them? Some things were better if they didn't push so hard.

If there was a Laura Folk, for example, she surely never lived in Port Gamble.

"Hayley," she whispered into the hole in the wall. "You awake?"

No answer.

"Are you up?"

Hayley murmured something about needing to get some sleep. "Big test tomorrow," she mumbled.

"Going to get the Scrabble."

"Why can't you just use an app?"

Taylor allowed a slight smile. Her sister was off in slumberland if she thought that even for a minute. "Doesn't work like that. Go back to sleep."

"All right. Good night."

Taylor grabbed her favorite fuzzy yellow robe, stuck her feet into her fleece-lined slippers and padded down the hall. She could hear her dad snoring and the insufferable wall clock ticking. It was after 1:00 a.m. Even though they were twins, Taylor didn't require as much sleep as her sister. She was a night owl. The darkness, the calming quiet, the sense of being alone resonated in her soul in a way that even Hayley didn't understand. From the base of the staircase, she looked out the front door window at the bay.

The water was still, glassy and very sad.

Taylor conjured up some memories of Katelyn and the last time she had seen her. They were riding the bus home the Friday before the holiday break. Katelyn sat in the front, her head leaning against the fogged-up window. In the din of the kids yammering about their holiday plans, Taylor remembered how she had tried to say hello to Katelyn but the other kids pushed her past her seat. They had locked eyes for only a second and Katelyn managed a smile.

A sad smile, Taylor remembered just then, though she wondered if her memory had been tainted by what happened on Christmas night. Her father told her that nothing turns a victim into a saint faster than their untimely and unexpected demise. After a crime took place, good and evil were always rendered in bold strokes.

She pulled the old, battered Scrabble game from the shelf and sat on the floor. The embers from the fire glowed eerily, and the warmth felt good. She quietly fished out the letters and arranged them on the carpet.

LEWD HOT ROD KOALA FURL SELF IVORY

Taylor clamped down her eyelids to shut out the ideas that she'd had about what words could be formed with the Scrabble tiles and what words she believed Katelyn might have wanted her to grasp. She and her sister didn't consider that they actually *spoke* to the dead—they merely felt that they could read an imprint of a moment left behind by those who crossed over. Although it was tougher to do, they could sometimes gauge the thoughts and feelings of those who were still among the living. The living were always tougher than the dead. She and her sister didn't know why for sure, but they agreed that perhaps it was because the breathing still had reason for lies and subterfuge. The dead, well, they just didn't have anything left to lose.

When Taylor opened her eyes, she found herself drawn to the word SELF. It was as if there was a pulsating energy in the word. The others, not so much. Next, she pushed all the words together and ran her hand across their smooth surfaces, mixing them without rolling them over.

"Talk to me, Katie," she said softly. "Tell me."

The Word YOUR pulsed from the mix. She studied the letter tiles spelling out YOURSELF.

Taylor closed her eyes again, and without any consideration for what she was doing, she smoothed out the tiles.

Her eyes popped open and the word FAVOR seemed to leap up at her. She set it next to YOURSELF.

She shut her eyes and tried again, but nothing. *Why is this so hard?* She closed her eyes once more, unaware that her sister had just entered the room.

"Taylor?" Hayley asked.

Taylor looked up, startled. "Geez, Hayley! Thanks for the warning."

"You should have dragged my butt out of bed."

"Your butt's too big to drag," Taylor said.

Hayley sat on the floor, facing her sister. "That means yours is too. We have the same butt, remember?"

"Don't remind me," Taylor said. "I see it every time you walk in front of me."

Hayley dropped the butt talk. She studied the letter tiles spelling out YOURSELF and FAVOR. "That's all you've got?"

"Yeah, I guess that's why you're here now. Give it a try."

Hayley closed her eyes and ran her fingers over the game pieces. When she opened them, she immediately saw the word WORLD.

"I feel something about that too," Taylor said, moving the tiles next to FAVOR and YOURSELF.

In the remaining letters—L I K L A H T E D O—Hayley saw the words HATE and KATE, but, while they seemed to play into the events of what happened to Katelyn, they didn't seem right.

She reached for the last of the wooden tiles and slowly moved them to spell KILL.

Without saying another word, Taylor arranged the remaining game pieces to spell out:

DO THE WORLD A FAVOR KILL YOURSELF

She looked up at Hayley. Even in the dim light of the living room, it was clear to see that the color had left her face.

"Are you thinking what I'm thinking?" Taylor asked, tears coming to her eyes. She hated when she reacted like that, but she couldn't help it.

"You already know I am thinking it," Hayley said.

Taylor rubbed her eyes dry with the sleeve of her robe.

"Someone wanted Katelyn to kill herself," she said.

Hayley started to gather up the pieces of the game, a game that would never, ever seem like fun again.

"Who would want that?" Taylor asked.

The sisters started toward the narrow staircase, lowering their voices to a whisper as they walked.

"Someone with a very black heart, that's for sure," Hayley said.

Taylor nodded. "Someone we're going to find."

"And we will make them pay," Hayley whispered. "Big-time."

It wasn't a threat, but more of a promise. All lives have a purpose. Taylor and Hayley Ryan knew whatever gifts they'd been given were powerful and they intended to use them for the right side.

For Katie.

CHAPTER TWENTY-NINE

The next morning, Hayley found their father in his office writing and drinking coffee, which, judging by the dark ring at the mug's midpoint, she was sure was left over from the previous day. Kevin Ryan was on a don't-disturb-I'm-in-the-homestretch-of-something-really-really-important work jag. It was Groundhog Day, and all indications were that this exact scene would be repeated until he was done.

"Got a minute?" she asked.

Kevin swiveled his office chair to face her. He hadn't shaved for two days and he was of the age where stubble wasn't cool, where it looked more bum than stud.

Not that thinking of her father in that way would ever cross Hayley's mind.

"What's up?" he asked.

Hayley hated when he talked like that, but this wasn't the time for a coaching session on which colloquial phrases were really in and which were used only on beer commercials written by completely unhip advertising copywriters.

"Dad," Hayley said, framing a lie, a small but necessary one, "I was reading about a case in Nebraska or Nevada about a woman who committed suicide because her husband said she was fat."

"I haven't seen that story," he said, glancing over at his idled keyboard.

"I saw it online," she went on. "The husband kept calling her names, leaving her bags of food with nasty notes."

"He sounds like a pig," he said.

"You don't know the half of it. Well, I've been wondering about him. I mean, can he be held liable for it?"

"I don't think so." Kevin slid his computer glasses down the bridge of his nose. "He mostly has to live with himself for being an ass."

"Isn't it like someone yelling fire in a crowded theater? You know, and causing someone to get trampled to death?"

"Not really. I mean, even if she were unstable and fat and he merely taunted her, that wouldn't mean he was responsible. After all, the woman in Nebraska or Nevada—"

"Maybe New Hampshire," Hayley said, adding a shrug for good measure.

"Right. Whatever N state she was from, makes no difference. The woman was an adult and responsible for her actions."

"But her husband urged her to kill herself."

Kevin, smelling a crime story, seemed more interested just then. "How so?"

"He told her to do it. Bullied her. He left her notes and told her to do the world a favor and kill herself."

"That's different," he said. "If she was vulnerable and he told her to do that... By the way, how *did* she kill herself?"

Hayley hadn't thought that one through. If she'd really read the story online—if there had been a story online—it would have mentioned the cause of the heavy woman's demise. For a split second she considered offering up something totally off the wall, like the dead woman ate a hundred waffles and died of a perforated stomach, but she refrained. She knew her dad would Google the case then.

Waffles + suicide. Hit search.

"She jumped off a roof."

"Wow," he said. "That's hard-core."

"Yeah, she hit the pavement and splattered like a melon," she said, adding a description that she knew he'd like.

"Watermelon?" he asked.

She shook her head. "Casaba."

"Nice, Hayley."

She hugged her dad before leaving him to do his work. She'd lied to him, but she'd made him smile too. She could tell that he loved the melon visual. She expected that he'd use that the next time he had the occasion to write about a jumper.

The body hit the asphalt and splattered like a melon… er… like a casaba.

CHAPTER THIRTY

People in Port Gamble knew the death of the Berkleys' daughter would make it nearly impossible for Harper and Sandra to survive what many already knew firsthand was a marriage on mudflat footing. Kim Lee told her daughter, Beth, that she'd seen Harper eating alone in a restaurant in Kingston. At first, she thought he'd been scoping the competition, though the concept of that endeavor so soon after his family tragedy seemed peculiar. When she saw him a second time sitting on one of the benches overlooking Puget Sound to Edmonds, at the landing of the Kingston ferry crossing, she had a better idea what he was up to.

He was staying away from Sandra.

"You know I'm not one to gossip," Kim said, as usual when gossiping, "but I have seen Sandra a few times in town and she looks terrible. I hate to say this, but I think she might be drinking heavily."

Sitting next to her mother on the sofa after dinner, Beth texted the info to Hayley and Taylor while promising complete discretion.

"Yeah, I don't like to gossip, either, Mom," she said, her thumbs still jabbing the message:

Sandra B is a drunk. Mr. B hates her.

Of course, Sandra Berkley knew what everyone thought of her. Her mother, Nancy, had made it abundantly clear the morning of Katelyn's funeral service.

"If you'd kept your hands out of the liquor cabinet, our only grandchild might still be alive," she had said.

Sandra could accept some blame but not all of it. She could also fire it back at her mom, telling her that if she hadn't squandered her granddaughter's college fund on a wine fridge, Katelyn might still be alive.

But she didn't. Sandra didn't say a word. She just pulled hermit-crab tight into herself. She no longer cared if she lived or died. And yes, she had a drinking problem, but right then drinking actually seemed to be helping. Feeling numb was better than feeling the sharp pain of regret and loss.

She sat on Katelyn's bed, a drink in her hand and tears streaming from her eyes. All around her were the memories of the daughter whom she'd lost long before Christmas night. How was it that they'd been so close once and then, nothing? Sandra loved her little girl. She had been the Girl Scout Daisy Troop leader only because she couldn't bear another woman taking the job and taking away time that she'd have with her little girl.

She'd taken Katelyn to every class, school function or retreat that was preceded by a school permission slip. They'd been two peas in a pod. *Inseparable.* As she sat there sobbing, it was hard to pin down just what it was that had caused the tectonic rift between the two of them. It could well have been her drinking. It could have been the fact that she and Harper weren't getting along. The restaurant was making money, but not enough to fuel the dreams Sandra had for herself.

For herself. For her family.

Sandra sipped her drink—rum, whiskey or vodka, whatever she had in the house. She no longer even bothered with mixers. As she tried to steady herself, her eyes landed on the laptop sitting on Katelyn's nightstand, a garage-sale discovery transformed with six coats of spray paint into a shabby chic table. She recalled how Hayley and Taylor Ryan had been standing over it the day they came to bring those awful cookies. She set her drink down and pulled the laptop closer. She plunked her shaky fingers against the keys, but when the window opened it revealed the need for a password.

Password? What in the world was Katelyn's password?

Suddenly, her heart rate accelerated. She swung her legs over the edge of the bed and sat up, trying feverishly to come up with her dead daughter's password. She hadn't a clue. KATIEBUG, a nickname Harper had called Katelyn when she was young? SKATELYN, another she had in elementary school when she rollerbladed everywhere in Port Gamble?

Nothing.

They never had any animals, so there was no obvious pet name to try.

Sandra pushed the laptop aside, took a big gulp from her drink and began to cry. *Hard.* A veritable river of tears. She rested her puffy, red face in her hands and let out a guttural scream. At that moment, she realized that she was, now and forever, alone. She dropped her hands, which were clenched hard against the comforter.

"Katie! Why did you do this? Why?"

Of course there was no answer, and as drunk as she was, Sandra Berkley knew there couldn't be one. As she picked up her glass for the last swallow, something caught her attention. It was on the floor, next to the bed. For a second, Sandra thought it was the handle of a toothbrush.

No, maybe a digital thermometer.

She dried her eyes on the sleeve of her blouse and extended her arm to reach it.

Her heart started to race faster.

What was that doing in Katelyn's room?

She held it close to her blurry eyes to make sure she was seeing correctly.

And she was.

It was a pregnancy test wand. Sandra couldn't believe her eyes. Maybe it wasn't a freak accident after all? Had Katelyn killed herself because she was pregnant? Sandra was reeling by then. She wondered why her daughter hadn't come to her, hadn't asked her for help. She clutched the wand like she could choke it away in her fingers. It was so unreal. So unexpected. So very, very shocking. She didn't even know Katelyn was having sex.

She was only fifteen! What is the matter with these kids today? Can't they wait to have sex until they get their driver's license and can go somewhere? Like what Harper and I did when we were sixteen?

CHAPTER THIRTY-ONE

Hayley Ryan and Colton James were in his bedroom—with the door open—as the teenager with a mass of dark hair proudly demonstrated an app that he'd finished programming the night before. Although Colton had been up all night, his energy level was completely unfettered. The app might not be a million-dollar idea, but it was definitely a viable one. He was hoping to make enough to buy a new car. Maybe he could convince his mom that the car she never drove could be traded in too. He was thinking big, and Hayley was suitably impressed.

"It is a simple idea," he said, "using existing police-scanner information that's already out there on the Net. I had to link up with a bunch of guys with servers in their basements. That was kind of tough, but I managed. I think they think I'm a lot older than I am."

Hayley sat on a stool next to Colton's ginormous computer screen. She inched herself a little closer than necessary to see, but that was only so she could be close to him. He smelled delicious. Like Colton.

"How does it work?" she asked, brushing a stray blonde lock from her forehead as she leaned a smidgen closer—close enough to brush against him a little. Sure they were dating, but nothing other than a once-a-week make-out session had transpired between the pair. She wanted to go further—not as far as they could go—but it just didn't seem like they were there yet. She liked everything about Colton, but she wasn't convinced she was in love with him.

Hayley wasn't sure what that real love really felt like. She tried to dissect it in the analytical way that she did with a lot of things. She tried to measure her feelings for Colton against the feelings she had for her mother, father and sister. Of course, those feelings weren't the same kind of love, and she accepted that she'd know when the time was right and if the feelings she had were of the depth needed for the most intimate experience she could imagine. She'd dreamed about it more than once, especially after they'd kissed the first time behind the twin 50,000-gallon water towers on the edge of Port Gamble's business district. She could still feel his lips on her from that encounter. All other kisses would be measured by the first one. She was glad Colton had been the boy of her dreams.

Colton flashed a big, white smile. "Users select the location that they want to keep tabs on. It allows them to listen in as the police, fire and other emergency responders chat in a monotone about people and their messed-up lives. I'm not kidding about messed up. Seriously messed up."

Hayley was interested. "Like what?"

"Like a guy was in trouble because his wife or girlfriend kicked him out of the house with nothing but his cell phone."

"So what's the big deal?" she asked.

"I mean *nothing*," he said, laughing. "Dude was butt naked."

Hayley laughed too. "Okay, that *is* messed up."

Colton's mom, Shania, appeared in the doorway. She was a pretty woman with dark hair like her son and the S'Klallam lineage that she could trace back to the days before Port Gamble was known as Memalucet. Though she seldom left the house, she never failed to dress up for the day as if she was going to the office or even a casual lunch out. Her clothes were almost all in earth tones. The only concession to glitz was the entwined ropes of liquid silver that wrapped around her neck. Colton confided to Hayley it was to hide a jagged scar, something his mom never, ever talked about.

"Colton?" she asked, her dark eyes heavy with concern. "Katelyn's mom is here. She wants to talk to you."

Hayley's mind stumbled a little on what Shania James just said. It was true that Sandra Berkley was Katelyn's mom, but, she wondered, if there was no daughter anymore, was she still a mom?

Colton and Hayley followed his mother down the hallway.

Shania lasered her eyes on her son and in mime-fashion mouthed the words: "She's been drinking."

Duh.

Sandra was a disheveled mess plunked down on the sofa in the front room. Her hair needed brushing, maybe even washing. She wore skinny jeans and a black cardigan sweater. On her feet were slippers, not shoes.

Yet it was what was sitting in her lap, gripped tightly by her chewed-to-the-nub fingertips, that commanded Hayley's full attention.

Katelyn's laptop.

"Hi, Mrs. Berkley," Colton said.

"Hi," Hayley echoed.

Sandra glanced up at the teenagers, then back down at the laptop. She locked eyes with Hayley briefly.

Hayley recalled the incident in Katelyn's bedroom. She felt uneasy.

"Hayley?" Sandra asked, never sure which girl it was and in that moment not really caring. "Colton. I'm sorry, Colton," she said, her voice soft and a little unsteady. "I know this will sound stupid."

The teakettle whistled from the kitchen.

Shania looked at Sandra with the compassionate eyes of someone who'd seen her own share of pain.

"Sugar and milk, if I remember?" Shania asked, turning to leave her son and his girlfriend alone with the mess of a woman who'd come calling.

"Yes," Sandra said, managing something of a smile.

That Shania recalled how Sandra liked her tea was a reminder of how they'd been close once, when their children were babies, and before the incident at the Safeway.

Shania left the room and Sandra held up the laptop.

"Colton, I want to know what's inside this thing," she said.

"What do you mean?" he asked, though he knew the answer. Her daughter was dead and she wanted to know more about the child that she'd lost. Most parents would probably do the same thing.

"I don't think I could do that," he said. "It seems kind of private."

"I don't want you to *read* what's in her laptop. I want to do that. I want to know everything I can, but I don't..." She trailed off, trying her best not to cry.

Her obvious pain made Colton feel uncomfortable. He hated seeing anyone cry, especially another kid's mom.

"You need the password, right?"

Sandra nodded. "That's right."

"You want me to hack it?" Colton said. "Seems kind of wrong to me."

"What's wrong is that Katelyn's dead," she said.

Shania returned with a couple of teacups on a tray. The smell of chai perfumed the air.

"You two want anything?"

"No, thanks, Mrs. James," Hayley said. "I'm heading home now."

Colton took the laptop and followed Hayley to the back door as she slipped on her jacket and they went outside. Though he was barefoot and wore only jeans and a Green Day T-shirt, he didn't seem to mind the chill. Hayley pulled her zipper up to her neck, bracing herself for the onslaught of the cold winter air.

"Okay," he said. "That was weird."

"Yeah, she looks terrible."

"I'm not really a hacker, you know that, right? People think because I'm playing with my computer all night that I could crack the da Vinci Code."

"You'll figure it out," she said.

"I guess I can try."

A large flock of Canada geese flew overhead, honking as they headed away from Port Gamble. Hayley wondered for only a second if Katelyn was somewhere up there too, watching, hoping, urging someone to tell her story.

Hayley looked around before planting a kiss on Colton's cheek.

"I have faith in you," she said.

"Nothing like a little pressure."

She waved at him and walked across the now snow-crunchy yard between their houses. Hayley knew Katelyn's password, but to say so would be too hard to explain to the boy she really, really liked.

No one, certainly no teenager, was normal or felt they were. Everyone wore a kind of mask that kept people from really seeing what—or who—was inside. Katelyn did. Starla did. And as she walked to her own back porch, Hayley Ryan knew that she and her sister kept things secret too. She didn't grasp all that they were or what they could do. She knew that even people she cared about—her father, her mother, Colton James—probably never could comprehend it.

After all, it happened to her and her sister, and *they* couldn't understand it.

CHAPTER THIRTY-TWO

Colton James's bedroom was one of three in house number 17, a light-yellow one-story with a low roofline that might have had one of the best views of the bay in Port Gamble, but otherwise was not so special. The house wasn't even really that old, having been barged over by the lumber company from Port Ludlow in the 1920s. His parents had the largest room, the one closest to the only full bathroom in the house. The other bedroom was used by his mom as an office. It had floor-to-ceiling shelving overloaded with catalogs that she'd collected in the years before the Internet became her lifeline to the outside world. Shania James, not surprisingly, did most of her shopping via catalogs. The UPS man and the FedEx lady had made so many trips to the James' house that both had been to Colton's birthday parties, family barbecues and other gatherings.

If one hadn't noticed that Shania James stayed in the house ninety-nine percent of the time, they'd never have thought there was anything strange about her.

Colton's own room was organized chaos. His often-away fisherman father had installed pegboard above the teenager's desk. Wires were coiled on hooks, and jars of teeny, tiny computer components hung above the workspace. Colton seldom used those things anymore; they were left over from the days when he built his own computers.

That was then. Now he was all about apps. He focused on coding, design work and learning the business of being an entrepreneur at age fifteen.

To see him hunched over his computer at night, Coke can at the ready, Cheese Nips open and available for serial consumption, was to witness a boy's true intensity. Code was beautiful to Colton. It was elegant. It was nearly a living, breathing thing.

And yet, Colton James was no geek. He was fit, handsome and could actually talk to adults while looking into their eyes. None of that "are you talking to me or the floor?" for Colton.

Colton's screen saver was a picture of him and Hayley that Taylor took on her phone when the three of them were out on his father's boat, the *Wanderlust*. The quality wasn't the best, but the look in Hayley's eyes was priceless to him. It was, he was sure, the look of a girl who really got him.

He scooted his keyboard aside and set Katelyn's laptop on the desk. He was plugging in the power cord when his phone buzzed.

Hayley: Break the da vinci code yet?

Colton: Just started. Give me 10 secs.

Hayley:):

Katelyn's laptop whirred on and Colton put on some music while he waited for the log-on window to pop open. Colton didn't like the idea of cracking Katelyn's password so her mother could do some postmortem eavesdropping on her life. Yet, he'd seen the tears in Sandra's eyes, the longing she had for what was never coming back, and he knew he had no choice. Password cracking was never really that easy. He knew a kid in school who used jailbreak software to crack his mother's password so he could get into the system and disable the Net Nanny tool that he'd found so humiliating.

"I'm not doing anything that bad," the kid had said. "Looking at porn is normal. It isn't like I'm paying for it on their credit card. It's free. They're like porn Nazis."

Colton thought about the last time he'd seen Katelyn. It was in the school cafeteria. She was sitting alone, looking over at the group of Buccaneers cheerleaders and the second-string players who couldn't manage a ride off campus. Starla was there, the center of it all.

"Hey," he had said to Katelyn on his way to the trash can.

She nodded.

"You got plans for the holidays?" he asked.

When he played back the conversation he knew that it was a lame attempt to engage someone he no longer really knew.

"Grandparents are coming over. Nothing great. You?"

"We're going out of town to spend some time with my dad's family in Portland."

"That's nice," she said. "Your mom going too?"

"Yeah. She's pretty freaked about it, but my dad's got a plan."

Katelyn smiled. "I like your mom."

Colton appreciated Katelyn just then. He could tell that something was troubling her, but no matter what it was, she still had it within her to be kind to someone.

Hayley texted again.

Hayley: Try team Edward. Just a wild guess.

Colton: lke twilite?

Hayley: LOL. Yes. Mine wz team Jacob. Don't tell any1!

Colton: About team Edward?

Hayley: About me & twilight. That wz a long time ago.

*

Hayley looked up from her phone and faced her sister.

"I don't like lying to Colton," she said. "Not at all."

Taylor nodded. "I know."

The two of them sat on the floor in Taylor's room, obsessing about Katelyn and what her mother had wanted to find on her laptop. Both girls knew the password as if it were their own. Somehow, when they touched the laptop, the password had imprinted on their minds.

"I just didn't want him to struggle too much," Hayley said. "Sure, he likes a challenge and he can do anything when it comes to computers. But, you know, we can help out, so why not?"

Taylor got up to fish a sweater from her bottom drawer. The walls of her bedroom leaked cold air like a crab pot leaked water, and she was freezing.

"Agreed," she said, pulling out a gray oversize sweater with pilled, stretched-out sleeves and a couple of missing buttons. It was a favorite cast-off of her dad's that she could never part with. "Totally."

"Your sweater needs a shave," Hayley said.

Taylor shrugged, and then put on a wicked grin, teasingly, of course. "I was thinking the same thing about your nasty legs," she said.

*

Colton typed in the suggested password and… *nothing*. He thought for a moment and figured that if TEAM EDWARD was Katelyn's password, she probably would have used a numeric sequence to make it less obvious.

That was easy to guess too. He typed in TEAMEDWARD23, the number for the Berkleys' house. He'd used his own house number tagged on the end of plenty of passwords over the years. It was always easy to remember.

The computer rumbled softly and the screen opened wide, baring all of Katelyn's secrets.

Got it, he thought.

No illicit software had been needed after all, and that made Colton feel a little better about what he'd been asked to do. It was one thing to password-crack a dead friend's computer; another to enlist a skanky Internet tool to do the deed. It seemed cleaner somehow to do it with a guess-and-go technique. Less criminal. Hayley had given him more than half of what he needed and that brought a smile to his face.

Colton: success. Now wot?

Hayley: Copy her hard drive. Everything. I'll explain l8r.

Colton: ???

Hayley: Katelyn wz in trouble. She's dead because of it.

Colton: WTF?

Hayley: Explain l8r. Promise.

CHAPTER THIRTY-THREE

Birdy Waterman, Kitsap County's forensic pathologist, had burned her tongue on coffee that she'd microwaved a minute too long. She looked out of the window of the green vinyl-floored kitchen on the main floor of the coroner's office. The old house, which had been converted to the county morgue, probably had an impressive view of the Olympic Mountains to the west. Trees and the Kitsap County Courthouse now stood in the way. She was swishing cold water in her mouth when her annoying assistant Terry Morris told her that a woman was there to see her.

"She's in a bad way," he said, sculpting his short faux hawk. "Wants to talk."

Dr. Waterman swallowed the water and pushed her disposable cup into the swinging lid of the kitchen garbage can. Without another word from Terry, she knew that it was the mother of a victim. Mothers can never let go. Fathers were different. Not all of them, of course, but most accepted scientific findings for what they were—clinical facts. Moms didn't.

Dr. Waterman didn't recognize the woman.

"I'm Birdy Waterman. Can I help you?" she asked.

Sandra Berkley was as she had been in the James' living room—a disaster. Her hair, disheveled. Her makeup, scrawled on, not applied carefully. She was thin where she should have had some fullness to her face. She was puffy where the contours should have been more sculpted. It was the face of a mother who'd lost her baby.

Dr. Waterman had seen that so many—too many—times before.

"Can I help you?" she repeated.

"I hope so," Sandra said, anxiously looking for a place to sit. Her knees shook just then.

"Let's go into my office," Dr. Waterman suggested, gently placing a hand on Sandra's bony shoulder as she led her to what had once been a bedroom but now functioned as her office. In addition to the louvered closet doors along the farthest wall, the ceiling light above her was the only other remnant of the office's original purpose. It was a glass fixture etched with figures of cowboys and their spinning lariats. It had been a child's room.

"I'm sorry," Dr. Waterman said, moving things aside to clear more space across her desk, "I didn't get your name."

"Sandra Berkley. My daughter was Katelyn."

Of course. Even though she'd only seen her laid out on her autopsy table, there was no mistaking the resemblance.

Dr. Waterman nodded. "I'm deeply sorry for your loss."

Sandra started to cry. "Thank you."

"Can I answer some questions for you?"

The words sounded flat, and not at all helpful, which was not the forensic pathologist's intention. It was merely the fact that no words could ever seem right. There was not a damn thing she could do for that woman. No one could.

Finally, Sandra spoke. "Was my daughter pregnant?"

A little caught off guard by the question, Dr. Waterman shook her head. "No, I would have noted that. It would have been in my report. Our exams are very, very thorough."

Sandra winced a little, squeezing tears from her eyes as she reached for a tissue from a box on the doctor's desk. Then she dug into her purse and pulled out a Ziploc bag containing the pregnancy test stick.

"I found this in her room. I thought… maybe that's why she might have killed herself… because she didn't want to disappoint me…" Her words trailed off into more sobs.

Dr. Waterman gently pushed the tissues closer.

"Mrs. Berkley, that wasn't it at all. I examined your daughter. As I recall it didn't appear that she was sexually active. Your daughter was more than likely still a virgin."

Sandra stopped her tears. "Then why would she have this?" she asked, waving the wand once more.

A somewhat startled Dr. Waterman shook her head. It was a very, very good question.

"No idea," she said. "Maybe she and her boyfriend messed around and *thought* she might be pregnant. I don't know. Kids are funny. When I was young, I almost believed you could get pregnant from a French kiss."

"If she had a boyfriend, her father and I never met him."

You wouldn't be the first mother who had no idea what her daughter was doing when she was out of your sight, Dr. Waterman thought.

"I know that none of this is easy and there's nothing I can do to make you feel better," she said.

It was all she could say.

Sandra Berkley stood. She was sad, hurt, and mad at the same time.

"I will *never* feel better again," she said.

"I understand, Mrs. Berkley. Really, to the best of my ability, I do." Dr. Waterman reached for a tablet and a pencil. She jotted down a phone number. "I know an excellent grief counselor in Poulsbo. Maybe you could talk to her? It might help."

"I don't want to talk to anyone," Sandra said, her voice louder than needed. "I want my daughter back. I want to watch her graduate from high school. Go to college. Get married."

Birdy Waterman let her go on. Nothing short of an AK-47 could halt the mother of a dead teenager as she grieved for all that had been lost.

CHAPTER THIRTY-FOUR

She may have been fueled by vodka or it might have been only the enormous sadness of her loss, but Sandra Berkley made a beeline for Katelyn's phone when she got home from the Kitsap County Morgue. *How could I not know my own daughter? How could it be that she didn't tell me?*

First on the list was Starla Larsen.

It didn't ring and went immediately to voice mail.

"Starla, this is Sandra, Katelyn's mom. Call me back when you get this."

A few minutes later she tried again, with the same results. Sandra had half a mind to just go next door and confront Starla face-to-face, but she thought better of that. She didn't want to fall apart in front of Mindee and Jake. They'd avoided her lately with the kind of sad, frightened look parents sometimes give others whose children had special needs, or had died—suicide or otherwise.

Next she tried Hayley Ryan.

She and her sister were nosy enough to snoop in Katelyn's room. Maybe one of them knew something.

Hayley was nearly done with the forensics book when she looked down at her vibrating phone. Her face went nearly white. It was as if she'd seen a ghost. In a very real way, with Katelyn's name popping up on the caller ID, it was a ghost.

"Hello?"

"Hayley, this is Sandra Berkley. I have something I need to talk to you about. Maybe your sister too. I've tried to reach Starla, but she's probably out running the universe."

There was genuine sarcasm in Sandra's voice. Hayley liked that. "What is it?"

"It's private. Can you come and see me?"

"Sure. Shall we come to the restaurant or your house?"

"I'm home."

"Okay, what's it about?"

"I'll tell you when you get here. Bring your twin."

Bring your twin. That didn't sound good.

Hayley hung up and went looking for her sister. Whatever it was, this was big. It had to be, because the last time the two of them had interacted with Sandra Berkley, she'd wanted to bite off their heads and toss them out of her daughter's second-floor bedroom.

Ten minutes later, Hayley and Taylor Ryan stood on the Berkleys' front doorstep, bracing themselves from the cold and for whatever it was Katelyn's mom wanted to say to them.

Sandra opened the door and wasted no time getting to the heart of the matter. There was no offer to take their coats, of a warm beverage, or anything like that. Not that they'd wanted anything, but still it was wham, bam, thank you, ma'am. She'd barely invited them in when she dropped the bomb.

"Who was my daughter sleeping with?"

"Huh?" Taylor asked, looking at her sister.

Hayley looked clueless.

Sandra had planted herself right in front of the twins and didn't step back. She was totally invading their personal space.

"Do you know who Katie was having sex with?" she asked, her eyes fierce and angry.

It was a look neither girl had seen from Sandra, who had always seemed so fragile.

Hayley shook her head. "As far as I know, she wasn't. And if she was, it was none of our business when she was alive."

"Or now, when she's, you know, not alive," Taylor said.

Sandra's eyes were stony. She was upset. Cold. Livid.

"*Dead* is the word you're looking for, Taylor," she said.

Taylor felt her face go pink. "Right. Dead. Well, we honestly don't know."

Sandra was on a mission. She needed to know. "Did she have a boyfriend?" she asked.

Hayley took that one. Taylor was unusually flustered. "She might have had someone she was talking to online."

"This is more than online," Katelyn's mother said, backing up and going toward the coat tree. She started fishing through her coat pockets.

"Damn," she said. "I can't find it."

"Find what?" Hayley asked.

"The pregnancy test she took," Sandra said, now digging through her purse but coming up empty-handed. "Must have left it in the car."

Taylor looked over at Hayley. She didn't say it, but she was thinking that nobody takes a test for having online sex. If people did, grocery and drugstores would be selling the kits by the cartful.

"Look, Mrs. Berkley," Taylor said. "We didn't know her that well. Not like we did when we were little. But I'm pretty sure Katelyn would have told you if she thought she was pregnant."

Taylor's words seemed to soften Mrs. Berkley's features.

"Maybe so," she said. "At least, I hope so."

She opened the door, which was their cue to leave.

As it swung shut, the twins looked at each other.

"What you just did was very nice," Hayley said as the pair hurried down the steps to the sidewalk in front of house number 23.

Taylor shrugged off the compliment. "That's not why I did it. It was the truth. Mrs. Berkley and Katelyn were close. Close enough to make me wonder what it would be like if it was just me and Mom."

"Instead of you, me, and Mom?"

"Right."

"That's a nice thought. Thanks for that."

"Oh, come on. Like you haven't wondered what it would be like as a singleton."

Just then they noticed Teagan, loitering in the alleyway with his BB gun and a coffee can that he'd been using for target practice. Both girls thought it, but didn't say it: *Who buys coffee in a can anymore?*

"Starla home?" Taylor asked.

"Yeah," he said. "The little B is upstairs."

"You mad at her?" Hayley asked.

Teagan lowered his BB gun. "Not really. Or maybe yes. She's always telling me what to do. Even when I'm not mad at her, I have to get ready to be mad."

He kicked the coffee can.

"Aren't BB guns illegal?" Hayley asked.

"You going to tell on me?"

"No. I'm just asking."

He shrugged. "I don't care if they are. It's fun to shoot stuff. One time I knocked a robin out of a tree. That was cool."

"Actually, that's not cool at all," Hayley said.

"Whatever. I'm going inside. Come on and I'll let you in."

CHAPTER THIRTY-FIVE

Teagan knocked on Starla's bedroom door and opened it before she had time to call out an answer. Brothers across the world routinely did that. Girls routinely got special treatment like that. No sister ever has to knock to get into her brother's room, that is, if she'd ever *want* to actually go into the gross, stinkfest lair that is usually on the other side of such a barrier.

Starla was sitting on the floor in that god-awful beanbag chair texting and listening to music. The room smelled of strawberry incense, and whoever thought that torching strawberries was a good idea was completely devoid of any good sense or scents. The only thing worse was tea rose incense, which Taylor was convinced smelled like a burning grandmother. Starla had taken to burning incense to round out what she called her "spiritual" side.

"Hayley and Taylor are here," Teagan announced.

"Oh, hi," Starla said, not looking particularly happy to see them. She reached up through her cascade of golden hair and pulled out her earbuds. "What's going on? You two look like crap."

Teagan disappeared into his room next door, and Hayley and Taylor went inside.

"What's up is that five minutes ago Mrs. Berkley just asked us if we knew who Katelyn was having sex with," Hayley said.

Starla didn't get up and the twins didn't sit. "Oh, that must be why she's been calling me," she said.

"So spill the beanbag," Hayley said. "Who was she sleeping with?"

"Sleeping with? A pillow is about it," Starla said. "Probably a blanket." If Starla had meant to be ironic just then, it fell flat.

"Honestly, you don't know?" Taylor said.

Starla's phone buzzed with a text, and, ignoring the two girls in her room, she went about the business of answering it. Without looking up, she said, "As far as I know she'd met that guy online but not in person. He stood her up."

"Right," Taylor said. "But how come her mom found a pregnancy test kit in her room?"

Starla looked up startled and then returned to her texting. "Beats me. I mean, maybe Katelyn was playing around more than we thought. Sometimes quiet girls are the wildest ones, right?" Turning, she specifically directed her gaze at Hayley. "How's Colton doing?"

Hayley smartly refused to take the bait. "Look, we thought you liked Katelyn," she said instead. "We thought that you'd want to know how she died. If she was pregnant, she might have felt there was no way out."

"No way but a suicide," Taylor said.

Starla shrugged slightly. "That seems dumb, but maybe."

"Or maybe she didn't want anyone to know because the guy that got her pregnant was someone older, someone she was protecting," Hayley said, a little proud that she refrained from saying something snarky to Starla in retaliation for the crack about Colton.

"But I don't know anything," Starla said. "I've got ten thousand messages to answer."

It was Starla's way of dismissing them, and it worked. Taylor and Hayley turned to leave.

Teagan emerged from his room as they were heading out.

"You were right, Teagan," Taylor said. "Your sister is a total B."

"The biggest B in the history of Port Gamble," Hayley added.

"No argument from me," he said with an undisputed grin on his face. "I heard you asking about Katelyn. What's up?"

"What's up?" Taylor asked. "She's dead, and we don't think she killed herself. What do you know?"

Teagan watched as Hayley hesitated in front of the door.

"Me? Nothing," he said. "She was depressed. I guess that's something."

Taylor pushed a little. Maybe the kid was more observant than his sister and actually knew something. "Did she have a boyfriend?"

He shook his head. "I think that's why she was depressed. She didn't have one."

Later that evening, Hayley and Colton looked at the screen on Hayley's computer. They'd opened up the files from the thumb drive, and with a few clicks went a little deeper, beyond the contents of the messages themselves to the source files. What they were seeing was baffling beyond belief. The IP address for all the messages sent to Katelyn came from the Larsens' house. All of them.

Including the "meet me in Seattle" message.

"Jake," Colton said. "That creep was stalking Katelyn."

"Jake," Hayley repeated. She avoided saying something stupid like the fact that she'd always had a "funny feeling" about Jake Damon, but she had. So had her sister. Beth too. One time the previous summer, Beth had complained that he drove by her house very slowly as she washed the car in the alley.

"Outside of Segway Guy, he's the creepiest person in Port Gamble. I'm glad that Jake's boning Starla's mom. She deserves it," Beth had said.

"That's harsh, Beth. Even for you," Hayley said.

Beth barely blinked. "That's me, I guess. Harsh."

As Colton scrolled through code, Hayley thought some more about Jake, and the pieces began to fall into place. It wasn't a perfect fit but the kind that inspired more digging. There had always been talk about Jake Damon and his supposedly lurid past.

No one really knew exactly what it was, and they assumed all sorts of nefarious possibilities—drug-running from Seattle to Alaska, motorcycle gang activity (derived from his first appearance in Port Gamble on a BSA Chopper) and even the suggestion that he'd been in prison (one of his tattoos looked suspiciously homemade). Hayley's dad took the bait on that one, but after computer research and a couple of phone calls, the only criminal activity that came up for Jake was traffic related.

And none of that involved a motorcycle gang.

Jake was handsome, kind of shiftless and never seemed to need full-time employment. When he hooked up with Mindee Larsen around the time her husband left town, most people saw him as an opportunist.

"Mindee's drowning her sorrows in a six-pack of steel," Sandra Berkley had blurted to Valerie when she and the twins were shopping the previous autumn at Central Market in Poulsbo.

Valerie had remained silent. The scene was too sad.

Sandra had the last word, though. "I know what kind of a guy Jake Damon is. I've seen the way he looks at our daughters."

Of course, Sandra knew something about drowning her own sorrows. Her idea of a six-pack had nothing to do with abs, either. In her cart were half a dozen bottles of Yellowtail Shiraz—on sale with a ten percent discount for shoppers who bought six.

Sandra Berkley had a lot to forget. And not all of it had to do with her daughter's death. No, Sandra's regrets went back almost a decade, and no amount of cheap wine could ever let her truly forget.

CHAPTER THIRTY-SIX

Moira Windsor never told anyone she was interviewing that she wasn't *exactly* an employee of the *Herald*. She was a stringer, a freelance writer. She thought that particular term made it sound like no one would hire her, so she never mentioned it when she was out talking with sources.

After speaking with Kevin Ryan, whom she thought was a royal jerk in the way he just brushed her aside, the pretty twenty-three-year-old returned to her aunt's house in Paradise Bay, just across the Hood Canal Bridge. The name of the place always made her wince a little when she told people where she lived. The view of the bay was lovely, but it was far from paradise. Her aunt was off snow-birding in Tucson, Arizona, and she'd left Moira to house-sit. The word *house* was a bit of a stretch. It was really more of a cabin with a woodstove for its sole heat source. Outside in the crusty snow were fourteen bird feeders, eight garden gnomes, and two bleach bottles cut and bent to allow the wind to spin them as they hung from the eaves.

Moira was sure that Savannah Guthrie never had to live like this.

She lined up two bottles of sparkling water, turned on some background TV and sat down at her computer to search for whatever she could find about the infamous Port Gamble crash. She'd grown up in Bremerton and had vague memories about it, but as a pudgy teenager back then she likely gave it two minutes of thought: *Wow, that's terrible! I feel sorry for those kids and their families!*

And then she went back to her life and her dreams of getting out of naval-gray Bremerton, the county's largest city.

With a cooking show playing in the background, she went onto the search engine and put in the words: "Port Gamble + Daisy + Crash."

The host was talking about ways to cut calories out of her "nice spice" Indian cuisine, but as a former fatty, Moira wanted to fantasize about the real thing. Bring on the fat! She guzzled her sparkling water and looked longingly at a bottle of red wine.

Seventeen articles popped up. She clicked on the first one that had appeared on the *Kitsap Sun* site.

HOOD CANAL BRIDGE CRASH KILLS FIVE

A Port Gamble school bus being used by a Girl Scout Daisy Troop for an ill-fated picnic at Indian Island careened over the Hood Canal Bridge yesterday afternoon, killing the driver and four girls, ages 5-7. Three children and an adult were airlifted to area hospitals.

Motorists on the scene indicated that the draw span had been retracted when the bus crashed in heavy rain and wind. State engineers say retracting the span is done to relieve pressure on the bridge.

"They were right in front of me," said Cindy Johnston of Bainbridge Island. "I was following them pretty closely because I could barely see. The rain was coming down so hard. In one second, the bus just disappeared."

Sustained winds of 50 mph, with gusts of 65 mph, were reported in the region by the National Weather Service.

The Washington State Department of Transportation and the State Patrol are investigating.

Moira knew that the crash had killed several people, but she thought it was only two. Four plus the bus driver... it was beyond tragic. She tried to process the depth of that kind of loss on a small town like Port Gamble. It had to have touched almost everyone who lived there.

She read the next article, which indicated that two children were recovered from the water as well as one child and an adult who'd been thrown from the bus to the bridge deck. The article also went on to say that the recovery of the North Kitsap School District's short bus and the bodies would likely take several days as the depth of the water was three hundred feet or more.

She clicked on another article, one from the *Daily Olympian*.

ELECTRICAL FAILURE LED TO FATAL HOOD CANAL CRASH

A spokesman for the Washington State Department of Transportation said today that the school bus crash killing five was a "tragic combination of the weather and an electrical fault that caused the span to open."

It had not been opened by the bridge tender, as previously reported.

Among the dead were Christina Lee, 7; Sarah Benton, 6; Violet Caswell, 5; and Emma Perkins, also 5. Also killed was bus driver Margie Jones, 29. Jones, according to the North Kitsap School District Records Office, was an exemplary employee. She was completing her master's degree in education and was working as an activity bus driver. She'd planned to teach next fall.

"She wanted nothing more than to do something for kids," said Barry Jones, her husband of five years.

Three of the survivors remain hospitalized. One, a 30-year-old Port Gamble woman, has been released.

Moira activated a few more links, some showing photographs of a barge transporting an enormous crane to the crash site, another as it raised the short bus out of the water, and finally a close-up of an exhausted pair of state divers standing at the rail. Their haunted eyes and grim expressions said more than anything a reporter could write.

Another article highlighted the joint memorial service held at Port Gamble's church.

She recognized Kevin Ryan in one of the photos.

Finally, she thought, as her eyes scanned the computer screen and the next article. The names of the survivors.

VICTIMS' NAMES RELEASED. TWO IN COMA

The names of the survivors of the Hood Canal Bridge bus accident were released this afternoon. Sandra Berkley, 30, and her daughter, Katelyn, 5, were thrown from the bus as it went off the bridge. Ms. Berkley suffered cracked ribs and abrasions. She and her daughter were treated and released from Harrison Medical Center, Bremerton.

The two other victims, 5-year-old twin girls Hayley and Taylor Ryan, remain hospitalized. Their parents issued a statement yesterday.

"Our daughters are fighters. Please keep them in your prayers. Believe in miracles."

The parents indicated that the girls are still in a coma.

Visibly shaken, Adam Larsen, 34, spoke to reporters outside his home in historic Port Gamble.

"We are grieving for the families who have lost their children and for the bus driver's family too. This touches all of us here. I doubt many of us will ever get over it."

Larsen's daughter, Starla, also 5, was a member of the Daisy Troop. She, however, did not go on the outing due to minor illness.

The last site Moira visited was one called *Kitsap Kalamities*, a forum devoted to—as its banner indicated—"happenings of the rotten kind, right here in our own twisted backyard."

There was nothing really new on the site. In fact, after skimming it, it was apparent that all of the content had been copied and pasted from other websites. Moira sniffed at that. It was the fate of journalism today. *Why do any legwork when you can just cut and paste?* Not her. Not Moira. She was going to do whatever it took to create something original. Notice-worthy. Star-making. And if her tip paid off, the Ryan girls were going to get her just where she needed to be.

Kitsap Kalamities was created by someone named Maxi Taxi using a WordPress blog. Moira clicked on the comments field and scrolled through the missives people posted, mostly of the "that sucks" or "your blog is Maxi Stupid" ilk. A few were more thoughtful.

One was very, very intriguing.

Sweet Data File 31: I'm not surprised those two survived. I knew them when they were babies. There was something scary about them back then. Something different.

Scary? Different? Babies? Moira looked at the name of the online commenter. "Sweet Data File 31". She typed it into Google, figuring that whoever used that handle had done so on more than one blog. Finding a person on the Internet was no different than going door to door asking for one little piece of information at a time. She likened it to digital legwork. One thing always led to another.

Moira sipped the dregs of her sparkling water and twisted the top of its understudy. She tipped it back and drank while her eyes studied the results of her search.

Sweet Data File 31 also posted on *More Than Words*, a site about slanguage and how words are evolving faster than ever.

Sweet Data File 31: I used to be a linguistics researcher—in another life—for a major university. I think changing language is a good thing. Human beings are creating all the time. New words are a solution to a genuine need.

Comments were closed on that site, so Moira moved on.

As the hands on the clock whirred around on her computer, which searched for more Sweet Data File 31 entries, the thought filled Moira's brain: *What's scary? Does it have to do with something I have been leaked?*

A farm-to-table site popped up, and its feature article, "Our Valley Is Green," was local, from the Kitsap Peninsula.

Sweet Data File 31: Every weekend I drive past the family farms between Bremerton and Belfair, and I am astounded that we don't have more farm stands. Come on, people! Local, sustainable, green is our food future.

Moira thought about it a moment and then posted a follow-up comment on the same thread.

News Star: Sweet Data, I'm Moira Windsor, a writer working on a big piece about the importance of farm to table. Would you like to talk to me for my story?

She added her email address and waited. She figured anyone lonely or self-righteous enough to post a comment like Sweet Data did would answer her comment. People like that always wanted to be in the paper. It was only a matter of time.

She looked over at the TV and saw that the chef was making some deep-fried apple dumplings. They looked so good she could feel her stomach trying to eat itself. She got up, went to the freezer, pulled out two Lean Cuisines (Butternut Squash Ravioli and Apple Cranberry Chicken) and headed for her aunt's obnoxiously large microwave.

Next, she looked up Sandra Berkley's number. She'd waited long enough to make the call. With the microwave beeping that her meal was ready, Moira quickly left a voice mail message.

"Mrs. Berkley, Moira Windsor calling from the *Herald*. I'm a friend of Kevin Ryan's and I'm working on a feature story about the ten-year anniversary of the Hood Canal crash and its aftermath. Of course, my heart goes out to you because of your recent loss. I'd like to talk to you for my story."

Satisfied that she'd sounded kind, authentic and deeply concerned, she ended the call with her phone number.

I was made for this job, she thought as she pierced a piping hot piece of cranberry chicken with a fork. *Just made for it.*

CHAPTER THIRTY-SEVEN

Sandra Berkley had taken her last drink. There was no point in it anymore. She went around the house and collected the partial-empties from their assorted hiding places. She recovered a bottle of vodka from under a stack of old towels on the bottom shelf of the linen closet. She found two—rum and whiskey—in the pantry behind the basmati rice bag that she'd purchased in bulk and doubted she'd ever use up.

There were six bottles in total, and she took them to the sink and poured out the remnants of each one until nothing remained.

Katelyn was gone. Harper was next door at the restaurant. She sat down and wrote out a letter. It was something that she'd wanted to do for almost ten years.

I want you to know that I'm so sorry… please forgive me…

Tears were streaming down her cheeks as she finished and signed her name. She folded the slip of paper and put it into an envelope.

*

It was after six thirty when Kim Lee finished her work in the mill office and began her precise and ritualistic practice of tidying up her desk. That was just how she was. Always the same, every day. Kim kept most things in order. As an accountant, that pretty much was her job. She closed her drawers, turned the locks, and got up to leave. In doing so, she noticed a small envelope in her in-basket. It had been addressed to her, care of the mill.

She used the letter opener that Beth had made in middle school, a red Plexiglas shark with a menacing jaw that cut through paper like a razor.

Kim started reading, and before she was finished, she was on her way out the door. Beth always complained that her mother was a slowpoke. If she'd seen her right then, she'd never dare to make that claim again. Kim's winter coat was left in the employee break room, but despite the cold wind off the water she didn't even notice. Four minutes later, she was pounding on her neighbor's front door.

"Open up!" Kim cried. "Please!"

No answer.

Kim went around the house, looking into the windows. The lights were on, but she couldn't see anyone home, yet she was sure Sandra had to be there or at the restaurant. Sandra's car was parked in back.

"Please! We need to talk!" Kim called out as she pounded her fist on the back door.

Footsteps! Good. Sandra hadn't done anything stupid. At least, not yet.

Finally, the door opened. Sandra Berkley stood in the doorway, her eyes outlined in red and her face blotchy. Her hands trembled as she let Kim Lee inside. She didn't say a word at first. Instantly, she started sobbing—uncontrollably so.

"Sit down, Sandra," said Kim, who was crying now too.

"I'm sorry," Sandra said. "I couldn't live with it any longer. I've never forgotten the screams."

"I know," Kim said, her own eyes welling with tears. "We all know."

"I heard Christina cry out for me as the bus started to sink. I just stood there. I didn't know what to do."

"You were in shock."

Sandra fought for some composure, but it was a losing battle. "I didn't even try. I just…"

"No one blames you," Kim said.

"I blame myself. I know what I did and didn't do. I know how I felt after."

Kim wrapped her arms around Sandra's shoulders as she tried to console her. The sobs came in waves. Sandra tried to speak in the breaks between her tears.

"I was glad, Kim," she said. "I was glad that Katelyn survived. I stood there listening to the screams, knowing that I had my daughter and that she was hurt but she was alive. She was going to live. And for what? She's gone now too."

"You've suffered so much, then and now," Kim said.

Sandra stopped long enough to lock her crying eyes on Kim's. "Forgive me, Kim."

Kim Lee shook her head. "No, no forgiveness is needed. You did all that you could."

"Did I? Really, Kim? Really?"

"I'm sure you did. No one knows how they will react in a moment like what happened on that bridge. No one. You did the best you could in a terrifying time."

"I don't know," Sandra said, looking for something that maybe Kim could finally give her.

"I know you did," Kim said.

The women talked a while longer. They cried; they hugged. Kim didn't tell Sandra that she had questioned why Katelyn had been spared, when Christina was taken. And even so, in that very moment in the Berkleys' house, no two women were ever closer, a bond so deep, born of such tragedy.

The Port Gamble gossip line, thought by many to be sublimely accurate, had failed miserably when it came to the true trouble reverberating in house number 23. The Berkleys' rows were not about a marriage crumbling because Sandra was drinking. It wasn't about a restaurant failing, or settlement money that had been squandered. It was a marriage falling apart because Sandra Berkley could not face what had really happened on the Hood Canal Bridge and the shame and misplaced guilt that came with it. Booze had been her medication. Anger had been her weapon against a husband who had wanted to help her work through her guilt.

*

After she was sure Sandra was going to be all right, Kim Lee left for home, shaken and relieved by the meeting. She composed herself before ducking inside. Beth was watching TV, texting, drinking a sugar-free Red Bull, and reading a book.

"You look completely trashed," Beth said, glancing at her mother. "What did they make you do now? Re-add everything five minutes before shift change? Your job so sucks."

Kim had hoped the short walk in the night air would take some of the puffiness from her eyes.

"Nothing ever adds up," she said, going into the kitchen. "Pizza tonight?"

Beth looked back down at her phone. "All right. I'll call it in. You always get thick crust because you think it's a better value because it weighs more. I like thin crust."

"Fine," Kim said, heading into the kitchen. She braced herself on the counter a little and steadied herself by taking in a deep breath. She unfolded the letter and read it one more time. After seeing Sandra, it no longer seemed like a suicide note.

I want you to know I'm so sorry that I didn't save your daughter or the other girls. Sometimes, I wish I could go back to that day and do it all over. I'd do things differently. Please forgive me. I don't know how much longer I can live with what I did. Sandra

Kim shredded the note and stuffed it down the garbage disposal. She turned on the water and, as the noisy contraption did its thing, she wondered if it was worse to lose a child or live with the guilt that yours had survived. She was glad that she never had to face that. Sandra's cross to bear weighed a million pounds.

Later, after a couple of slices of thin-crust pizza and some distracted conversation between mother and daughter, Beth excused herself to her bedroom and texted Hayley and Taylor.

Beth: Mom is stranger than normal 2nite. Boss prob yelled @ her. Wish i had her probs. Her life is so easy.

Hayley: Tell me about it. They keep saying that things r harder in the "real world" but they have no idea how f'ed up it is @ kingston.

Taylor: def the worst.

As Kim Lee placed her head on the pillow, she was transported back to that day almost ten years ago, standing on the Hood Canal Bridge as the sirens wailed and all the mothers cried. Seeing Sandra hadn't brought it all back because it had never really left her. She, like all the other moms, hated that damn bridge. Just hated it.

CHAPTER THIRTY-EIGHT

Some bridges, like the nearby Tacoma Narrows or its far sexier cousin, the Golden Gate in San Francisco, are a marvel for their stunning beauty, arching over dangerous waters or defying gravity as they connect two high points over a deep chasm.

The Hood Canal Bridge is a marvel too, though not for how it looks. It literally floats atop the water for which it is named as it carries Washington State Route 104 across Hood Canal and connects the Olympic and Kitsap Peninsulas. At the time of its construction in 1961, depths of more than three hundred feet made it impossible for a suspension bridge to be built there. So it floats. Concrete pontoons hold up the roadway just above water level.

Fifteen thousand cars cross it every day, its drivers and passengers thinking nothing more than how beautiful the Olympic Mountains are, with the eagles soaring overhead, and the occasional submarine cruising for the navy base in Bangor.

A few families cross the bridge and remember the darkest days of their lives. The Ryan family was one of those. Valerie Ryan in particular couldn't stand driving over the span. It was the primary reason why she went back to school to complete her psychiatric nursing degree. All of those jobs were on the Seattle side of the bridge. She didn't want to find herself crossing Hood Canal for the mundane reason that her job was there.

The girls knew about the accident, of course, but traversing the bridge on those rare trips to Port Townsend or Port Angeles brought the occasional questions about what happened that rainy, windy March 21 years ago. For some reason, the girls sought clarity of only one detail—not of what happened but of exactly where it had been.

Taylor, in particular, seemed to hone in on the spot where the draw span connected with the main bridge deck.

"It was here," she said when she was seven and they were heading home from a visit in Port Townsend.

"Somewhere around here, yes," Valerie had said.

"No," Taylor said, "it was right *here*."

Hayley looked at the water. It was glass that late afternoon.

"She's right, Mom. Right at that spot where those birds are floating. That's where it happened."

Valerie glanced in the direction of gulls bobbing on the surface as their car sped past. She didn't like to think about it at all. She wanted everyone to just forget it.

"I don't remember," she lied. "But yes, right around here."

Kevin's eyes met his daughters' in the rearview mirror.

"Look at the snow on the mountains," he said. "Must have had a storm last night."

The girls turned their attention to the view on the other side of the bridge. It was a distraction, and they knew it. Inside, both understood that their mother and father were as damaged by the events of the crash as they were.

For as many people who'd lived and died in Port Gamble, the number of the dead buried in the Buena Vista Cemetery was exceedingly tiny. Among the more notable was Gustav Englebrecht, the first member of the United States Navy to be killed in action in the Pacific. His death was less heroic than foolish. He met his maker during an attack at Port Gamble in 1856 when he hoisted himself up over a log to get a better view of the battle at hand only to be finished off by a young man from the S'Klallam Tribe.

There were older graves there too. Early settlers, workers who died at the mill, and so on. And, mixed in among many, there was also a modest plaque—one so small, worn, and faded that unless one knew of the legend, you'd never be able to decipher the inscription:

PETER O'MALLEY, 15,
was interred in the sea on April 22, 1792.
He is now in God's hands.
May he rest in eternal peace

According to the story, which had been passed on for generations, poor Peter had died from cholera and was laid to rest in a salt-cod crate coffin that had washed atop a sandbar. However, when three young S'Klallams forced open the mysterious crate, all that was inside was a silver crucifix, a tornado of flies and an acrid, hideous odor. The smell of death. Soon after, the oyster beds died and the seabirds stopped nesting there. People began to say that the site was cursed. They called the place Memalucet, or empty box. Those with a more twisted frame of mind called it Empty Coffin. Decades later Port Gamble was plotted there.

On a day that many also consider cursed, Buena Vista Cemetery received a row of little girls' graves, under a gigantic maple tree at the edge of the bluff looking toward the floating bridge across Hood Canal. Christina Lee was first, then Sarah Benton, Violet Caswell and Emma Perkins. Other than the obvious differences of the dates of their births and their names, all gravestones were identical in their design. Carved in relief from the black and white granite was a sleeping lamb and a phrase in simple script:

Only a Short Time Here
With God Forever

For years after, visitors came to the cemetery and left toys and flowers for the little girls. One time, someone left a complete Barbie dream house and a Ken doll. Another deposited a tiny porcelain tea set. All of those things were gathered up and stored in the museum's archives, with the understanding that no display would be made until the youngest of the survivors turned twenty-one years old. History was full of tragedy, but, as the archivist pointed out, it didn't need to be shoved into the faces of the living.

Although it never faded from the memory of those who lived in Port Gamble, people did find ways to move on.

Visitors who came to the Buena Vista Cemetery to pay their respects never knew that one of the little girls' graves was empty. Kim and Park Lee refused to bury their daughter Christina there. It was too cold and windy, and its location was too much of a reminder with that awful bridge off in the distance.

Instead, they had Christina cremated and kept her ashes in an urn in their living room.

Park Lee was among those who could never forget the loss of his firstborn daughter. The mill supervisor died when shrimping in the choppy waters of Hood Canal the year after the tragedy on the bridge. The sheriff's investigation closed the case as an accidental drowning. His wife, Kim, knew better. When the county authorities returned his personal effects, Kim noticed something missing from his wallet—Park's fishing license. She knew there was no way he'd have gone shrimping without that. Park was very strict about doing things the right way, the legal way.

At thirty-four years old, Park Lee simply could not face his hurt anymore.

Kim arranged photos of her husband and daughter on a shelf above the TV in the living room. On either end of the shelf, she placed two turquoise and gold cloisonné urns. One held the remains of her daughter; the other, her husband.

They'd been up there so long that Beth no longer begged to spread the ashes on the shore because she thought it would be fun and dramatic. After a time, weeks would pass before she even noticed that the urns were there.

It was just her and her mom and that was all it was ever going to be. And while Kim tried hard to make her daughter feel special, Beth never really felt it.

Once, in a moment of deep introspection and personal clarity, Beth admitted to Hay-Tay that the reason she never stayed with anything very long was because "none of it seems to work."

"What do you mean?" Taylor had asked as the three of them walked across the field by the wedding pavilion. It was summer and a bridal party was being photographed along the edge of the bluff overlooking the water.

"I'm not blaming my mom," she said. "I guess I get that the love she has for Christina and my dad is stronger because they're dead. It isn't like she gets any do-overs with those relationships. She can fantasize and romanticize."

"People do that, sure," Hayley said as the girls sat in the freshly mowed grass, not caring that their butts would turn green.

"Sometimes I just want to tell her, 'Hey! Look at me! I'm still here!'"

Taylor touched Beth on the shoulder. "She knows that, Beth," she said.

They watched as a young eagle tussled with a gull overhead.

"On some level I get that," Beth said. "It's just hard when half your family's in urns, you know?"

The parents of the dead girls and the husband of the bus driver received financial settlements from the state, though each of them would have traded the money for their loved one's life any day of the week. After lawyers' fees, the sum was nowhere near the hundreds of thousands reported by the Seattle media.

Kim Lee squirreled away every dime and watched her nest egg grow, like the accountant that she was. She could have cashed it out any time she wanted and moved away. Anywhere—even Fiji. But she stayed put because Park and Christina considered Port Gamble home. Though they were completely portable, they weren't going anywhere.

The Berkleys used their windfall to finance and refurbish the Timberline, a restaurant that they'd never own because no historic buildings in Port Gamble could be sold to anyone.

When Katelyn was in seventh grade, Sandra and Harper confessed to her that the college fund she'd thought she'd have for her pain and suffering had been spent on a new car and the first restaurant.

"Don't worry, baby," Sandra said. "Your grandparents are going to take care of your college education. They've promised."

The disclosure had brought some relief. Katelyn was sure Starla would get some fabulous scholarship to a top-tier school, while she'd need to pay her way to get there.

"I trust you, Mom," she had said. "I know you'd never let me down. You or Dad."

CHAPTER THIRTY-NINE

The morning after Colton found his way into Katelyn Berkley's computer, he drank a glass of orange juice and ate two thick slices of cinnamon toast that his mother made. Shania James slathered on the butter and sugar nearly to the point of complete calorie overload, but that's the way her son liked it. He'd been thinking all morning about Katelyn, her mother and whatever it was that was on her laptop that Sandra had wanted to see. As he ate, he watched from the window for Hayley and Taylor to emerge from their house so they could huddle at the bus stop.

He left Katelyn's laptop and a Post-it note with her password on the kitchen table. Sandra Berkley said she was going to come by later in the morning to pick it up.

"Did you look at any of it?" Shania asked.

He shook his head. "Not really," he said. It wasn't a lie. He hadn't. "Seemed a little invasive to me."

Shania nodded in the direction of the Ryan girls and Colton got up.

"Yes," she said, "I think it would be. But I think if something happened to you, I'd probably do the same thing."

He zipped up his coat, grabbed his backpack, and went for the door.

"I guess I should start deleting all the bad stuff I'm into when I get home tonight," he said, deadpan. "You know, so you don't have to dig through all that ugly."

"No need," she teased. "I've already installed a secret Net Nanny on your PC. I've caught up with all your ugly already."

Colton was fifteen, too old to hug his mom, but he wanted to just then. He never had any doubt that she was always on his side.

"Bye, Mom," he said.

The sky had cleared overnight, which brought temperatures down to well below freezing. Hayley, Taylor and Colton met in the alley. The girls were zipped up and prepared for the Arctic. To humor her mother, Taylor wore what Colton knew was Aunt Jolene's vomit scarf. Hayley had on a bright red scarf with a four-inch black leather fringe. He'd been with her when she bought it, and she had told him it was both cool and functional.

"Which is very difficult to achieve," she had said.

Colton handed over the thumb drive. "All of Katelyn's info is on this," he said. "Emails, saved chats, Word docs."

Hayley took the thumb drive and zipped it into her pocket.

"Now are you going to tell me what's up with that?" Colton asked.

They were nearly at the bus stop, where a few other kids were waiting.

"I have a feeling that Katelyn would never have committed suicide," Hayley said, thinking about how she was going to say the next part.

"We both do," Taylor said, cutting in. "It's either an accident—"

This time it was Hayley's turn to cut off her sister. "Or a homicide," she said.

"You've been reading too many of your dad's books."

"Maybe so. But suspicion is a good thing," said Taylor, the daughter who had never cracked a Kevin Ryan paperback in her life.

The bus came into view, and the space between the kids tightened as they lined up to get on board out of the cold.

"How's that?" Colton asked, hoisting his backpack over his shoulder.

"Keeps things interesting. And we need that in Port Gamble," she said.

Colton nodded, but deep down he knew that was far from the truth. Port Gamble was a small town, certainly, and those who didn't live there might think it was a sleepy little place. Yet the truth was almost every household had been the victim of something. Starla's dad, Adam, left town without so much as a word; Beth's father drowned; Katelyn was dead; and then there was what had happened to his own mom.

Exactly what it was had never been a topic of conversation around the James' household. And as much as he loved his mother, he loved her enough not to say a word about it. Whenever he saw the scars on her neck, he pretended they weren't there.

Later at school, between algebra and history, Colton ran into Starla—a rare occurrence because they spent most of their passing time in their separate pods, his orange, hers blue. It was even more unusual that Starla was alone, away from her usual group of mean-girl admirers and the straggler or two who wanted to be part of the group—until Starla had the poor girl picked off like a weakened zebra.

"Hi, Colt," she said.

"Hi, Starla." Colton tried to remember the last time she had spoken to him privately. Was it seventh grade? When she pretended to like him, when all she really wanted was for him to do her computer science homework? Like the biggest idiot in the universe, he had done it.

Starla edged a little closer, drawing him over by the teacher's resource room, where it was quiet.

What does she want now?

"You doing okay?" she asked him.

"I'm fine," Colton said, "but what about you? Are you doing all right?"

She was full-on Starla just then. She smelled good. Her eyes were done up in such a way that they looked anime-big. "It has been really hard," she said. "My mom mentioned to me that Sandra dropped off Katelyn's laptop for you to hack."

The reason. Starla was ten times more efficient in getting to the point than she had been in middle school, Colton thought.

"Yeah," he said. "She did."

"Were you able to get into it? You're pretty good at that kind of stuff."

Colton knew she was using him again, yet he still blushed a little. *Why did she have that effect on him?*

"Thanks. I guess. But yeah, I was."

"Really."

"Yeah. *Really.*"

Starla inched a little closer. She looked concerned, interested. She was kind of good at that, and just maybe had a future in movies. Make that TV.

"What did you find out?" she asked. "She was pretty messed up, wasn't she?"

Colton thought a moment before answering. There was always a risk in telling Starla something. Information was her currency. Gossip. Truth. Whatever she could use, she did. She was, Colton knew, an info-parasite.

"Messed up, maybe," he said. "But not half as much as the SOB who was sending her those taunting emails."

He wanted to tell her that the sick SOB who sent them was her mom's boyfriend, but he didn't.

"Wow," she said, her eyes no longer as large, but shuttered a little as if she were concentrating on something important. Or as if she were trying to narrow her focus on Colton to see just what it was that he knew. "That's totally scary."

Colton brushed past her. "Yeah." He didn't look back at her anime eyes. He just went to class, letting Starla think about what he'd found on her dead friend's hard drive.

*

Moira Windsor ate a couple of mint-flavor Tums she had fished out of the Paradise Bay house's medicine cabinet. She had eaten too much. Too fast. She heard the ping of a new email being delivered and quickly returned to her computer.

From: S. Osteen
To: Moira Windsor
RE: Farm to table article

Ms. Windsor, I got your email about the farm-to-table story you're doing. I'd be glad to assist you in any way that I can. I see buying local food as a key to our future longevity on this planet. Please feel free to call me or email me if you'd like to meet. I live near the Bremerton Airport.

Moira picked up her phone and tapped out the telephone number provided. After a few pleasantries and some confirmation about what she wanted, Savannah Osteen invited her to come over.

"When can I come? I'm kind of on deadline."

"Anytime," Savannah said. "I work out of my home."

Moira pounced. "How about today?"

Savannah paused, thinking it over. "Today's fine," she said.

"How about now? I'm not doing anything and I can be there in half an hour. I was thinking it would be a nice day for a drive."

"Partly sunny days like this are a treasure this time of year," Savannah said. "Sure, come on over."

She provided directions and the address, and Moira was out the door.

*

About the time the Port Gamble High School students were looking for their second latte of the day, pathologist assistant Terry Morris made a run to the Albertson's store on Mile Hill Road for maple bars, because he loved those better than anything and could easily eat two on his morning drive to the Kitsap County Morgue. He didn't care how sticky his fingers got, because he could just lick them clean in the parking lot. Who cared if anyone saw him? He wasn't a people person, which is why he selected a career in the coroner's office. He'd figured he might be a dead-people people person.

That sticky, sweet maple bar run took longer than he'd planned. Terry wasn't good at planning, period. He wasn't really good at being the pathologist's assistant either, but he'd been hired and was on three-month probation. He was already getting the vibe from Dr. Waterman that he wasn't exactly winning her over.

He tossed his greasy bakery bag into the trash by the morgue's back door and looked inside through the window.

Good, Dr. Waterman wasn't in there hacking away through the first autopsy of the day.

Terry was late for the autopsy of a burn victim from a house fire in Bremerton. *But not too late*, he thought, *since it hadn't started.*

He was glad he had those maple bars. Hanging around a smelly corpse might kill his appetite for lunch.

He went upstairs, where Dr. Waterman and the county office administrator were conferring about something in the kitchen. Terry scurried past to put away his things, wiping his hands on his trousers along the way. He hoped she didn't notice he was late.

But she did.

"Glad you made it into work today," Dr. Waterman called out from the kitchen.

"Car trouble," he lied.

"I have some things bagged and ready for shipping to the state crime lab," she said. "Please get them processed and meet me downstairs in the autopsy suite. Everything's on my desk. Let me know if you have problems managing that, all right?"

What a hag, he thought, though he didn't say it out loud.

"No problem, Doctor," he said, thinking that a real doctor would be helping living people, not literally picking their brains. But, hey, that was just him.

He found four bags labeled with the case information for Robin Ramstad, a gunshot victim found in a wooded area outside of Port Orchard. The incident was before his time, which was just fine with him. Terry didn't know much about it, and, frankly, didn't care.

He started boxing up the evidence for shipping when Dr. Waterman called out again.

"Heading downstairs," she said. "See you there when you're done."

Terry scowled inwardly. He hated how passive-aggressive she was. She was always telling him what to do. She was so bossy.

It didn't occur to him that she was bossy because she actually *was* his boss.

"Be right there," he said, shoving a fifth bag into the box, before sealing it with strapping tape and signing the chain-of-custody paperwork.

He rushed downstairs, his hands still sticky and his annoyance still in full force.

What escaped him was that the fifth item, a Ziploc bag containing a pregnancy test wand, had nothing to do with Robin Ramstad.

CHAPTER FORTY

There was no getting around it. Starla Larsen wanted everyone out of her way. She practically stiff-armed the kids in the hall as she rummaged in her hobo for her cell phone. The look of determination and pure venom in the cheerleader's eyes would have made a two-year-old cry for her mother. Teenage girls at Kingston High School? Pretty much the same result. Starla was just that scary right then as she hurried out the door and over to a hedge of evergreens near the bridge that served as the school's entryway. Her heels stuck in the mud, and that only made her madder.

"Look," she said into her phone, her eyes nervously scanning the scene. "This thing went too far, and I'm afraid someone is going to call me on it."

Starla turned her back to the school courtyard filling up with the onslaught of kids as they meandered toward the cars in the lot. She faced the hedge and listened to the person on the other end of the line. Her lips were a straight line, and her eyes narrowed in anger. In that moment, maybe for the first time in her life, no one would have said Starla Larsen was beautiful. Maybe not even reality-TV pretty.

And since she was so pissed off about what the other person was saying, she probably didn't care what anyone thought about her appearance just then—likely another first-time occurrence.

"Don't tell me that it wasn't our fault. I already know *that*. I never wanted anything like this to happen. I'm putting the blame on you!"

Starla pressed the phone tight to her ear and balled up her other fist. If a kitten had the misfortune to walk by, she might have stomped on it with her four-inch heels. She was *that* irate.

Whoever was talking to her didn't have the opportunity to say much. Starla, it seemed, was on a roll.

"The biggest mistake I ever made was to trust you. If this goes any farther, you're the one who's going down for this. No excuses! I have too much to live for and I'm not about to have you F it up!"

She lowered her phone and turned around.

Taylor and Beth were coming toward her.

"Starla," Beth said in that direct way of hers, "you look pissed off. Someone steal your pom-poms?"

Starla barely looked at either girl as she retracted her heels from the muddy grass, making a sucking sound that only served to make her angrier.

"Don't even go there, you emo-freak," Starla said, her voice as controlled as possible. She said nothing else and never looked back.

"Wow, she looks like crap," Taylor said, stating the obvious.

"I almost feel sorry for her," Beth said. "She's really going through something. Maybe she hates her highlights."

Taylor tugged at Beth to get to the bus for the ride home. "I have no idea what's up," she said, in what she knew was a big lie.

Savannah Osteen lived in a log cabin in the middle of wooded acreage near the airport. While the location was indeed remote, the mosquito-like buzzing of private planes could be heard overhead as they dropped lower for landing. The aircraft was an audible reminder that even in the woods, there are people hovering, watching. Savannah's cabin wasn't one of those Daniel Boone affairs, all mossy and drafty, but a decidedly modern one with a steep roofline and made of perfectly peeled pine logs. Anchoring it from the ground to the sky was a river rock chimney

that looked like it might even be made of real rocks. Which it
wasn't, of course.

Moira Windsor edged her pewter compact car under a gnarly
grove of cedars that formed a canopy, nearly blacking out the late
afternoon sky.

"Moira?" a voice called out.

Moira turned in the direction of the voice. "Savannah?"

"Yes. I'm back here, in the aviary."

Moira followed the sound to a large, fenced pen with a ten-foot-
high ceiling of chicken wire. Inside, a woman in her late thirties
was huddled next to a wooden crate. Suspended above the crate
was a heat lamp sending an eerie splash of orange over its contents.

Savannah motioned for her to come inside the pen.

"Dumb idea to raise pheasants in the middle of winter," she
said. "I don't know what I was thinking."

Moira unlatched the gate and walked over. She bent down a
little and looked inside at a dozen or more small birds huddled in
one disgusting mass and pretended to be interested.

"They're pretty," she said. "I'm sure they'll be all right. Spring
will be here soon enough."

"I hope so," Savannah said, looking up at her visitor and
smiling. Up close, she was a pretty woman with corkscrew hair
that was more gray than brown. She wore slim-fit jeans; a heavy,
tan Carhartt jacket; boots; and a pair of garden gloves with the
fingertips nipped off.

"Let's go inside and talk about farm to table, and I'll tell you
how my pheasants fit into that scenario," she said, lowering the heat
lamp a little. The birds peeped loudly and scuttered from the light.

"Oops," Savannah said, raising the lamp a touch. "Don't want
to cook them. At least, not yet."

"No, not yet," Moira said, acting as if she was excited, though
she couldn't care less. She wanted to talk about something completely different from these disgusting birds. Besides, farm to table

made no sense to her. Everything she ate came from a box or was shrink-wrapped.

The place was spotless, which surprised Moira. She figured an old hippie—if that's what Savannah was—would be a grungy pack rat with recycling stations in every room and ugly eco repurposed items like a bucket made into a lampshade. But the house wasn't. Instead, it was clean and bright with furnishings upholstered in creams and grays.

After Moira removed her boots and jacket, she could see that Savannah was neat, maybe not exactly stylish, but not some Boho wannabe with a trashed-out house. A coil of silver chains swirled around her toned neck. Ten silver bangles ran up each wrist.

Savannah offered coffee, not herbal tea, which also surprised Moira. There was no small talk about sustainable resources, the dire situation with South America's rain forests. They engaged in some casual chatter before Moira made a confession of sorts.

"I lied to you on the phone," she said, once they settled at the kitchen table, a large Douglas fir crosscut topped with quarter-inch-thick glass.

"You're not from the paper?" Savannah said, her tone indicating some skepticism and maybe even a little understanding.

"Not exactly," she said and looked away.

"Blogger? That's okay. I understand."

"No, I actually *am* from the paper. I'm just not doing a farm-to-table story."

Savannah perked up a little. She didn't seem alarmed, only a little interested.

Moira wondered if there was marijuana in the coffee. *This woman is so calm. I could be an IRS agent or a serial killer and she wouldn't bat an eye.*

"Is Moira your real name?" she asked.

"Yes, yes, it is. I'm sorry. Do you want to see my driver's license?"

Savannah shook her head. "No. But tell me exactly why you are here?"

Moira took a deep breath and started to tell her about Katelyn's death and how her editor had told her that Katelyn was in the terrible crash on the Hood Canal Bridge.

"You remember it? The one that killed the driver and four little girls?"

The look on Savannah's face clearly indicated that she did. Actual words weren't necessary. But the former language researcher answered anyway.

"Yes, I remember it very well."

Just then, the air in the room thickened considerably. Moira Windsor knew whatever words she chose next would likely make or break the interview. In that moment, it was clear to both parties that what they were talking about was far bigger than merely an update on an accident and the lives of the survivors.

"I saw your posting on the *Kitsap Kalamities* site," she said, waiting.

Savannah sipped her coffee. "Yes. I'm sure you did."

"It was an interesting comment," Moira said.

Savannah set down her cup and looked out the window toward the aviary. "I knew I shouldn't have posted it. I even emailed the site owners and asked if they'd remove it."

"They didn't, you know."

Savannah nodded. "Right. They didn't. That's really why you're here."

"What did it mean?"

"It meant that I'd had too much ouzo," Savannah said, somewhat sheepishly. "Greek dinner party in Seattle and… I don't know how I got home and, even worse, how I managed to type that comment. I'm not denying that I did it, because I did."

Moira kept her eyes on Savannah. "I know you did," she said.

Savannah turned her attention back to her coffee and took a sip.
"What did you mean by it?" Moira asked again.

Savannah took a breath and faced the reporter. Her face was grim.
She's going to talk. Good. Tell all.

"I was a researcher years ago, for the linguistics lab at the University of Washington," she said, now fidgeting with her fingertips deep within the back of her tangle of hair.

Moira flipped open her reporter's notebook.

"I don't think I want you to write about this," Savannah said.

"About what?"

"About what I'm going to show you."

For some reason, unclear to her just then, Moira's heart started to race. She was not a woman given to much fear, but, right then, she felt some.

"Are we in agreement?"

"Yes," Moira said, knowing that she was being completely deceitful.

Savannah had trusting eyes, and Moira felt sorry for her. She knew that Savannah was going to give her something she considered precious. She also knew that the woman wanted to. She wouldn't have put that comment online, with or without too much ouzo, if she had wanted to hold it inside forever.

"You were saying?" Moira said, prodding.

"Yes, I was saying that I was doing a study on early talkers at the U. I was a field research assistant. My job was to tape children in their home environment."

"Those children who, what, spoke at a very young age?"

Savannah nodded slowly. "Right. As early as six months."

"I don't think I started talking until after I was almost two," Moira said, feeling a little stupid for the admission.

"Many kids *don't*. But in order to better understand how the brain develops and what external forces shape speech, we were sent out to record children who exhibited the propensity for early speech."

Moira wanted to write it all down, but this disclosure was all off the record. She prayed right then that she'd remember everything Savannah Osteen was telling her.

"So the Ryan twins, Hayley and Taylor, were in the study?" she asked.

"Yes, Hayley and Taylor." Savannah paused, and it looked like she was going to cry, but somehow she appeared to shake it off and recompose herself. "They were beautiful little girls, really sweet. And smart too. Smart beyond their years, no doubt."

"It sounds like they were gifted," Moira said, thinking of her sister Maizey, who was in the gifted program for six years and really wasn't—as far as she could tell—any smarter than she.

"More than gifted," Savannah said, leaving the words to dangle in the air.

"You said something was scary about them. That you weren't surprised they survived the crash."

Something resembling a smile crossed Savannah's lips, but it was more a nervous reaction than the result of a pleasant memory. "I did say that, didn't I?"

Moira leaned closer. She was going in for the kill. "You did. Yes, you did."

Savannah played with her bangles, moving them nervously up and down her wrists. She wasn't going to rush, but she was going to talk. Finally, after a few beats, she spoke.

"It has been fourteen years," she said, her voice quiet. "I've never shown this to anyone."

Savannah got up from the table and indicated for Moira to follow her to her TV, hidden in a barn board cabinet in the living room. She retrieved an old Sony VCR player, layered in dust, from under the console.

"I keep this relic because it is the only way to play the tape," she said. "It isn't like I play it all the time, mind you. But I have watched it once or twice a year since I left the university."

The VCR powered up and Savannah inserted a tape.

"I didn't know they made tapes that big," Moira said, reaching for her phone.

"Half-inch. The quality for major productions at the time. Calling someone?"

Moira shook her head no. "Silencing my phone," she said.

Savannah pushed PLAY.

The video predated HD and it had indeed degraded over the years. Not as bad as those old-timey movies they showed late at night, but there were gaps, scratches and pops. The camera moved back and forth before finally landing on a pair of baby girls dressed in matching blue outfits. Their hair was faint, downy, and blonde. It was lunchtime, or maybe dinner.

"That's Hayley on the right. Taylor's on the left," she said, touching the screen to indicate which girl was sitting in which blue high chair. Savannah was on the video too, looking quite lovely with dark hair and no wrinkles.

"Look at what they are doing," Savannah said, her eyes fixed on Moira.

"Eating pasta?" Moira leaned closer, but she still didn't see what could possibly be the big deal.

Savannah pointed to the screen. "See how Taylor is reaching into her sister's bowl and looking at the camera?"

"Yes, I see it. But I think if I had a twin sister I'd be battling her for more food all the time." Moira was surprised by her disclosure because it was so very, very true.

"Hang on," Savannah said. "It was a lot easier to see when I was in the room. I zoomed in. Watch now."

Someone nudged the camera and it went a little blurry before being refocused.

The girls were eating alphabet pasta in a light tomato sauce. Both were looking at the camera as it panned down to the tray in front of Hayley.

Moira looked up, her eyes wide as she took it all in. "It has to be some kind of trick," she said.

Savannah turned off the VCR and faced Moira. She was expressionless now. She'd shared something that had traveled from place to place with her wherever she went. It was a tape that she'd watched countless times. It was something she considered both wonderful and frightening.

"It wasn't and it isn't," she said, her eyes landing above the TV.

Moira looked up at several photographs. They were pictures of Savannah when she was younger, maybe the same age Moira was right then—early twenties. The girl next to Savannah was blonde and blue-eyed.

"Is that… ?" she asked.

Tears came to Savannah's eyes. Just the mention of her sister brought back a stabbing pain.

"My sister, Serena. Yes, that's her."

"What… what happened to her?"

Savannah shook her head. She wasn't going to go there right then. She didn't think she had to. "You already know, don't you, Moira?"

Moira stood. She felt the air suck right out of the log house. It seemed to happen so fast. All of a sudden she felt like she was going to faint. But she didn't. *She couldn't.*

"Does anyone know about this?" she asked.

Savannah pushed PLAY on the recorder again and the old machine clunked into action.

"You mean does anyone *else* know about it?" she asked.

A second or two passed and a fourteen-years-younger Valerie Ryan came into view.

"That's the mother," Savannah said. "Valerie Ryan."

Moira knew that already. She'd seen her at the pizza place in Poulsbo, but she didn't say so. "I see," she said.

On the screen, Valerie picked up the plastic pasta bowls and paused, her eyes meeting the camera fleetingly. As she moved the bowls to take them to the kitchen, she dragged Hayley's across the tray, leaving a red smear and a clump of pasta.

Moira had seen enough. Her heart was pounding. Hard. She started to leave, fumbling for her purse, her car keys.

"I quit the university after it happened," Savannah said.

Moira knew that the *it* referred to what happened to Serena, not the message on the tray.

"You won't write about this, will you?"

"Are you serious? If this is real, this changes everything."

"I'm not sure what you mean by everything, but, yes, it is real. But you can't write about it."

Moira didn't even answer Savannah as she started for the door. She felt scared and elated at the same time. Her info was true. She hadn't believed the source at the time, but Savannah Osteen had confirmed it. She was onto something big—bigger and far more dangerous than she really knew.

CHAPTER FORTY-ONE

Hayley and Colton were sharing a Portobello sandwich—*her* favorite—at the Port Gamble General Store after school. They'd been talking nonstop about missing Hedda and Taylor's jealousy over the time they spent together. But mostly about Starla, what was on Katelyn's computer and who had sent her the messages. Before Katelyn died, they'd have talked about going to a movie in Silverdale, what they were reading, the merits of the Like It size at Cold Stone or the latest lame musical trend.

Important stuff? No. Such topics, however, fueled the kind of conversation that allowed them to be critical, even snarky, about things that weren't really important to anyone.

All of that changed when Katelyn Berkley was espressoed to death in her bathroom.

When Hayley's phone buzzed, she reflexively reached for it.

It was a text message. Her eyes widened and she spun her phone around so Colton could read it.

Beth: Jake got fired from Bellevue schools 4 what he did w/a kid. Wz asking abt Starla's family & heard it from some1 who told some1 else whose dad used 2 work w/him.

"Holy crap!" Colton's eyes darted back to Hayley's.

"No kidding," she said.

Hayley remembered Starla once saying that Jake was a janitor before he became her mother's personal handyman.

"What did Jake do with a student?" Colton asked.

"I have no idea," she said.

"Something disgusting, probably. Guy's a total creep."

"I'm going to find out what Jake did," Hayley said. "Google the number for the Bellevue School District."

Bellevue was a suburb east of Seattle that was known for its gargantuan mall and an endless stream of luxury cars. It was also Jake's home before he slithered over to Port Gamble.

"Done," Colton said, pulling it up on his phone. "But they can't tell you anything about a fired employee."

Hayley dialed the number and was quickly routed through to the human resources department. A woman with a chirpy voice who identified herself as Karen took the call.

"My name is Brenda Monson," Hayley said, turning away from the din of the restaurant and facing the mill through the window. "I'm doing an employment backgrounder on a former district employee."

"Name?"

"Jake Damon, D-A-M-O-N."

"Hold on," Karen said, typing his name into a computer. "Yes, he worked here."

So far so good.

"Can you tell me the circumstances of his departure?"

"I'm sorry, we're not able to do so. District policy. What company did you say you were with?"

"I didn't," she said, looking out over whitecapped Port Gamble Bay. "Wind over Water. We're a small company providing educational services to disadvantaged kids in North Kitsap."

Colton smiled. Disadvantaged kids was a nice touch.

"Pretty over there," the HR representative said, her voice trailing off a little.

"Are you still there?" Hayley asked.

"I'm not supposed to say anything, but…"

"I won't tell anyone, Karen. It must be important because you're hesitating."

Karen let out a sigh. "I could lose my job, but I'm sick of how our policies protect the worst among us." She paused before continuing. "His e-file says something about being let go for an inappropriate relationship."

That was all Hayley needed to hear. She thanked her and ended the call.

"He was fixated on Katelyn," Hayley said.

Colton had a worried look on his face. "Enough to kill her?" he asked.

Hayley wasn't sure. "Let's find out," she said.

When she got home later, Hayley made a beeline for her sister's room with the information she and Colton had learned about Jake. Taylor was lying on her bed with a book.

"You've got to be kidding," Taylor said, pulling out her iPod Touch's earbuds with a single yank.

"I am definitely not kidding."

"How could you?"

Hayley knew that her sister wasn't referring to the fact that she'd uncovered vital info: that Jake had been run out of his last job. No, it was because she'd uncovered it with Colton.

Taylor didn't hide her emotions well. She probably couldn't even if she really tried. "Why are you doing this? Leaving me out?"

Hayley sat on the edge of the bed. "I'm not leaving you out of anything. You're being way too sensitive here."

Taylor pushed her sister away. "Great. Now, you're making me feel like a freak because I'm angry at you. No one can get mad at Hayley. Always so perfect."

"Don't talk like that," Hayley said. "You're being stupid."

"Stupid? That's great. Thanks for that, too."

"You know what I mean."

Taylor shook her head. "I'm just sick of Colton and you, that's all. I'll get over it. I guess." She crossed her arms over her chest, holding in the feelings that were making her hurt, mad, embarrassed.

"I'm sorry, Tay."

"Forget it," she said. "Forget it for now. Let's concentrate on Katelyn and who's responsible for her death. I might be mad at you and Colton right now, but it's nothing compared to how I feel about that jerk Jake Damon."

Hayley and Taylor knew they had to do something. They just weren't sure *what* or *how* they should do it. They found their dad in his office in front of his computer. He took off his glasses and swiveled around in his chair to face them.

"I know that look. You two look like you've got something to say," he said.

Of course he knew it. It was the look of any teenage girl (in this case, times two) with something BIG to tell. In that split second before either spoke, Kevin Ryan hoped whatever it was wasn't that big.

With Hayley looking on, Taylor said, "Dad, we think that Jake was stalking Katelyn."

Kevin looked confused. "Jake? Mindee's Jake?"

"Yeah," Hayley chimed in. "That's the one."

The girls sat next to each other on the window seat.

"Stalking? What do you mean by stalking?" he asked.

Hayley, again, took the lead. "He was emailing her."

"What do you mean?" Kevin asked again, pausing for a moment while he processed what was said. "And just how do you know any of this?"

Neither wanted to tell their father just how they were sure of it. The idea that they were able to draw information from people or even inanimate objects was too much for their dad, a man who saw things as either black or white, true or false, real or not.

"Mrs. Berkley asked us to get into Katelyn's laptop," Taylor said. "She was worried that something was up. She didn't know what. She just had a feeling, Dad, you know... the kind of feeling parents sometimes have when they think their children are in trouble?"

Kevin knew that feeling too. One time when the Ryans had been vacationing in London, the twins were separated from their parents at King's Cross station. In that moment, he and Valerie both had the agonizing fear that they'd never see their girls again. Of course, the family was eventually reunited, though it was some agonizing eight hours later. Nevertheless, there was no doubt among any of the Ryans that emotions were often more powerful than reason.

Bad things happening are the exception, Kevin always insisted, not the rule.

The girls were relieved. Their dad wasn't asking too many questions. It seemed like a good time to drop the other bomb.

"Dad, did you know that Jake was a janitor for Bellevue schools?"

"Custodian, I think," he said. "They like to be called *custodians*, and yes, I think I'd heard that."

"Did you know he got fired?" Hayley asked.

Kevin clearly didn't. "For what?"

"He was fired for having an inappropriate relationship. My guess is with a student."

"That's pretty sick, if it's true."

"It's true, all right."

"How do you know?"

"I called the district and they told me..."

"Wait a second. Even if he had been let go for something like that, why would they tell you?"

"She lied and said she was his new employer," Taylor said. "But she had no choice. Who knows what Jake might do next?"

Kevin didn't like the fact that Hayley had lied. He didn't like that Taylor was acting all worried about Jake attacking other girls. What he did like, and what he could respect a little, was the fact that Hayley had kind of gone undercover with that little ruse. He'd have hugged her right then, but he knew that that was the wrong message.

"We'll deal with your tricking the school district out of confidential information later," he said. "Right now, we have to let Chief Garnett know what we know."

Taylor produced a stack of documents that until that moment Kevin hadn't even noticed she was carrying.

"Here are some of the emails, Dad," she said.

He took the papers, his eyes taking in each disgusting word.

"We've also got some chats that she saved," Hayley said.

"I see that," he said, still immersed in the pages. "How do we know it came from Jake?"

"Colton tracked the IP. All emails came from the Larsens' place," Hayley said.

"The guy's a pig," Taylor said. "Dad, he pushed her into killing herself. Told her how great she was, beautiful, smart… then dropped her like a hot rock. He told her she was stupid and should do the world a favor and kill herself. Isn't he guilty of something?"

"He's guilty of incredibly bad judgment and of being a scumbag, but Internet bullying, harassment, I'm not sure. There are laws on the books in some states, but not all. And most haven't been tested."

"What are you going to do?" Taylor asked.

"Only one thing we can do," Kevin said. "We've got to get this to Annie."

CHAPTER FORTY-TWO

Beth Lee texted Hayley and Taylor at the same time with the news that Jake Damon had been picked up by the Port Gamble Police. The twins were watching TV downstairs, not talking to each other. Taylor resented Hayley and Colton for going off on a Jake dirt-finding mission without her. Not cool. And there was no saying when they would forgive each other. One time, they didn't talk for five days—and that was over a sweater that Hayley had stained with cranberry juice.

Accidentally. Honest. Really!

Beth: Mom's dorky friend Nina works there. Says Jake was wanted on an outstndng warrant for dui.

Taylor: Did they arrest him for killing K?

Beth: No. Not yet. Nina says that he's been questioned about stalkng her, but he denied it.

Hayley: He's such a liar!

Beth: Yeah, but kind of cute.

Taylor: OMG! U think a sleazy guy like that is cute?

Beth: Don't blame me. I <3 me a bad boy.

Hayley turned to her sister and they burst out laughing.

"Can you believe her?" Hayley asked.

"No," Taylor said, her smile fading. "And I'm still kind of mad at you."

Savannah Osteen crawled onto her couch knowing she had made a very big mistake. She pulled an old poly-filled comforter up to her neck and allowed her tears to tumble.

Whenever she told anyone about her sister's death, it was like the creation of a fresh wound—a rusty knife into her stomach. Hurt poured out of her. Regret, shame, and guilt too.

Savannah could never let go of her sister and how she'd loved her more than anyone—more than her mother, father, older brothers. When Serena came home from the hospital, it was like getting a real-life baby doll. She was pink. Straight-haired. *Perfect.* Their mother let Savannah bottle-feed her and bathe her. She was, Savannah believed, her baby too.

Because of her, her baby was gone forever.

To lose Serena as Savannah had and to have missed the opportunity to save her was a tragic event that shaped the rest of her life. She quit the university, got involved in drugs, and went from boyfriend to boyfriend. She'd only come out of the darkness the year before she posted the response on the *Kitsap Kalamities* website.

Curled up with the comforter, Savannah knew she had made a grave error sharing that videotape with the reporter, but she couldn't help herself. She had wanted to tell somebody for the longest time. Someone who didn't know her and wouldn't judge her.

In doing so, she had unleashed something that she hadn't meant to.

Just then she made a decision. Her pity party was over. Savannah threw off the comforter, dried her tears, went to her computer and found Kevin Ryan's website. She hit the CONTACT button. An email window opened and she started typing a message.

She hoped that it wasn't too late.

A message from the Washington State crime lab was waiting for Dr. Waterman when she returned to her desk from her autopsy suite. The note made absolutely no sense. She dialed the lab and got a tech on the phone.

"The pregnancy test kit you sent in with Ramstad came back negative, no presence of hCG. Picked up a trace of blood, though. We typed it though, AB. Nada else," said the lab tech, a cheerful woman named Paris who always made sure that everyone knew she was named for the French capital, not the plaster.

Dr. Waterman slid her glasses down her nose as she searched for the Ramstad folder.

"There must be an error," she said.

"Nope. Pretty clear. That gunshot victim, Robin, wasn't pregnant."

"I should hope not," Birdy said.

"What's with that?" the tech said.

"She'd be the first man to have a baby."

Paris wasn't so sure. "What about that guy in Oregon? The one I saw on *Good Morning America*?"

Birdy knew what she was referring to but ignored the impulse to say another word. Instead, she thanked Paris and hung up, a flash of recognition coming to her. She moved her hands over her desk, feeling the covering of file folders for the pregnancy kit that Mrs. Berkley had waved at her when she came to the morgue.

It was nowhere to be found.

Terry! He must have sent it into the lab by mistake.

She didn't know whether to fire him or hug him right then. His error was an answer to a tormented mother's prayers.

Katelyn wasn't AB. She was type O. The test kit didn't belong to her.

Dr. Waterman felt so relieved. In a job that seemed only to relay the worst possible news to a loved one ("ten broken ribs" or "sixty-one stab wounds to the chest" or "strangled with a bungee cord"), she had something that would bring comfort, not additional pain. Sandra Berkley would be comforted to know that Katelyn hadn't cut her out of every important thing in her life. Dr. Waterman immediately phoned her and explained how her assistant's mistake had inadvertently brought information that she thought would console her.

At least a little bit.

"Are you sure about this?" Sandra asked, clearly overjoyed that her daughter had not hidden a pregnancy.

The forensic pathologist said she was positive.

"I only have one question…"

"I know the question, but I don't have the answer. Whoever thought she was pregnant was AB. That's about all I can say."

It was early evening. The Ryans' dinner table had been cleared and the girls were upstairs doing their schoolwork, though Hayley said she really didn't have any.

"I'll just do some sympathy homework for you, Tay," she said, trying to worm her way back into her sister's good graces.

Taylor begrudgingly thanked her. She had to write a paper for art class.

"Can't you just do a drawing or something?" Hayley asked.

"I wish. I thought art would be easy. This teacher is actually making us write papers on technique. I'm doing mine on chiaroscuro."

"Yum… I love churros," Hayley teased.

Downstairs, things were quiet. Valerie had gone out to gas up her car so she wouldn't have to do it in the morning, and Kevin went into his office to catch up on email.

He was pleased to see two fan letters in his inbox. The first was from a woman in Alabama who said she'd never written to a "real life" author in her entire life, but after reading Kevin's *Handsome as the Devil*, about Dylan Walker, a charismatic serial killer who stalked women and girls in the Northwest, she felt compelled to do so.

The next one was from S. Osteen. Her tone was too familiar for a mere fan letter, which he instantly knew it was not.

From: S. Osteen
To: Kevin Ryan
RE: WARNING!

Mr. Ryan, hopefully you remember me. I observed your girls for the linguistics project from the U. I'm Savannah Osteen. I have done something terrible, and I wanted to warn you. I apologize for it, and I truly hope no harm comes to you or your family. I showed a reporter named Moira Windsor a tape I made when I was there filming your girls. Maybe you know what was on that tape. Maybe you don't. I know Mrs. Ryan does. Please forgive me.

Kevin could feel his heart sinking. He hit the PRINT button on his computer and fumbled for an aspirin in case he had a heart attack. Sweat collected above his brows and wicked in his shirt under his armpits.

Val, hurry home. You've got to see this.

*

Upstairs, Taylor reread her paper for art class. There had been a two-page requirement, and she'd managed to meet that by using a fourteen-point font. She was sure the teacher would call her on that, but she'd done her best. She knew other kids would basically wiki their whole paper, but she'd tried to do them all one better by using web sources from other sites, including the

Metropolitan Museum of Art. The New York City museum was hosting a traveling exhibit from Italy called *Chiaroscuro: Our World in Light and Dark.*

The wiki kids were so lazy. It really didn't take any more time or effort to actually use a search engine to find something beyond the very obvious.

Taylor popped her head into her sister's room and told her that her "sympathy" homework could end.

"Good," Hayley said, "because I've been Facebooking for the last hour anyway."

"Thanks for the support," Taylor said as she made her way down the hall and downstairs to their dad's office, where the networked printer commanded a little table next to the door. She noticed the bathroom door was shut and wondered if the dinner she'd made—a kind of beef stroganoff without beef—had made him sick.

Taylor picked up her report and returned to her bedroom to proofread. On her computer screen, she could never find the mistakes that spell-checkers missed. Somehow they just leaped off the page when it was actually a *page.*

She pulled out a yellow highlighter and positioned it to mark whatever she needed to fix.

First page, perfection. Not a single mistake, grammatically, thematically, or otherwise. The second page, not so much. She'd switched the first name and the surname of the Italian artist. She wasn't too hard on herself. It could happen to anyone.

Underneath was a third, and ultimately devastating, sheet of paper.

It was an email to her father and she almost didn't bother reading it. But the subject line caught her attention: *Warning!*

Before she even finished reading she had it in her sister's face.

"Holy crap," Hayley said. "What's she talking about?"

Taylor shook her head. "Dunno, but let's ask Dad."

As they went downstairs, they could hear their mother and father talking by the kitchen sink in slightly hushed tones. Valerie had just gotten home from filling up the car. She hadn't even removed her coat. Her face was ashen, her eyes pinched together in worry. Kevin, who had his back to his girls, noticed Valerie's eyes track the twins as they entered the room.

"Hi, girls," he said, turning to face them. He wasn't a very good actor, but he tried valiantly just then. He put on a smile. "Great dinner tonight. Mom and I were just talking about how you both are giving her a run for her money when it comes being Top Chef around here."

Taylor held up the email. "That's not what you're talking about, Dad," she said.

He looked at the paper. "Where did you get that?"

"She picked it up from the printer by mistake," Hayley said.

Taylor spoke up. "Mom, Dad, what is this woman…" She looked down at the paper. "What is Savannah Osteen talking about?"

Kevin took the paper and pretended to give it a cursory read. Its contents were already burned into his memory. If a radio game show host called just then and asked for a word-for-word recounting of the "worst letter you've ever received" for a $10,000 prize, Kevin would be able to start spending the cash right then.

Instead, he lied.

"I don't know," he began, clearly struggling before gaining some steam. "Nothing. She's a nut. I get letters like this every day from people who want to marry me or want to kill me."

Valerie studied Hayley and Taylor. It was clear that Kevin's blame on a crazed fan was a complete failure.

"Girls, I think we should all sit down for a moment and talk," she suggested.

Taylor glanced at their father, who was still muttering about the crazed fan. "I agree, Mom. Let's talk."

Hayley joined her sister and peered at their father, who now looked embarrassed and a little irritated.

Valerie led them to the old pine kitchen table, finally peeling off her coat and setting it along with her purse and keys on an empty chair.

"I'll go first," she said, while Kevin, paper now folded discreetly in half, slid into a chair next to her. It was happening so fast, he wasn't exactly sure what his wife was going to say.

Valerie began by reminding the girls of their short stint as subjects for the University of Washington study.

"We've mentioned that," she said, "remember?"

The girls nodded.

"We were exceptional, right?" Taylor said.

"In every way, of course. Just like me," Kevin said, meaning it, but also trying to lighten the mood in the kitchen a little. "And your mom, yes, let's not forget her." Ordinarily, he didn't mind tension because it was a great motivator—but not when it came to his family. His attempts to smooth things over fell completely flat.

Valerie went on to talk about the protocol for the study, how excited they'd been to have the university learn more about language development by studying the girls.

Hayley smiled a little. "We did say some crazy stuff, didn't we?"

Taylor cut in. "Yeah, remember 'levee split poop'?"

A look of recognition came over Hayley. "I'd forgotten that one. That was one of our classics."

"So what's with this Savannah?" Taylor asked, guiding the conversation back to the email she'd accidentally retrieved from the printer.

"I didn't have my training back then," Valerie went on, "but looking back now, I can clearly see that she had some serious emotional problems."

"Very unstable," Kevin added. "She just kind of fell apart on us. She was supposed to come back to do more follow-up sessions and she just vanished. Quit the program. The university. We never heard from her again."

"As I recall, neither did the university," Valerie said. "You made multiple calls there, didn't you?"

Kevin nodded.

"What happened to her?" Taylor asked.

"Who knows? With the kind of work your mom and I do, we probably know better than any family around that the world is full of misfits, tortured souls, and the wholly unbalanced," Kevin said.

"Why is she talking to Moira Windsor?" Hayley asked, knowing the answer.

Kevin looked away. "Moira's writing an article and wants info on you two."

Taylor spoke up. "So what does that have to do with Savannah?"

Kevin looked at Valerie. She wasn't answering, so he did. "You know that the ten-year anniversary is coming up," he said. "We've talked about that."

There was no need to say *what* anniversary. In the Ryan household there was always... *IT.*

Valerie: I have a conference in Port Townsend Thursday and Friday... crossing that bridge only makes me think about IT.

Taylor: Tell me about how you and mom stayed by our sides at the hospital after IT happened.

Hayley: Even though I have no memory of IT, every time a short bus goes by I wonder about IT.

Kevin: IT almost cost us everything.

"Someone at the *Herald* probably tipped off Moira about the anniversary and the tragedy of Katelyn's death. Linking all of you together, though none of it is related whatsoever," he said.

"Talk about someone trying to capitalize on a tragedy," Taylor said, looking at her father. Despite the seriousness of the moment, it was a playful poke at her dad's true-crime writing.

"Thanks for that, Tay," he said.

"What video is Savannah talking about?"

"She taped you girls," Kevin said. "You know that. I asked the school for a copy after she quit, but they never got back to us."

Valerie smiled as a happy memory crossed her mind. "Yes, we wanted it because we didn't have the money for a video camera back then. It would have been nice to have. You girls were so tiny."

Kevin suggested a slice of Dutch apple pie, like it was some worthy distraction from the conversation that was really going nowhere. Hayley got up to get the plates.

Taylor looked at her mother directly, without saying a word. She was playing the old chicken game, a stare down, just to see what she could read in her mother's eyes. Valerie turned away first.

*

Later that night, Hayley and Taylor talked through the outlet cover.

"I hate it when they lie to us," Hayley said in a soft whisper.

Taylor rolled over to get closer to the outlet. "No kidding," she said. "I felt like calling them on it."

"Me too. We're going to have check out Atlanta Osteen," Hayley said, deliberately using an incorrect first name.

"Savannah," Taylor said.

"Whatever," Hayley went on. "I hate it when parents name their kids for the states the moms got pregnant in."

"It's a city."

"Okay," Hayley said. "I hate when parents name their kids after cities too. Geographic names are just plain dumb."

"Remember how we had four Dakotas in fifth grade?"

"Good night, Taylor."

And though they were joking a little, both girls felt very uneasy about what had transpired that evening—the email, the discussion with their parents. There were things about their own lives that were foreign to them. Undeniably, there was some irony to all of that. On separate occasions, Colton and Beth had remarked about how open-minded their parents were. Hayley and Taylor knew there was an invisible wall there too.

Some things were hidden behind a curtain. But no more. Not if they had any say in it.

When word got around to everyone else in Port Gamble (thanks, Beth!) that Jake Damon had been picked up in conjunction with the death of Katelyn Berkeley, tongues wagged in the way they do in small towns where everybody has an opinion about someone else's business. Jake had few fans to begin with. Most people were sure he was nothing but a male gold digger, though with Mindee Larsen, he was surely digging in a depleted mine. Although she never told anyone, her husband, Adam, had disappeared with more than the remnants of a fraying marriage. He'd taken more than a hundred thousand dollars, which had been her inheritance from a distant and very, very rich uncle.

Sandra Berkley went up to Katelyn's bed, where she'd been sleeping for the past three days, and called her husband to let him know that Jake had been arrested. Harper was staying in a Kingston motel, saying he needed some space to sort things out.

"Are they saying he killed our daughter?" he asked.

"No. They really won't say why, only that he's been arrested. I'm not sure."

"Should we go down there?"

"No, the police say not to. They say they are working on things and the gossip around town is way out of hand."

"I hated that guy."

"I know."

"I miss you," he said.

"I miss our daughter," she said.

Sandra hung up and thought about what Dr. Waterman had disclosed. *AB blood?* That was not the most common of blood types. She knew someone who had that type.

Starla Larsen did.

Sandra remembered how Katelyn once remarked on it when she and Starla had typed their blood in middle-school biology. They were cleaning the grills in the restaurant and Katelyn had wanted to talk about Starla.

"No one else in our class had AB, Mom. Only she did. Doesn't it figure?"

Sandra wasn't sure what her daughter was getting at. "How so?" she asked.

"She's so special, Mom. Everything about her."

CHAPTER FORTY-THREE

His hair slicked back with a shellacking of hair gel, Jake Damon sat on a concrete cot in one of two holding cells set up in the back of the Port Gamble Police Department. For a man arrested on charges that he'd had an outstanding DUI—a man who was likely the stalker of a teenage girl—he was remarkably composed.

"You need anything?" Chief Annie Garnett, a S'Klallam Tribe member, asked.

"Just an apology," Jake said.

"I was thinking about a candy bar or something," she said.

"I didn't do anything wrong," he said. "You'll see."

"You have a history, and we have the IP address tying you to the emails and chats sent to Katelyn," Annie said.

"IP address? I don't know a thing about that. What history?"

"Bellevue," Annie said. "We're getting the personnel papers about your dismissal."

Jake blew up, his neck veins popping like roots under blacktop. "That? You think that's some big deal that got me canned?"

"It involved an inappropriate relationship with a student, Jake."

Jake regained his composure a little and shook his head. "Boy, are you going to look stupid."

Annie had heard that before. So far she'd never looked stupid.

"We'll see about that," she said.

Jake stepped up to the bars of the holding cell. "No, you will. The 'inappropriate relationship with a student' that got me fired was because I gave money to the kid and his mother. Their house burned down. They had nothing. I wrote 'em a few checks. It was against district policy because I didn't go through channels. That's why they fired me."

"I'll need to verify that," Annie said, turning away.

"You'd just better," he called out.

Annie stopped and did an about-face. "Okay, if it wasn't you, then who was tormenting the girl next door?"

Jake looked in her eyes and shook his head. "I have no idea," he said. "Your information is crap."

Even though she was wearing a silver mini and her go-to strappy heels, Mindee Larsen couldn't turn a single head with her good looks as she arrived at the Port Gamble Police Department. Forget that it was the dead of winter and such a getup was so, so wrong. But the truth of the matter was, no one was looking at Mindee because she was hot, pretty or anything like that at all. They watched her every move because she was the girlfriend of the man in the holding cell, an Internet stalker who'd pushed fifteen-year-old Katelyn Berkley to the brink, and then coldly shoved her over its cruel edge.

Chief Garnett led Mindee to her office. It was a comfortable space, as police chief offices go. The walls were decorated with citations and S'Klallam tribal artwork. Behind her was a bookcase full of case files—perfectly ordered and complete. Most crimes in Port Gamble were property crimes, and those were usually solved in short order.

Annie knew Mindee quite well, at least on a professional basis. It was Mindee who did the chief's hair—color and cut. From the very beginning, the chief had liked Mindee. She liked her over-the-top sense of style. She didn't consider herself a Native American version of RuPaul, but if Annie had the body for a silver mini she'd be shopping at Forever 21 instead of Lane Bryant at the mall.

If only.

"Annie, just so you know, Jake could not have done this," Mindee said, planting herself in a visitor's chair across from the chief.

The chief offered her some coffee, but Mindee declined.

"I just bleached my teeth and they're still a little porous," she said.

"I know you care for Jake," Annie said. Coming from any other cop, the words might have felt condescending. Not Annie Garnett. With all that she'd been through to get where she was, Annie never forgot what it felt like to be on the sad side of things.

Mindee nodded and searched her purse for a tissue.

Just in case.

"I love Jake, yes, I do," she said. "After Adam left me… I don't know what I would have done without him in my life."

"Understood," Annie said, her slightly deep voice resonating a kind of calmness that was needed right then. On occasion, Mindee could be a bit of a train wreck and she needed to be handled with some care. "You know why he's here. And since you've come in, I'd like to ask you some questions, all right?"

"He didn't do anything," she said quickly and decisively.

A deputy passed the open doorway. When she caught him looking at her exposed thigh, Mindee brightened a beat. Finally someone noticed how sexy she was. *What more did she have to do to get any attention around Port Gamble?*

"How does he get along with your kids?"

"Fine. He gets along with them just fine. Okay, maybe they have some issues. But nothing out of the norm."

"What kind of issues?" Annie asked, her voice soft but unmistakably authoritative.

Mindee crossed her legs and pushed the balled-up tissue to the edge of Chief Garnett's desk. The hairstylist was signaling that she was moving on and the conversation wasn't going to last much longer.

"Just issues," she said. "You know… the kind any kids have when a new man comes into their mother's life. He didn't try to be Adam. But as far as Starla and Teagan could tell, he was a replacement for him. Which he wasn't."

"All right. Did you ever see him do anything inappropriate?"

The word *inappropriate* hung in the air. It was the word law enforcement used instead of the more, well, appropriate word *sleazy*.

"You mean around me?" she asked.

"Yes, but also around your kids, around Katelyn?"

Mindee shook her head adamantly. "Never!"

The next question was the ringer in its directness, and Annie Garnett knew it. It was the kind of question that one never wanted to ask a friend—or even a hairstylist, for that matter.

"Did Jake touch the kids?" she asked, her eyes fixed on Mindee's.

The words hurt, and it was clear on Mindee's face. It was like she stopped breathing for a moment.

"You're offending me now, Annie. I don't like your tone or what your question implies."

Annie knew that. "Sorry," she said. "I have to ask. It's my job."

Mindee went for her purse and her keys. "No," she said, quite convincingly. "He absolutely did not."

"Mindee, we have evidence that suggests Jake was stalking Katelyn."

She turned to leave but thought better of it. "What evidence?" she asked.

Chief Garnett got up and faced her, weighing every movement, every single tic.

"Emails," she said.

Mindee didn't like being backed into a corner, but she didn't blink.

"What emails?" she asked.

Again, there was a flat expression on Annie's face as she said, "Sent to Katelyn."

"Why are you being so vague here? I've cut your hair for years."

"Fine," Annie said. "Emails that originated from your house."

Even under her carefully applied dusting of Bare Minerals powder, it was easy to see that the blood quickly drained from Mindee's face.

"I don't know what you're talking about, but I'm leaving now. I'm going to have my lawyer get Jake out. He's a good man. He's no stalker!"

With that, Mindee turned on those strappy heels and left the police department. It was a good thing that it was after work. If it had been in the middle of the day, the woman sitting in the number-two chair at the Shear Elegance salon might actually have gotten those scissors shoved deep into her eardrum.

Mindee Larsen was fit to be tied—and not in a good way.

CHAPTER FORTY-FOUR

Mindee braced her head against the steering wheel of her car outside her house. Her world was unraveling. She remembered how the Katelyn mess had started, and she wished—no, *prayed*—she could go back in time to undo things. She'd been drinking that evening, and while she knew that was no excuse, it was the only one she had. She grabbed the steering wheel and let out a quiet scream.

That day. That moment of truth. If only...

Starla was hovering over her mother as she had pushed the SEND button.

A little tipsy, Mindee had leaned back and sipped her wine, her glass just about empty.

"Who are you going to get to meet her in Seattle?"

Mindee looked over at Starla, the vision of what she'd been meant to be when she was growing up in a modest south Seattle neighborhood—before she got pregnant by Adam and was forced to drop out of college. Mindee hadn't always dreamed of cutting hair. In fact, her dreams, both day and night, had always been of other women fussing over her.

Like they do and will always do for Starla.

"No one," Mindee said, tilting her empty glass to indicate that Starla had better fill it. "That would be too over-the-top."

Starla shook her head and took the glass. "Like this isn't?"

"We want to teach her a lesson, don't we?"

"Yeah, but what lesson is she going to learn from going to Seattle and finding that her fake boyfriend doesn't exist?"

"The best kind of lesson, Starla. The kind she won't ever forget."

As the memory replayed, Mindee steadied herself before getting out of her car and going inside.

This was, she was sure, the worst day ever.

She had no idea just how bad it really was.

*

Starla cornered her mother in the kitchen. In doing so, she effectively blocked Mindee from the refrigerator and the wine that was beckoning the frazzled hairstylist from behind the shut door. Mindee wasn't happy about that, but Starla didn't care. They were in big trouble, and it seemed it was getting bigger all the time. Mindee had just returned from the police station, upset and shaky.

"Mom, we've got a colossal problem here, and I want to know how you're going to fix things."

Mindee tried to push her daughter away. "Me? How am I going to fix this? This whole thing is *your* fault. You wanted me to make Katelyn pay."

Starla's blue eyes were cold even when she was merely miffed. This time they shot out a stream of liquid nitrogen.

"You can't be serious, Mom," she said, standing her ground. "You know damn well that you came up with the idea to make her a fake boyfriend. And then you wrote that creepy note: 'Watching you.'"

Mindee took another step, and there was barely room to do so. Refrigerator magnets and the bric-a-brac they held fell to the dingy floor.

"Do not use foul language with me," she said.

Starla would not back down. It was as if someone had substituted lesser quality pom-poms and tried to trick her.

"Like, really? After all you've said and done, you're going to blast me for my language? I'd laugh if I wasn't so mad at you already!"

Mindee managed to wriggle away. "Exactly how would you have me fix this?" she asked, once more eyeing the fridge door.

The question was a fair one. What exactly could she do? Jake was in a holding cell for something he didn't do. Katelyn had been very fragile. And it was true that she might be dead because of how they had emailed and taunted her over that stupid beer-and-cigarette photograph she handed over to the principal for revenge. What had seemed like only a pinprick of revenge had turned into one enormous gash.

"You know, Mom," Starla said, looking for words that would hurt and resonate, "I used to think you were pretty and stupid; now I'm thinking you're just pretty stupid."

Mindee, however, remained stone-faced. Her daughter was at least a little bit right.

"I have to tell the truth. The whole truth," she finally said, starting toward the door.

Starla stopped her mother. "The whole truth?" she asked. "Wait a sec. Not the *whole* truth."

Mindee knew what Starla was getting at. Starla in a very real way was Mindee's creation, the girl she wanted to be. The girl other girls dreamed of being. She'd put everything she had into Starla, and she wasn't about to pull the plug on her ambitions.

"Not everything. Don't worry. I'll take the blame here. I'll leave you out of it."

"Even if you have to go to jail?" Starla asked in a manner that both suggested a possible outcome but also a kind of contract between the two. She'd seen her mother cheat her no-good boss, Nicola, out of tips a time or two. She'd seen how she'd once told Jake she was going to visit a sister in Tacoma—when the truth was that she had no sister in Tacoma but rather an old flame she sought to rekindle.

As Starla and Mindee gathered their things, Teagan appeared in the doorway. He was visibly upset by the conversation coming from the kitchen, the latest in many from which he was routinely excluded.

"I heard what you were talking about," he said.

"Fine," Starla said. "Then you'll know what *not* to talk about. We're going to the police. Mom screwed up big-time and she's going to do what's right. For once."

Mindee hooked her purse on her arms. She looked weak, ready to crumble.

"Yeah, your sister is right," she said.

Teagan stopped her. "But it isn't right for you to take all the blame."

"Let Mom handle it," Starla said, trying to untangle mother and son. "You can come with us or you can stay here. You choose."

Teagan put on his jacket, his gloves and his hat.

The same things he had worn that night.

Teagan despised his family, but doing the right thing seemed like a step toward something better than the direction in which they'd all been going since his father abandoned them. He'd been unable to sleep, pay attention in class or do anything whatsoever. He needed to come clean. He needed to save himself.

Because he couldn't save Katelyn.

Teagan looked at his mother, his eyes welling with tears and the muscles in his throat so taut he could barely speak.

"Mom," he said, "there's something you should know."

God knew where Hayley was, though Taylor had no doubt *who* she was with. Colton, of course. It was always Colton. Her mom was in the master bedroom working on her least favorite task in the world—paying bills. Her father was in his office Skyping with a spiky redhead with a bird-beak nose, who insisted she was the daughter of Richard "Night Stalker" Ramirez.

As if that were something worth telling the world about. Jeesh! Anything for fame.

Taylor poured herself a glass of water and sipped it at the kitchen table. A digital clock made to sound like an analog clock ticked away the seconds as she thought about Jake's arrest, Katelyn's death and the reporter from the *North Kitsap Herald* who seemed to lurk around Port Gamble like a crime groupie.

She texted her sister and waited for a reply. Nothing. For the first time, she noticed a copy of her dad's magazine called *Justice*; it was open to an article about weapons.

Taylor sipped her water, her eyes gliding over the glossy pages. She was just about to dismiss the rag, thinking *Vogue* was so much more interesting, when a headline leaped out at her. All thoughts of haute couture dropped away, and a dark feeling swept over the fifteen-year-old. She could feel the hairs on the back of her neck begin to rise. There was something wrong about those *words*—something that wasn't the least bit funny. The letters appeared to pulsate on the page.

Taylor shifted in the kitchen chair. Her heart rate started to accelerate. She could feel something happening, a feeling that drew her eyes to the article for further scrutiny.

Taylor finished her water and reached for a pen and the cube-shaped notepad next to the kitchen phone that only rang with robocalls around election time. No one ever called a house phone anymore.

GUNS: THE KEY TO JAIL

The words shifted and moved across the small square of paper. Taylor had experienced that before, but never with such velocity. The movement was so fast that it almost made her sick. It was as fast as a merry-go-round at nano speed, a spinning bottle in Truth or Dare whirling in a blur, or the wheels of an overturned car spinning in a ditch.

The frenetic movement was probably necessary. So much was at stake.

The words that formed were unmistakable, and suddenly Taylor knew what happened to Katelyn.

She just knew.

JAKE. HE'S NOT GUILTY

Jumping from her chair, Taylor looked up at her mother who appeared while all that was happening on the square of paper.

"I thought you might find that article interesting," Valerie said, her words oddly tentative. "I left it there for you."

Taylor pushed herself from the table and headed for the door. "Thanks, Mom," she gasped.

Valerie reached for Taylor's shoulder, but missed.

"Where are you going?" she asked.

"Nowhere," Taylor said, her eyes catching her mother's briefly. "I don't have time to talk. There's something I need to do."

*

She ran as fast as she could. Cold puffs came from her lips like a steam engine. Taylor Ryan wasn't sure what she was going to say or what would greet her. But she had to get to the Larsens. The Larsens' car disappeared down the dimly lit street just as Taylor reached house number 21.

A voice came from behind her: "What just happened here?"

Taylor spun around. It was Hayley and Colton.

"Where were you?" Taylor asked, eyeing her sister warily. "I texted you four times today."

Hayley pulled her coat closer and fanned out her scarf. "Studying," she replied.

Taylor resisted the urge to roll her eyes just then. "Whatever," she said. "The Larsens have gone to the police station. I just missed them."

Colton shifted on his feet, taking a slight step away from Hayley. It was as if he were trying to show that whatever their relationship was, they were not one of those joined-at-the-hip couples who clung together like handbills tacked on telephone poles. A little space between them was just fine.

"Jake's going down, big-time," he said.

"I'm not so sure about that," Taylor said.

Hayley studied her sister right then. She telegraphed something, and if Taylor had wanted to, she probably could have grabbed the feeling. Instead, she started walking.

"I know Jake is a creep, but I don't think he did this," Taylor said.

"Did *what*, specifically?" Colton stopped, and the girls did the same. On the sidewalk in front of the Timberline, they huddled, acutely aware they'd just passed Katelyn's house.

"Killed Katelyn," Taylor said, her voice almost a whisper. "He didn't do it."

The disclosure had Colton's interest. He cocked his head, and his dark eyes flickered as he asked, "And you know this because… ?"

Hayley looked on, but stayed silent.

"I just know it. I can't say how, I mean," Taylor replied, pausing to find the right words. She knew that, whatever her reasons, whatever the source of what she knew, he wouldn't be able to understand. No one would.

"I just don't think he did it."

She could have said she was *certain* he didn't do it, but certainty coming from the pages of a magazine seemed too lame to share—especially a magazine as dumb as *Justice*. Besides her dad, who reads that anyway?

CHAPTER FORTY-FIVE

Under the watchful eye of Annie Garnett and the stony faces of his mother and sister, Teagan Larsen slumped into a chair across from the Port Gamble police chief. The boy who wanted nothing more than to be the man of the house after his dad left suddenly dissolved into tears. If the thirteen-year-old had been on the cusp of adulthood a moment before, all of that was gone.

"I'm sorry," he said. "I'm really, really sorry."

Mindee was crying too. She'd set all of this in motion, and the outcome had been devastating to everyone involved.

"Honey, this is my fault," she said.

Starla didn't say a word. She'd seen enough cop shows to know that every utterance she made could be used against her. Starla didn't intend to go down with the ship. She, more than anyone, had something greater to lose.

My brother is a loser. My mother, a damned hairstylist. A second-chair stylist at that!

Chief Garnett patted Teagan on the shoulder, not so much to comfort him but to keep him focused on what she had to say.

"Teagan," she said, "I need you to tell me what happened."

Teagan looked up with flooded eyes. "It was an accident. I swear it was."

"Do we need a lawyer?" Mindee asked. It was the first indication that she knew that whatever it was that had transpired in Katelyn's room was potentially the subject of a criminal investigation.

Apparently, it had slipped her mind that they were sitting in the office of the Port Gamble police chief.

"Up to you," Annie said, somewhat coolly. "We can get to the truth either way. Teagan, what do you want to do?"

"I want to talk," he said. "I want to tell Mr. and Mrs. Berkley that I'm really, really sorry. That what happened was my fault, but it was an accident."

His word choice was interesting: an accident, but his fault.

Annie waited for Teagan to look up. There seemed to be no guile in the boy's damp eyes just then. Whatever he was about to disclose was going to be the painful truth.

Every rotten detail.

"Then you need to tell us what happened, okay?" Annie asked.

Mindee spoke up again. Her eyes were puffy from her own tears. Her voice creaked a little with the emotion of the moment. She had so much to answer for right then, but now it was her son's turn and she was worried.

"Are you absolutely sure he doesn't need a lawyer?" she asked.

"If it was an accident, there's no need for it," Annie said.

Mindee turned to Teagan, who up to that moment had barely looked at his mother or sister. When he did, there was no doubt what he felt about either one of them. He'd been living his life alone in house number 21. Starla was caught up in the wonderland she'd created of her own life, and her mother had dragged Jake Damon into her bed. Everyone was so busy doing whatever it was they'd wanted to do to make themselves happy. Teagan had been left to his own devices.

He'd always liked Katelyn. A lot.

Teagan looked at the chief. "I used to think that maybe, you know, if we were both the same age we'd hook up. Be boyfriend and girlfriend."

Teagan took a gulp of air.

"When I saw those notes Jake was writing to her—at least I thought it was Jake—it made me so mad. I mean, he already had my mom and then he was going to steal Katelyn away from me too. Forget that."

"Steal her away?" Mindee said, now touching her son's shoulder. "She wasn't interested in you, Teagan."

Teagan shot his mother a frosty look and removed her hand. "Mom, you don't know anything about me or Katelyn or anyone. Not even your precious Starla."

"Don't drag me into this," Starla said. Not surprisingly, the first words out of her mouth were meant to preserve her character in a very messy situation.

"Your pregnancy started the whole thing," he said.

Mindee gasped.

Starla shook her head. "I'm not pregnant."

Teagan shrugged; it was a dismissive gesture and it brought a smile to his face. It wasn't often that Starla squirmed.

"Maybe you're not now," he said. "But you thought you were."

Starla looked at her mother before glowering at Teagan.

"You'd better not be," Mindee finally said.

"Oh, shut up, Mom," Starla said. "I wasn't pregnant. And I'm not pregnant."

Annie steered the conversation away from the mini family feud.

"What about the pregnancy, Teagan? What did that have to do with anything?" she asked.

Teagan grinned a little more. In that, the worst moment of his life, he'd found something that brought a smile. "I found that gross pregnancy test kit in the trash. Mom makes me take out the garbage because I'm a boy, and the garbage is too nasty a job for a princess like Starla. Like she ever lifts a finger around the house anyway. And Jake? He never does anything but come over to hook up with my mom, so I guess he's too beat to do anything."

"Don't talk about Jake like that," Mindee said.

"Mom, do you ever hear yourself? You put Jake, Starla, anybody ahead of me," Teagan said.

Mindee, heeding some of her own advice, kept her lips zipped.

Annie pushed a can of soda in front of Teagan and the boy took a sip.

"That's interesting, Teagan, but what about the pregnancy test?" Annie asked. "What did Katelyn have to do with it? I thought you said you found it in Starla's trash."

"I did," Teagan said. "I thought it was funny. I thought if I took it over to Katelyn's she and I could, I don't know, get closer because we could share something nasty about Starla. I logged on to the account and read the emails and chats that Jake... I mean, my mom was doing. By the way, Mom, you're really twisted to do that to her."

Mindee's face turned a deeper shade of red. It was a harsh statement and she'd deserved it.

"I know," she said, stumbling over her monosyllables. "I went a little Mama Grizzly that night."

She didn't want to say she was a little drunk on boxed wine when she'd started the emailing. That would make her sound even more pathetic than she was.

"Go on, Teagan," Annie prodded.

Teagan swallowed the rest of his drink and asked for another. His mom would never let him have two cans of pop at home, but this was the police station and she wasn't in charge.

"My mom spent all her money for Christmas on Jake and Starla, and I was pissed off."

Mindee unzipped her lips. "That's not true! I got you several wonderful things."

Apparently, it was difficult to keep them closed.

"Do you mind, Mindee?" Annie said, cutting her off once more. "This isn't about how fair you are to your kids, but I suspect if you were fair in your attention to them none of us would be sitting here right now."

"Yeah, Mom," Teagan said, clearly enjoying the focus on his mother's child-rearing expertise—or lack thereof.

"What happened next, Teagan?"

"I pretended to be Cullen Anthony and messaged Katelyn and told her I wanted to come see her. That I promised to come and I had a surprise Christmas present for her."

"The pregnancy test kit?" Annie asked.

"Right. I didn't tell her that because I didn't want to ruin the surprise. She said her grandparents were going to leave early and I should come over at about nine. She'd leave the window unlocked. She told me how to climb up the trellis, which I already knew, because I had done it before. She didn't know it. But I did. I guess that makes me sound like a perv, but I never spied on her. I only looked in her window when she was gone. You know, to see what she was reading or whatever so I could be a better boyfriend."

"A secret boyfriend," Annie said.

"Yeah, secret until I guess she realized that I cared about her."

"So you went over there that night…"

CHAPTER FORTY-SIX

Teagan Larsen put on his coat, gloves, and stocking cap (which in his mind was spelled *stalking cap*). He stashed the pregnancy wand inside his pocket, a little grossed out that his sister had actually peed on it, and said goodbye to his mom. Apparently enthralled by Jake, who was poking the log in the fire, she didn't seem to care that her son was going out in the darkness on Christmas night.

Teagan told himself repeatedly that Katelyn would revel in the idea that Starla was pregnant, or thought she was, and when he pretended that he was the one who had been messaging her, well, he was sure Katelyn would forgive him. She'd see him as more than the boy next door. She'd see him as a true friend, and maybe, he hoped, as something more.

The only cars in the alleyway were Harper's and Sandra's; the grandparents had come and gone. A dog barked from the woods, and Teagan could hear one of the neighbors from across the road calling a cat.

"Here, kitty, kitty," the woman's voice said in a voice that easily carried over the cold Port Gamble night.

Maybe some coyote found your stupid cat, Teagan thought.

Teagan was grateful for the gloves as he climbed hand over hand up the trellis, hoping that the ancient wood structure would still support his wiry frame. He wasn't afraid of heights, but he was afraid of falling, making a lot of noise and looking like an idiot.

He hoisted himself up and worked his way over to Katelyn's window, the only one of several on the second floor emitting any light. It was ajar. He pushed it, and in a second, was inside.

Her room. Katelyn's beautiful, almost *magical* room. He'd never been in there before—except in his imagination when he pictured her typing answers to his messages. That was a fantasy. That was a dream. This was all very, very real. It smelled like Katelyn—pretty, light, sweet. Not like his sister's room, which always smelled like burning incense.

Her spiritual side, he thought. *What a joke!*

Not Katelyn. She was spiritual. Like a lot of people who'd suffered great hurt, she never forgot how that felt. She could understand the pain of others because she'd been there herself. She was a fighter, and everything she had was because she was able to dig herself out of it. Starla thought she was on the rise, but Teagan was sure that it was Katelyn who was the true star.

And he was in her bedroom. Her wonderful, freaking awesome, amazing bedroom.

He could hear the water running in the bathroom, and he followed the sound. Each step closer, closer. He wasn't sure that he was ready to see her naked, but he was positive that must have been something she had wanted.

Why else would she have let him come over?

The faucet stopped and the sound of her in the water beckoned.

Before opening the half-closed door, he drew in a breath. Katelyn smelled of jasmine bath salts and scented candles. It was the scent of a young woman. Not like his sister. Not like his mother.

A sweet, young woman. A woman who wanted him there. Invited him there.

He pushed the door open. And just like that, the fantasy was over.

"Teagan!" a stunned-beyond-measure Katelyn called out. "What are you doing here?"

She moved her arms to hide her breasts and sank lower into the water, trying desperately to cover herself. Her long dark hair, which had been clipped up out of the water, became unfurled and soaked as she swiveled around.

Teagan started to shake. "You asked me to come over," he said. "That last message was from me."

Katelyn was angry and embarrassed—and the punk kid next door was frozen in fear.

"No, I didn't! Teagan, get out of my bathroom! You little creep!"

What? Teagan couldn't quite grasp what Katelyn was saying. It was at odds with how he felt about her—and how he was sure she felt about *him*.

"I brought you Starla's pregnancy test. She thought Cameron knocked her up. We can report her to the school or something."

He held out the test wand to prove what he was saying.

But Katelyn didn't seem to care.

"Do you want me to scream?" she asked. "Get out of my bathroom!"

Teagan became frantic. This wasn't how he thought it would be.

"I love you, Katelyn," he said.

She turned in the tub, sending some water to the floor.

"You are seriously f-ed up, Teagan. You need help. I get that. But get the hell out of here!"

Teagan was embarrassed, confused, ashamed. All of his emotions were in a Magic Bullet and were spinning around and around. He moved forward, closer to the tub. He'd wanted to tell her he was sorry. He wasn't going to touch her.

"Get out!" This time she was loud. Not loud enough to wake up the neighborhood, but loud enough to get him into trouble.

He was going to be in trouble. His sister was going to make fun of him. He was going to get yelled at by his mom. Jake was going to hit him again.

And yet he stood frozen, unable to move.

*

"It happened so fast," Teagan said to Chief Garnett. "It was so, so fast, but at the time, it happened in slow motion. Really."

The chief's office was pin-drop quiet.

Annie looked over at Mindee and Starla, their grim faces easily betraying their own shame and guilt over what had occurred. A lot of what the boy said was true. In fact, all of it. But what he had to tell them next was the most important part of the story—the part that would keep him out of juvenile detention in Port Orchard… or wouldn't.

Teagan had started to tear up some more, which Annie considered a good sign. Whatever happened in that bathroom in the house next door, it had not occurred without a heaping measure of regret and hurt. Teagan might have been a bit desperate and a pervert-in-training to climb up that trellis to Katelyn's bedroom, but he likely wasn't as bad as the kid who sets fire to the family dog or the one who trolled the neighborhood for an open window to get a peek at a girl undressing.

"Okay," the boy said. "I just stood there a second, not really knowing what to do. I thought she wanted me there. I really did. She was so mad at me."

*

Katelyn was completely pissed off. "Get out of here, Teagan!"

"But, I thought…" Teagan tried to find the words that would turn all of that moment into something better. Something he'd imagined.

"You thought wrong!"

Seeing that he wasn't going, Katelyn fumbled for the towel on the vanity adjacent to the bathtub. Once she got a hold of it, she jerked it toward herself. In that terrible moment, the towel caught the electrical cord on the espresso machine. In a second, but again, seemingly in slow motion, the machine cartwheeled into the bathtub.

Although she saw it coming, Katelyn didn't have time to scream.

In those hideous split seconds, the water hissed and Katelyn jerked in the bath like a fish on a line fighting that brief battle for its life. And then the lights went out.

"Katie?" Teagan called out.

No answer.

"Katie?" he tried again.

He bent down, embarrassed to get so close to the naked girl next door but needing to know what he could do to help her. Her eyes were open, staring at him in the ultimate staring game, one that he knew for sure he couldn't win.

*

"She had soap on her face and in her eyes. I turned on the water and tried to rinse it off, thinking… I don't know… thinking that maybe she'd be all right. But I kind of knew that she wouldn't be."

"Then what did you do?" Annie asked.

Teagan looked over at his mother and sister, then back at the police chief. He was shaking then, no longer a grown-up wannabe, but a kid who'd have done anything right then to turn back time for a do-over.

But with Katelyn Berkley's death, there was no do-over.

"I heard her mother calling up the stairs, and I got out of there as fast as I could. I swear I didn't mean for anything bad to happen. I just wanted a girlfriend."

"I'm really proud of you, Teagan," Annie said, meaning every word. "I know that telling me all of this was really hard to do, but you got through it. You did a good job in being truthful. That's something that's been in short supply around Port Gamble these days."

She looked at Mindee and Starla. It was a long, searing look and the message was easily understood.

"Teagan's not going to be arrested, right?" Mindee asked.

"If his story's true, not likely," Annie said. "He's not, but *you* might be."

Mindee's jaw dropped. "Me? What did I do?"

"You and your game," Annie said with obvious disdain, "lit the fuse here. You might not have meant for any of this to happen, but your online taunting of Katelyn Berkley instigated her death. Plain and simple. It'll be up to the county prosecutor to decide what kind of blame, if any, to lay at your feet, Mindee."

CHAPTER FORTY-SEVEN

For a half hour, the girls whisper-argued through the outlet about the Larsens, their dad's email from Savannah and whether or not to ask Colton for help. Taylor knew that something serious was up, but she deplored the idea of calling him into the scenario. They could take care of things on their own. They'd done it before. And they could do it again.

"I never figured you'd ever go damsel-in-distress on me," she finally said in a little dig that felt good.

"It isn't about going to him because he's a guy," Hayley said.

"Your Prince Charming. Ugh! Your boyfriend. Whatever."

Hayley tried to let it bounce off. "Look, we can argue about it, but the bottom line is that we need help. He's got a learner's permit, and we don't. Plus his mom's car is sitting right there. Do you have a better plan? Because we need it now."

Taylor didn't, so Hayley texted Colton.

EMERGENCY!

*

A breathless Colton hurried down the hall and through the kitchen to meet the girls at the back door. He was wearing a ratty Kingston High T-shirt and slightly shrunken, highwater sweat pants—pajamas that he'd just as soon not have Hayley see. His mom asleep, the house was still quiet.

Taylor had been crying.

"What's the matter?" he asked as he let them both inside.

"We don't really know," Hayley said. "Something's going on."

He shut the door and led them to the living room, motioning them to be quiet since his mother was sleeping.

"Is it about Hedda?" he asked.

"No," Hayley said, looking at her sister.

"Jake?" Colton's black eyes were awash with worry. "He's still in jail."

"We're not sure, but that's not why we're here. That reporter, Moira, is causing all sorts of problems. She's working on a story about the crash… about some things related to the crash."

"About *us*," Taylor said.

It was coming too fast at Colton. "What about you?" he asked.

The girls had agreed in advance that they could trust Colton, but it still was too big, too scary to share. Long ago, they both decided it would be better if no one knew. Ever.

"Some gifts should be shared but the source never revealed," their grandmother had once said.

"Like giving a ham or something to a poor family?" Taylor asked.

"Like that. Sort of. Shared, but never revealed."

As the three teens conferred in the living room, Shania came down the stairs in her pretty, pale-blue bathrobe, the color of a robin's egg.

"It's very late," she said, in a way that was more comforting than confrontational. "Is there something I need to know about?"

She looked at Hayley, Taylor, and finally at her son. It was clear, by the way in which she wore her emotions on the surface, Taylor would be the one to speak.

Her tears started up again. "Mrs. James, I'm sorry. I'm sorry that we came over."

"You girls are like family. You're always welcome here."

She pulled them in the direction of the couch and sat them down. Colton remained standing.

"Mrs. James, this has something to do with the crash," Taylor said, talking as fast as she could. "Some reporter is writing about it, and she's talked to someone who is upset about what she told her."

Shania told Taylor to slow down.

"Take a breath," she said, confused about where the conversation was going. "Tell me more."

Hayley took over, telling Colton's mother about how Katelyn's death and the ten-year anniversary had inspired Moira Windsor to do some kind of an update.

Shania nodded. "I'd been thinking about the anniversary. I do every year as spring approaches."

"My mom does too," Taylor said, back in the conversation.

Of course she does, Shania thought. *She almost lost you both. More than once, in fact.*

"A researcher evaluated us when we were little, and the reporter is going to put it in the story. Medical stuff about us. Private things."

Hayley didn't mention that the researcher had done the study prior to the crash, and she was grateful that neither Colton nor Shania asked about it.

"What does your father say? Your mother?"

"They want us to leave it alone. But I know they are worried too."

This time, Colton spoke up. "She sees this as her big story. She won't listen to reason."

"She's been Internet-stalking us," Hayley said.

"Mrs. James, we need to get out of here tonight. We need to get to the researcher's place and see what she's talking about. We don't want to read about ourselves in the paper," Taylor said.

"Colton's dad will be home tomorrow. He can take you."

Hayley pushed. "We have to go *now*."

Shania looked at the clock over the mantel. It was after eleven. *A reporter digging into the past was no good. How far back had she gone? What did she know?*

"We can't go anywhere right now," she said.

"Please," Hayley said. "Please. I can't explain it, but this is important. If information about us gets out…"

"I can drive them," Colton said.

Shania didn't like the idea at all. "You don't even have your learner's permit," she said.

Colton cocked his head a little sheepishly. "I do. Dad and I got it. We didn't want you to worry. Besides, Mom, you've let me back the car in and out of the alley. I can drive."

"No. Wait until tomorrow."

"Mom, can't you see? There's no waiting. I'm taking them. This is about their lives, not like we're looking for a ride to the mall to go to the movies or something."

"He's right, Mrs. James," Taylor said, a little surprised that she'd gone from hating Colton's involvement to appreciating and needing his help. "He really is. Please let him take us."

Shania James went for her keys.

"I knew you'd understand," Hayley said.

"No," she said. "Colton's not driving. I'll take you. Your parents will kill me if Colton drives. They'll only give me the cold shoulder if I do. I can live with that."

"But, Mom, you don't drive anymore."

"It's like riding a bike," Shania said. "I'm sure I'll get the hang of it. But you'd better buckle up, everyone. No promises how smooth it will be."

She started up the stairs.

"I thought you were going to drive us?" Colton said, calling up after her.

"I am, but there's a good chance I'll get pulled over, and if I do I'll be damned if I'm going to be wearing this robe—favorite or not. You should get dressed too."

Taylor turned to Colton, her eyes wide.

"When was the last time your mom got behind the wheel?"

"She hasn't driven since."

"Why is she doing it now?"

"Don't you know?"

Both girls shook their heads.

"Mom always said that you two were special, special in a way that some people can never understand. She would do anything for you."

Hayley looked puzzled. "What did she mean by that?"

He shrugged and headed toward the stairs. "I'm guessing we'll find out tonight."

CHAPTER FORTY-EIGHT

Even in the darkness of night, Shania James couldn't conceal her anxiety as she led the trio of teens to the old Camry parked in the alley behind the house. Her legs looked like wobbly sticks, ready to snap with each step. Aside from the Christmas trip during which she was blindfolded and heavily medicated, Shania hadn't been out of the house for years.

The car keys that she retrieved from the kitchen's junk drawer shook like a jingling tambourine. It had been a long time since she held those keys; a Lucite red heart dangled like it had that afternoon so many years before. She remembered looking it at, sparkling happily in the worst moment of her life: the time she plotted whether she could summon the courage to gouge the eyes out of her attacker's face.

She looked around nervously, and her son put his hand on her shoulder.

"Mom, you don't have to do this."

"I can and I want to," she said. "Give me a second. Every time I go outside, the world seems so much bigger than I remember."

Shania took several deep breaths and steadied herself before proceeding.

She opened the driver's door and looked down at the seat and the steering wheel.

Colton wondered what it was that she felt right then. Was she thinking about that afternoon when Colton was a baby? Was she thinking about her attacker? Was she thinking about what she did to save her life? And Colton's?

"I can do this," she said a second time.

Colton helped his mom into the driver's seat. Taylor and Hayley slid into the backseat, while Colton went around to the other side to get in next to his mother.

"You've kept the car so clean," Shania said, trying to take herself out of the moment, out of what she was about to do—and where she was sitting.

"Like you asked, Mom," he said.

She smiled. But if ever there was a plastered-on smile, Shania James was wearing one just then. The keys and the Lucite heart jangled some more as she turned the ignition and put the car in gear, first in reverse by mistake, then in drive. It felt so strange and yet oddly beautiful to drive again, like a foreign language she managed to recall. Shania drove slowly, very slowly, down the alley and onto the highway. She gripped the wheel like she wanted to choke the life out of it.

Just maybe she did.

"There," she said, trying effortfully to stay focused on the roadway in front of her and not on the reasons why she hadn't been in that car. "I'm driving."

Colton looked back at Hayley and Taylor. Neither said a word.

Hayley couldn't have spoken just then if she had wanted to. The movie playing in her mind was a horror show of unimaginable depravity. A half-naked man. A knife. A scream. A baby's scrunched-up face as he cried out. *Colton's face!* A struggle. Another scream. In one flash, she saw Shania's face, younger, prettier, as she mouthed the words: *Help me.*

"Are you all right?" It was Taylor nudging her twin.

Hayley nodded. "Think so."

"I feel it too," Taylor said. "Just so you know."

"I know you do," she said.

Colton read the directions off the Google Maps printout that Hayley had retrieved from her pocket, and Shania James did what she had to do. She had to protect the girls. Outside of the safety of her house, Shania recalled the promise she had made—a promise that lay dormant until it finally bubbled back up to the surface that night. Agoraphobic or not, Shania had no choice but to drive into the darkness of Port Gamble. Toward what? She wasn't sure. No one in the car was.

*

The woods of Kitsap County were creepy enough in daylight. Add a wicked February wind and the black of night and it is the stuff of dark fairy tales, the kind of place where only a fool would wander. Shania pulled the Camry up the gravel driveway to Savannah Osteen's cabin. A porch light blazed and the heat lamps of the pheasant breeder sent a red glow over the sword ferns at the forest's edge. The long shadows from the headlights turned every low-hanging cedar and fir bough into a crouching figure, moving in the wind.

A criminal.

An attacker.

Someone who would do evil.

A light in the kitchen turned on. Then another in the living room. As Hayley, Taylor, and Colton got out of the car, Savannah Osteen appeared in the doorway.

"Who's there?"

"Hayley and Taylor Ryan," Hayley called out. "We need to talk to you."

Colton went to his mother's door and opened it. "Mom, are you coming?"

"Just a minute," Shania said, doing all that she could to steady herself. "Let me catch my breath."

"Thank you for bringing us," Hayley said, hugging her.

"Honey, don't thank me," she said. "At least, not yet. We don't know exactly where this is going."

The log cabin was warm, and stepping inside from the cold night air brought some relief. Shania had kept the air conditioner going full blast on the way from Port Gamble because she was sweating profusely and thought it would help her from passing out.

Savannah looked at the girls, one at a time. Back and forth.

"You don't remember me, do you?" she asked.

Neither did.

"I'm sorry, Ms. Osteen," Taylor said, "but, no, we don't."

"You were babies; of course you don't. Extraordinary babies."

For a second it felt as if the gathering were some kind of reunion. The kind of occasion in which a teacher meets her class years later to survey the results of the seeds she'd planted. Yet that wasn't quite right, of course.

"What is it that Moira Windsor thinks is so newsworthy?" Hayley asked.

Savannah stared at both girls intently. As she scanned their faces, she wondered out loud. "You girls don't know? Or is it that you don't want to say?"

The former linguistics researcher put her fingers to her lips. She didn't like the way her words came out and apologized. "I'm on your side, and I'm sorry for that. I'm sorry that I showed Moira the tape."

Hayley wasn't sure she'd heard correctly. "The tape?"

Savannah nodded. "Yes, that's why you're here… Taylor?"

"I'm Hayley," she said, glancing at Taylor. "And this is Colton and Shania James."

"Hello," Savannah said before getting down to business. "Yes, it's about the tape."

Savannah told the girls about how she'd come from the University of Washington to videotape them for a language study.

"It was supposed to be ongoing," she said. "Some kids were going to be followed until first grade. You two probably should have been."

"We were that good?" Hayley asked. "I mean that *proficient*."

"You were good, very good, but not more so than many other kids in the study."

"Then what's the big deal with this tape? And why did you stop coming around? My dad said you dropped us."

Savannah picked up the tape and inserted it into the old Sony VCR; it clunked into position. She hit the POWER button. Then PLAY.

"Watch," she said. As she had with Moira, Savannah provided a running narration, telling the girls what they were seeing and how the study was conducted. The tape started to play, and familiar bits of their home came into view. The framed embroidery that their grandmother had done after the girls came home from the hospital hung behind the girls and their high chairs. It said:

EXPECT A MIRACLE

They could hear their mother's voice saying something off-camera.

"They can feed themselves," she said.

Savannah looked at the TV and then turned to face the audience of four on the sofa behind her.

"See what Taylor is doing?" she asked.

Shania leaned forward. "Yes, I see it," she said. Up until that point, Colton's mom hadn't said much of anything.

"I don't get it," Colton said, looking at the frozen image of the two babies, the pasta on the tray. "What's the big deal?"

Savannah pointed to the screen and Hayley, Taylor, Colton, and Shania got up from the sofa and moved closer to see whatever it was that was written there. It was astonishingly clear. Seventeen tomato-coated letters spelled out five words:

TELL SERENA NOT TO GO

Savannah ran her fingers under the words. "See?" she asked.

They all did by then, but no one said anything. It was amazing, strange and scary at the same time. It was something that could have been faked, of course, but no one in the log cabin even considered that.

It was real. Frighteningly real.

"Who's Serena?" Shania asked, without a hint of shock in her voice that the twins had left a message on the tray table of the high chair.

"My sister," Savannah said, indicating the framed photograph above the TV.

Taylor and Hayley didn't say a word. They just stared.

"Not to go where?" Colton asked, parroting the phrase seen in the videotape. "Where was she not supposed to go?"

Savannah stepped away from the TV and melted into the sofa. Alone. She scrunched up her body a little, as if she were trying to protect herself. That was exactly what she was doing; it was clear to all four of her visitors.

"Don't go where?" Colton repeated.

Still quiet, Hayley and Taylor had a sense where this conversation was going—not in specific terms, but in the outcome. They glanced over at Shania, and she smiled warmly, comfortingly at them.

She knew.

"She had a blind date," Savannah said. "Some guy her friends fixed her up with. He went to our church." She stopped talking. It was clear that she was on the edge of a very bad memory, a place that she'd been many, many times, and despite that could not soften its hold on her.

Colton prodded her to continue. "And?"

Savannah moved her gaze from Colton and looked up at her sister's portrait as she spoke, as if her eyes could see her.

"His name was Larry Milton," she said, her words now clipped by emotion.

The name brought a chill into the room. It was almost like the fire was extinguished and the doors swung open, though that hadn't happened at all. Not for real.

Larry Milton.

Everyone in the Pacific Northwest knew the name. Outside of deadly charmer Ted Bundy, Larry Milton was likely the most notorious serial killer in a state that for some reason had more than its share of such predators. He stalked and murdered several young women before being convicted of killing two college girls in Pullman.

Larry Milton was definitely in the Infamy Hall of Fame.

"Your sister was killed by *him*?" Hayley asked in disbelief.

Savannah studied the teenage girl. She was blonde and pretty like her own sister. A few years younger than her sister had been at the time of her death, yes. But nevertheless, Hayley and Taylor were both reminders of a tragic loss.

"You know she was," Savannah said, locking her eyes on Hayley. "You and your sister warned me."

"That food message thing was random," Colton said, almost wishing it to be true.

Savannah shook her head. "I let myself think that for a while. But it wasn't," she said, turning to face the twins. "The two of you were working together. You were both trying to help me do something to save her. I just dismissed it." She stopped as a tear rolled down her cheek. "She was dead two days later, and I could have stopped it."

Colton wanted to ask what happened to her, but he thought better of it. The woman with the corkscrew hair and sad face was falling apart right in front of their eyes.

"I'm glad you came. I'm glad you're all right," she said. She got up and went for the tape, pulling it from the VCR. "I never should have showed that reporter this."

"You didn't give her a copy?" Shania, who'd been mostly silent, asked. Savannah shook her head. "No, this is the only copy."

"Good," Colton said, snatching the tape.

"Hey!" Savannah called out, lunging at Colton.

He held the tape from her, like a game of keep-away.

"You care about these girls," he said. "You said so yourself."

"Give it to me," she said.

Colton pushed her, and Savannah slumped back down onto the sofa. It wasn't a hard shove, but the fact that he'd knocked down a stranger drew a gasp from his mother. What he did next, however, shocked everyone in the log house.

"I don't want to see this on *Entertainment Tonight*," he said. Without another word, he spun around, opened the woodstove, and shoved the tape inside.

"Don't!" Savannah cried out.

But it was too late. Too, too late.

"Sorry about the carbon monoxide and the other toxins in the plastic," Colton said.

Savannah sat back down and buried her face in her hands. There was nothing she could do. In a very real way, deep down, she was glad that the tape was gone. It had been like a finger pointing at her for almost fifteen years. As she looked back up and watched it melt, then burn, a sense of relief came over her.

Hayley hugged Colton. Taylor had wanted to do the same. Both understood his reasons for destroying it.

It was for them. To protect them.

"Who else has seen it?" Shania asked.

"No one," Savannah said. "Just you four, me and that reporter."

"Why didn't you show it to the university?" Taylor asked.

Tears came once more to Savannah's sad eyes. "Because…"

Shania sat down and put her hand on Savannah's knee. "Why?" she asked.

Although tears flowed, somehow Savannah pulled herself together and picked out the words she needed to say.

"Because I was ashamed," she began. "*Guilty*. My sister was dead, and anyone else probably would have heeded the warning. I was operating under the assumption that logic should rule the day, not emotions. I messed up. What was on that tape was real. It wasn't some mumbo-jumbo carnival game. Somehow you two sensed what was going to happen to Serena. Have you done that since? I mean, of course you have."

Neither Hayley nor Taylor answered. They might have if Colton and Shania hadn't been standing there.

"My sister's death is my shame, and it will be until the day I die," Savannah said.

"You couldn't have known," Hayley said.

Savannah nodded. "But *you* knew. You were babies, and *you* knew."

"We *were* babies," said Taylor. "We didn't know anything."

Savannah didn't seem convinced. Even in her shock and grief, she was able to process the past like the researcher she once had been.

"Your age has nothing to do with it, then or now."

"I don't know what you mean," Taylor said.

Savannah shook her head and dried her tears. "Of course you do. Everyone on the bus went into the water and died. But not you two."

"I don't like where this is going," Colton said, actually meaning every word.

"Nothing like what happened with you when we were babies has ever happened since," Taylor said.

Savannah remained unconvinced. "*Really?* That surprises me."

"Be surprised then," Taylor said.

As they sat there, the tape dissolved into the red and orange coals of the woodstove. The only trace that it had burned was a ribbon of dark soot along the top of the glass panel that allowed a peek inside.

"Really," Hayley said, looking at Colton and hoping that he didn't think she was some kind of freak, because she wasn't. She and her sister did see things differently from others, but they figured they likely weren't alone in that regard. Sure, they were special, but not any more so than anyone else who could pick up on the hidden hurt, the secret worries, and the dark plans that others foisted upon the unsuspecting.

While the five of them huddled around the woodstove, all could agree that its contents shouldn't be disclosed, but there was that reporter and her ceaseless need for attention and recognition.

How in the world would they convince her to forget about it?

CHAPTER FORTY-NINE

It was after 2:45 a.m. when Shania, Colton, Hayley and Taylor got back into the car. For the first few moments, no one said another word. Even after what they'd seen on the video and heard from Savannah Osteen with their own eyes and ears, it seemed as if there were no words to convey whatever anyone was thinking. Hayley caught Colton's dark eyes in the rearview mirror. He'd protected her and her sister by getting rid of the tape.

But what did he think of her now?

"How do we solve a problem like Moira?" Taylor asked.

In another time and place, Hayley might have teased her sister with singing some corrupted lyrics from their mother's all-time favorite movie, *The Sound of Music*.

How do you crush a reporter with your hands?

But not then. She resisted the temptation. She kept her mouth shut.

"Let's go talk to her," Colton said, looking first at his mother before turning to face the girls.

Shania didn't answer. She merely looked at her son and nodded. Her eyes were focused and free of the shock of the others in the car.

"When?" Taylor asked.

"Now," he said.

"Now? It's literally the middle of the night," Hayley said, looking at her phone, grateful that their parents hadn't discovered they'd slipped out of the house.

Shania put the car in gear—the *wrong* gear—and it lurched forward into the fringy bank of cedar boughs.

"Sorry," she said, releasing a small laugh, a laugh that was almost a therapeutic exhale. "A little bit harder than riding a bike. I agree with Colton. We need to get to the reporter's house."

"We don't know where she lives," Taylor said.

Colton held up another Google Maps printout. "Oh, yes we do," Colton said. "Moira must have left this at Savannah's. We just have to follow it from here to her place in Paradise Bay."

"We have to reason with her and tell her to back off," Hayley said.

"That's right," Shania said.

The Camry headed up the highway, on its way to the seemingly wrongly named Paradise Bay.

Valerie Ryan's eyelids popped open at 3:21 a.m. No sudden noise. No flash of light preceded it. Just the gentle and predictable unshuttering of her sleeping eyes as they had done countless times over the past decade.

Valerie lay in bed looking at the big, fat digital numbers on her bedside clock: *3:21. March 21.* The first day of spring, the day when her daughters and the others from the Daisy Troop plunged over the side of the bridge into the choppy waters of Hood Canal.

Without waking Kevin, she got up and slipped on her bathrobe, a Christmas gift from her daughters the year before. That night, she felt a compulsion to check on the girls. It was as if she was being called to do so, quietly, maybe in the way that dogs can only hear certain whistles.

Valerie crept up the stairs and turned the low knob on Hayley's door. Moonlight flooded the room, and it was clear that the bed was empty. Racing to Taylor's room across the narrow landing of the staircase, she saw that Taylor's bed was empty too.

Where on earth were they?

Her brown eyes puddled, but Valerie Ryan didn't cry. And then she felt it: a mother's intuition. She touched Taylor's pillow, still molded with an imprint of her head.

Are my babies okay?

Lights from a distant neighbor's house sparkled against the black water of Paradise Bay as the tide slowly, sluggishly shifted in the stillness of the night. Shania cut the headlights and pulled into the driveway. No one in the car spoke—partly because there was no making real sense of what they'd seen, but also because they'd wanted to catch Moira off guard.

"I'm calling her," Taylor said, as she pressed her ear to her phone. "Ringing now."

"Moira Windsor? I know this is late. It's Taylor Ryan," she said.

"Taylor Ryan? Really?"

"Yes," Taylor said. "You've been calling."

"Yes, I have. I want to talk to you."

Taylor delivered the understatement of her life. "You've really been a pain—like some kind of stalker. Stalking us! Leaving annoying messages! Bothering our friends. We're kind of pissed off. But, yeah, my sister and I will talk to you."

"That's great," Moira said, indifferent to anything other than what she'd wanted. "When?"

"How about now?"

"Okay," Moira said. "I'd rather do it in person, but fine. I'll put you on speaker so I can take notes."

Taylor smiled; as nervous and tired as she was, she loved every moment of this.

"You don't understand," she said. "We're here. At your house. Right now."

A curtain in the window by the front door parted a sliver, then widened. Moira peered out over the gravel driveway toward the idling Camry.

"So you are," she said. "Hang on. I'll let you inside."

Colton got out, but his mom stayed in the car. A trail of exhaust curled from its tailpipe into the cold air.

Moira, fully dressed even at that ridiculous hour, opened the door and came down the steps, squinting into the light from the car. She could see the teenagers silhouetted in the light. The scene was eerie and beautiful.

Hayley immediately recognized Moira as the young woman who'd been arguing with their father at the pizza place.

"I've seen you," she said. "You were yelling at my dad."

"Actually, he was doing the yelling," Moira said.

Why hadn't their father said something about Moira that night? What had she said to him if she wasn't a fan wanting a free book?

"Who's that?" Moira said, indicating Colton.

"My sister's boyfriend," Taylor said. For the first time, the words felt good instead of acid-reflux inducing. "His mom is here too."

She looked over at the car, still running. Shania had rolled down the window and moved her hand. It wasn't a wave—just an indicator that a person was there.

There was no need to be friendly. This wasn't about that at all.

"Just what do you want with them?" Colton asked, now standing slightly in front of both girls. He was clearly on their side of things.

"This is between us," Moira said, looking at the girls, bypassing Colton's glaring stare. "And they know what I'm after."

"What are you talking about?" he asked, his warm, angry breath leaving puffs of white vapor in the air.

"Do you mind? This has nothing to do with you." She looked at Colton and then turned back to Hayley and Taylor. "I saw the tape," she said.

"So what?" Taylor said. "Tape's gone."

Moira looked puzzled. "Gone? How so?"

"I burned it up," Colton said.

"You're a lot of trouble, aren't you?" Moira stared hard at Colton, annoyed that she had to deal with anyone other than the twins. She took a breath and held out her phone. "Savannah's tape might be gone. That is, if you were stupid enough to burn it. Doesn't matter to me. I made a copy. Not the best quality, but good enough."

"I don't believe you," Hayley said. "Show me."

Moira looked down at her phone and pressed a button to start the video. The image was minuscule, but it was good enough to see the pasta message. "Then you'll talk to me?" she asked.

"If you have the video, what choice do we have?" Taylor asked. Taylor was stringing Moira along, of course. She would never talk to her. *Never.*

Moira brightened a little, glad that things were going her way. "None. None that I can see. By the way, do you know what I'm thinking now?"

Hayley wanted to say something about how there were no synapses firing in Moira's head, but she actually did know what she was thinking.

So did Taylor.

"You need to leave us alone," Hayley said.

Shania tapped the horn, and the teens looked over at the car. Moira turned too, but the clouds blocked the moon and it was hard to see in the dim light.

A dog started barking, or rather, yapping. It was a very familiar bark-yap.

Hedda!

Taylor lost it right then. "You're the one who took our dog? You took our effing dog?"

She pushed past Moira, nearly shoving her to the ground, and rushed up to the porch. Her eyes were darts of anger. Colton was at her heels.

Stunned by being strong-armed, Moira steadied herself. "It wasn't like that. I *found* her. I was going to bring her back to your place tomorrow."

"You are such a big liar," Hayley said.

Moira started to sputter. "I promise. I was. I was going to bring her back. I saw on your Facebook wall that she was missing."

Taylor opened the door, bent down and picked up the dog—the laziest, fattest, ugliest doxie in the history of the world was in her arms. At that moment, no one could have taken that dog from her.

"What a liar!" Taylor repeated. "We're getting out of here."

Hayley tugged at her sister. "Wait! What about the recording?"

"I don't care," Taylor said. "I don't deal with people like that."

"I'm sitting on the story of stories," Moira said. "And I'm going to tell the world about you. About what you two can do."

"Just shut up, you psycho dog-stealer!" It was Colton. "Shut it!"

"Wait! We can work something out!" Moira said. Her voice was pleading, desperate. She didn't want to lose this opportunity. She *needed* to talk to those girls. "You can trust me to do a good job!"

"This isn't about a news story, and you know it," Taylor said.

Moira was frantic, spinning around and trying to figure out a way to get them to stay. Her bright eyes flashed with fear. Everything she needed, wanted, had to have, was slipping away.

"Don't leave! You'll be sorry if you do."

What came out of her mouth then were the words of truth. Whatever she wanted, it was important enough to threaten them.

You'll be sorry if you do.

Just then, the headlights were adjusted to the bright setting and the Camry's engine revved. Hayley, Colton and Taylor turned to face the car.

It started across the driveway, gaining speed.

Moira opened her mouth to scream, but nothing came out. It was just that quick. She was over the hood, then down on the ground and finally, over the embankment to the water below.

What had Shania done?

"Mom!" Colton said, nearly crying at the shock of what had happened. "Mom, what did you do?"

"Get her phone and get her laptop out of the house. Don't touch anything else."

Colton locked eyes with his mother and nodded.

Shania had just done the unthinkable, but it was apparent that she had, in fact, thought of everything.

It took only a second and Colton found the laptop on the dining table amid a nest of empty sparkling water bottles and a half-empty bottle of wine. He snatched up the computer, yanking it from its power cord as he hurried back to the car. While Colton was inside, Hayley recovered Moira's phone in the gravel of the parking area. She shoved it into her pocket.

Instinct told her to look for Moira, but when she scanned the water below the bulkhead, she saw nothing—not even a shore bird. Just the ripples of the tide. Moira was dead and gone, and Hayley, scared and worried, felt relief.

And that bothered her. *Deeply.*

It happened so fast. Like gas poured on a bonfire. *Whoosh!* In less than a minute after Moira was pitched into the black waters of Paradise Bay, the stunned teenagers had piled into the backseat of the car. Hedda was safely in Taylor's arms, already asleep despite the horrific turn of events that had just occurred. Hayley leaned into Colton, breathing hard, scared and unsure. He took her hand and gripped it.

Shania looked in the mirror, her sad, dark eyes assessing each of the kids.

"Take a deep breath," she said. "All of you. It had to be done." Her voice was full of emotion. "I had no choice. I protected what had to be protected. There are things she should not know… or repeat to anyone. I made a promise to Valerie all those years ago…"

The teenagers looked at each other, unable—or unwilling—to speak. Each knew what the other was feeling inside. They were breathing hard, their eyes wide with shock. All three were scared to death over what they'd done, but deep down they were glad that Moira was gone. As Shania James had said, there was no choice.

It had to be done.

POSTMORTEM

After the flurry of police activity that had marked the weeks following the winter holidays had finally died down, Port Gamble began to return to its more sedate (at least on the surface) and familiar mode. To outsiders, it once more appeared to be the pretty town on the water with the happy faces of visitors and residents, all enjoying views of a stunning bay as spring took over the ice and snow.

Most who lived there, however, wouldn't really say that it was quite the same as it had been before Katelyn Berkley's unfortunate double-tall-skinny death in the bathtub. For many, things were very, very different.

Harper and Sandra Berkley sublet the remainder of the lease on the Timberline and made plans to start over in a place where there weren't as many memories. It wasn't thoughts of their beloved daughter they were running from, but the recollections of living next door to the hurt and hate that had caused her death. They knew that Katelyn's resentment of Starla had been the spark of the tragedy, but it was easy to lay the blame squarely on the occupants of house number 21. The hatred Sandra had for Mindee, Starla and Teagan had a strange effect on her. She was able to use that emotion to replace the other that had marked her life since she stood on the Hood Canal Bridge, saving only her own child.

Hate felt better than regret. Better than guilt or shame.

The Berkley house was rented three days after it went up for lease—fast by anyone's standards, especially considering what had occurred in that upstairs bathroom. A new girl named Amanda O'Neal moved into Katelyn's bedroom and was working her way into the circle of friends at Kingston High.

Next door, a vindicated Jake Damon stood by button-pusher Mindee Larsen, though he was about the only one in town who really did. Mindee tried her best to prove that she was sorry for the cruel game that she had initiated to such a tragic outcome, and she was grateful when the Kitsap County Prosecutor's Office gave her probation for her relentless cyberstalking of a teenage girl. She never told anyone that Starla had been involved too. Teagan was required to attend two years of counseling sessions to deal with what he'd done. It had, of course, been a terrible accident.

Starla turned her mother's evil plot and her brother's freak-show infatuation with Katelyn to her advantage, causing even more Kingston High teens to fall at her feet in awe. In envy.

"My dysfunctional family is part of my backstory," she said. "A messy backstory is essential to true stardom. Ask just about anyone in Hollywood."

Moira Windsor's body was recovered and her death was also ruled accidental. The Jefferson County sheriff's department reported that while her blood-alcohol level wasn't beyond the legal limit had she been driving, it apparently was much too high to walk with sure footing. They concluded it was the booze that had caused her to tumble down the bank to her rocky death in Paradise Bay.

Neither Colton nor his mother talked about what happened that night. In fact, a week after Moira died, people in town noticed that the old Camry was gone. Shania James had donated it to a children's charity in Tacoma.

When Kevin Ryan called the *North Kitsap Herald* to launch his new book, he mentioned Moira's name to offer his condolences to the editorial staff. They'd never heard of her. If she had been working on a story, it wasn't for their newspaper.

Or maybe any other paper at all.

Hayley and Taylor continued to talk through the outlet between their bedrooms. They knew they had to keep quiet about Shania, but everything about that night kept resurfacing in their thoughts during the weeks after the incident. They were relieved their secret was safe. But did the ends justify the means?

They continued to get the feelings and visions that had been a part of them long before that plunge off the bridge. Whenever they could, they revisited what occurred when they were five years old and fighting for air in the icy waters of Hood Canal.

Sometimes they talked about it, speculated, even made jokes. Other times, new details emerged in dreams, bits about Shania, their mother, Moira and someone else, someone sinister they couldn't quite see. Taylor had one that came over a series of consecutive nights the week after Teagan confessed to sneaking into Katelyn's bedroom.

That dream again. Official-looking papers. A file. One word:

REVENGE

She rubbed her eyes and leaned over to whisper to her sister on the other side of the wall.

"Going to get a drink," she said. "Want anything?"

"What time is it?" Hayley asked. Her voice was groggy from what had to be a much sounder sleep than her twin's.

Taylor sighed. "Late. Too late."

"You aren't going to guzzle some water to recall something," Hayley said.

"No," Taylor said. "Just thirsty."

Hayley smiled and turned to roll back into the cozy slumber of the bed she shared with Hedda that night. "Good," she said. "We've had enough drama around here for a while."

Hayley was right, of course. And yet, as Taylor started down the stairs, she knew that the deep chill that came with that terrible December was the start of something dark and dangerous.

She could feel it.

A LETTER FROM GREGG

I want to say a huge thank you for choosing to read *Beneath Her Skin*. If you enjoyed it and want to keep up to date with all my latest releases, just sign up at the following link. Your email address will never be shared and you can unsubscribe at any time.

www.bookouture.com/gregg-olsen

I come from the rainy and murderous Pacific Northwest near Seattle. We know a thing or two about murder here because we've had some of the most notorious serial killers call our neck of the woods home. I can look across the water from my home and see the city where Ted first killed a girl. Gary Ridgway, the Green River Killer, dumped several bodies in a cluster within a mile or two of where I worked at the time. And better (or worse) yet, Robert Lee Yates, a serial killer from Spokane, dumped a body one road over from where I live today.

Here's the thing… my characters are rooted in experiences I've had as a true crime writer. Hanging out with cops, talking to victims of crimes and living in a wonderfully dreary place, are the creative forces behind my novels.

I hope you loved *Beneath Her Skin* and if you did I would be very grateful if you could write a review. Reviews are your way of introducing other to books that have intrigued or maybe even scared you. ☺ I'd love to hear what you think, and it makes such a difference helping new readers to discover one of my books for the first time.

I love hearing from my readers—you can get in touch on my Facebook page, through Twitter, Goodreads or my website.

Thanks,
Gregg Olsen

greggolsenauthor

@Gregg_Olsen

@GreggOlsen

www.greggolsen.com

ACKNOWLEDGMENTS

Thanks to the usual suspects: agent Susan Raihofer of the David Black Literary Agency, and readers Tina Marie Brewer, Maizey Nunn, Annette Anderson, Mary Anderson, Hannah Smith, Jessica Wolfe, Anjali Banerjee, Randall Platt, Shana Smith and Jim Thomsen.

I am grateful to the awesome Bookouture team: Claire Bord, Laura Deacon, Radhika Sonagra, Alexandra Homes, Chris Lucraft, Alex Crow, Kim Nash, Noelle Holten and Natalie Butlin. To my copyeditor Janette Currie, proofreader Maddy Newquist and, last but not least, cover designer Lisa Horton. Each of you are innovators and masters of disciplines and programs that are unrivaled anywhere in the world. Thank you all!

On a personal note, I can't ignore the contributions of my family. We've traipsed through crime scenes, looked for body parts in the woods and had some killer conversations—literally—with people on either side of homicide. Thanks and love to Claudia, and our girls, Marta and Morgan, for sharing my life of crime.

Made in the USA
Monee, IL
13 January 2024

51716734R00171